CU00923469

break away

Ellie Grace

"Sometimes, all it takes is finding
something to fight for..."

Ellie Grace

Break Away

Copyright © 2014 by Ellie Grace

All rights reserved.

No part of this publication may be reproduced or transmitted in any form or by any means, electronic or mechanical, without express permission from the author, except by a reviewer who may quote brief passages for review purposes.

This book is a work of fiction. Names, characters, places, brands, media, and incidents are either the products of the author's imagination or are used fictitiously. Any resemblance to actual events, places or persons, living or dead, is entirely coincidental.

Cover Design by Sarah Hansen of Okay Creations
http://www.okaycreations.com/

Interior Formatting & Design by Angela McLaurin, Fictional Formats
https://www.facebook.com/FictionalFormats

ISBN: 978-0-9914060-3-6

For everyone who's helped me along the way.

prologue

Olivia

For the first time since I'd arrived at the office, I glanced up from the piles of reports and spreadsheets that littered my desk and checked the time. It was already almost noon, and despite the fact that my morning coffee and muffin were practically untouched, it was also time for my lunch break.

It never ceased to amaze me how quickly time went by while performing the menial office tasks that went along with working at an investment firm in New York City. My official job title was "Assistant Analyst," which was really just a fancy term for someone who pushes paper all day and takes care of all the tedious duties that all the higher-ups were too busy and important to do themselves. I'm not sure what I had originally planned to do with my business degree, but being a glorified secretary wasn't exactly what I'd had in mind.

I'd been working at Chambers International for almost a year, since graduating from New York University. Investment banking wasn't something I was particularly interested in, but my fiancé,

Steven, was a senior analyst at the company, and his father also happened to be the CEO. Oh, and his grandfather was the company's founder. Needless to say, Steven had planned his whole life around working there and eventually taking it over, so when he suggested how great it would be for us to work together, I eventually agreed. He ended up proposing to me a few days later, leaving me to wonder if he was motivated by love or by the fact that I had finally added myself to the grand equation of his life.

Of course, Steven's office was upstairs with the other big-wigs and executives, so we didn't actually work together or see each other aside from the occasional lunch when his schedule permitted. Not that I minded. I wasn't working at his family's company because I wanted any handouts or special treatment. The truth was, I had taken the job because it was convenient, and I hadn't known what else to do.

I normally ate lunch by myself in the employee cafeteria, but today I decided to call up to Steven's office and find out if he wanted to join me. The phone rang only once before his secretary answered in her usual cheerful tone.

"Good afternoon, Steven Chambers' office. How may I help you?"

"Hi, Lynn, it's Olivia," I said. "Is Steven available by any chance?"

"No, hon, I'm afraid he's not. He went home for the day… said he wasn't feeling very well and thought he might be coming down with the flu."

"Oh, no problem. Thank you, Lynn." I hung up. That was strange; he hadn't mentioned that he was sick, and normally nothing could keep him out of the office. I hoped it wasn't anything too serious.

I made my way down to the first floor, but instead of going to the cafeteria, I decided to go to our apartment to check on Steven, stopping at a bistro along the way to pick up a bowl of his favorite chicken noodle soup. He was always making comments about how "cold" and "distant" I was, and even though he claimed to be joking around, I had the urge to do something nice and prove him wrong.

After greeting the doorman of our building, I stepped into the elevator and made my way up to our apartment on the fifth floor. Steven moved into this exclusive apartment complex when he was first hired full-time at the company. At the time, I was still a junior at NYU and hadn't wanted to move from the cozy, on-campus apartment that I shared with my roommate, Nora. However, after graduation when Nora moved back home to South Carolina and Steven and I got engaged, moving in with him made the most sense.

I still hadn't adjusted to living in such an elegant place and being a part of the glitzy lifestyle that Steven had always known. It was an entirely new world for me, and I would probably never get used to it. The only way of life I'd ever known was penny-pinching to make ends meet, shoebox apartments, and always earning my own keep. I didn't like Steven to pay my way, but he insisted on it. I did my best to reciprocate by always taking care of him—cooking his meals, cleaning the apartment, doing his laundry, ironing his shirts and basically catering to his every need. He seemed to like it that way.

I would have preferred paying rent.

Still, I was grateful to Steven. He'd come into my life and taken care of me when I had no one else. So no matter how much I hated cooking and cleaning, I would always do it for him.

The summer after I graduated high school, and only a month before I was to begin my first year at NYU, my mother died in a car accident. I'd never known my so-called father; he left when I was three, and we never heard from him again. My mom was an only child and lost both of her parents when she was young, so she was all the family I had. We moved around a lot while I was growing up. My mom would relocate to wherever there was work available, and since we were never in one place for an extended period of time, I'd never had any true, lifelong friends who stayed in touch. When I lost my mom, I was all alone.

As devastated as I was when my mom died, I began college in the fall as planned, mainly due to the simple fact that I hadn't had anywhere else to go. I went through the motions of school and classes, but it was all a haze. I'd become completely numb to everything around me. My roommate, Nora, was a big help, but she had her own problems. Within the first couple weeks of school I'd met Steven at the college library. He was a junior at the time and, unlike me, seemed to have his whole life together. He was determined, and always seemed to know the right thing to say. All of a sudden, I wasn't so alone anymore. He took care of me and was there for me when no one else was.

So, I became the person that he needed me to be.

I stepped off the elevator and into the hall that we shared with one other apartment. Letting myself in quietly, I slipped my heels off and set them down next to the door before making my way across the apartment. It was quiet, and I assumed that Steven was either resting in the bedroom or working in his home office. Before I had a chance to check, the bedroom door opened, and he walked out with a towel wrapped around his waist, his normally perfect hair all mussed up.

"Olivia, what are you doing here?" he said, closing the door tightly behind him. "Aren't you supposed to be at work?" A look of panic flashed across his features as he positioned himself between the door and me. His surprise was odd considering that our apartment was only a fifteen-minute walk from the office. It wasn't like I worked across the state and a quick trip home was out of the question.

"I'm on my lunch break," I explained. "Lynn told me that you went home sick and I wanted to check on you. I brought you some soup from that place downtown that you—"

I stopped mid-sentence when I heard the sound of the shower turning on. Before I had a chance to comprehend what was happening, a woman's voice called out from behind the closed bedroom door.

"Stevie! What's taking so long? Get your sexy ass in here so I can lather you up, you dirty, dirty boy…"

The door flung open and out waltzed an attractive brunette holding a towel that did little to hide her nakedness. She stopped in her tracks when she saw me, her cheerful expression morphing into fear. Steven was still standing there like a statue, all the color draining from his face as his eyeballs moved back and forth between me and the whore as though he was desperately searching his brain for some kind of explanation that didn't involve him being an asshole.

"Well, *Stevie*… apparently you have been a dirty boy," I spat out, anger boiling inside me. Was this seriously happening? He could have at least found a more original way to reveal himself as a cheating scumbag. I mean, come on. The whole situation was just so… cliché. I honestly wasn't sure whether I wanted to yell, cry, or laugh out loud. Maybe I really was a frigid bitch after all.

"Fuck, it's not what it looks like," Steven said, fumbling for words. He inched slowly toward me as though I were waving a loaded gun around and threatening to blow them both away.

I scoffed, rolling my eyes in disgust. "Don't be an idiot, Steven. It's exactly what it looks like." Finally moving from the spot where I was standing, I stormed into the bedroom and grabbed a small duffel bag from my closet, haphazardly packing the few things I had that meant enough to take with me. My closet was full of fancy clothes and expensive shoes, but I had no intention of taking any of that stuff with me. Steven had bought it all for me for the various parties and events that we'd attended over the years, and I didn't want anything from him anymore.

"Olivia, I'm so sorry," Steven said, slowly coming up behind me. "I was stupid and I let her seduce me, but I swear to you, it was a one-time mistake, and it meant nothing. You've been so distant lately, and after more than four years together, you still won't let me in. I was frustrated and upset. But it will never, ever happen again. I promise to make it up to you. Please, don't go. I made a mistake. We'll fix it and move on."

"You're seriously going to try and blame me for the fact that you couldn't keep it in your pants?" I asked, clenching my fists at my side. "That's the worst excuse I've ever heard! You are a pitiful excuse for a man, and I can't believe I wasted four years of my life with you. Go to hell!"

There was a flash of anger in his eyes, and I knew I'd struck a nerve. I'd never raised my voice to him like this, and Steven was someone who was used to always getting what he wanted. From everyone.

"Where are you going to go, Olivia?" he sneered. "In case you've forgotten, I'm all you've got!"

I zipped up the duffel bag and stood inches away from his face, glaring at him with narrowed eyes. "As far away from you as possible. I'd rather have no one than be with you."

Throwing my pitiful little bag over my shoulder, I turned and walked out of the room, muttering a sarcastic "good luck" to the woman still cowering in the hallway on my way out. I grabbed my purse, left my engagement ring and cell phone (that Steven paid for) on the counter and walked out the door without looking back.

Maybe I *had* always been a little bit closed off, but it was for good reason. Men were scum! Just look at my so-called father. He had claimed to love my mom and me, but at the first chance he got, he abandoned us. I never wanted to suffer through that kind of pain and heartbreak, which was why I'd chosen someone exactly the opposite of my dad. Steven was supposed to be the safe choice. After growing up in a state of constant change and instability, I had vowed to live my life differently. The reason I'd been so attracted to Steven in the first place was because he was predictable, uncomplicated and risk-free. I thought I would always know what was coming with him. Turned out I didn't know him at all.

I kept waiting for the crushing pain to hit me, but it never came. I felt angry, hurt, confused and slightly terrified about what I would do next, but somehow I also felt strangely relieved, like a weight had been lifted.

Unfortunately, I had no idea where the hell I was going or what I was going to do. Steven was right about one thing; I really didn't have anyone else.

chapter one

Olivia

I'd been in the car for almost fifteen hours now. When I first got on the road, I hadn't known where I was going. But after driving southbound for a while, I realized that there was only one place I wanted to go. The last place that had ever felt like home.

Charleston, South Carolina.

I'd never actually lived in South Carolina, but my mom was from Charleston and I'd spent time there with Nora when we were on break from school. There was something about the area that immediately drew me in. I couldn't explain it. Maybe it was because I felt a connection to my mom there, or maybe it was simply because the city was so beautiful, but as soon as I'd arrived there for the first time, I just had this feeling—like it was where I was meant to be. It was comforting and peaceful, and somehow being there put me at ease. Since my mom and I had moved around so much over the years, I'd lived in my fair share of places—Pennsylvania, Ohio, Maryland, Virginia, New York—but none had ever felt like home.

After leaving Steven's apartment, I'd wandered around the city for a while trying to decide what I was going to do. All I had was my purse, a few toiletries and a change of clothes. I didn't even have a cell phone anymore. Eventually, I'd hailed a cab to take me upstate to Scarsdale, where my mom and I had lived before she died.

All our stuff, including the old Honda she owned, was sitting in a storage unit there. I could never bring myself to go through it or throw any of it away, so I'd been paying for the storage until I decided what to do with it. Everything from my old life was in that unit. I hadn't wanted to bring any of it to Steven's—it never seemed right to have it there. I kept those two parts of my life separate. But now that I'd left my "new life" behind, it was all I had.

My old clothes were still there, and even though they were from when I was a teenager, I would have to make do until I could buy new stuff. I had started to sort through one of my mom's boxes, but it was too much. As soon as I opened it, the smell of her perfume hit me, opening a floodgate of memories that crashed into me like a freight train. It was amazing how a scent could transport me back in time and make me recall certain moments with absolute clarity. It brought me back to when I was a little girl, watching my mom as she sat at her vanity and got ready for work, dabbing a small amount of perfume on my wrist and my neck, just the way she did it. It made me feel so grown up.

I'd closed the box after I found what I was looking for. I left most of her stuff behind until I actually had a safe place for it, other than the trunk of the car. The only thing I'd wanted to bring with me was a pair of her earrings. They were beautiful, antique diamond drop earrings that had belonged to my grandmother. No matter how tight money was, my mom would never sell them. They had been special to her, and for some reason, I wanted to have them with me.

After loading up the car and saying a silent prayer that the old hunk of junk would still start, I hit the road, ready for a fresh start.

Once I'd decided on a destination, I drove straight through, making only a few stops along the way for food, bathroom breaks and a quick nap at one of the rest areas. I'd also grabbed a paper and thumbed through the classifieds in search of an apartment near Charleston. I knew that Nora was there and I could probably stay with her, but I wanted to do this without anyone's help or handouts. I never wanted to be dependent on anyone ever again. I needed to know that I could survive on my own.

The only apartment that I could afford was in Folly Beach, just outside Charleston. I called the number and arranged to see it the following morning.

After driving more than four hundred miles on I-95, I was desperate to see anything other than the same two-lane highway lined with trees, advertisements for fireworks and stands offering the area's famous handmade woven baskets. When I finally turned onto the exit for Charleston, I was full of nervous, excited energy. It wasn't long before I arrived in the city and saw the familiar cobblestone streets, live oak trees, and historic antebellum houses. It was still fairly early in the morning and the streets were quiet, not yet bustling with cars and crowds. It was like arriving in another time period, one that was enchanting and perfectly simplistic, a seamless blend of past and present.

I crossed the small bridge into Folly Beach and found the address that the woman had given me on the phone. It was a two-story house that sat on the edge of one of the river inlets. There was a small dock on the water and a hammock under the shade of tree. It was paradise.

As I climbed out of the car and stretched my tired limbs, a woman about my age came down the outside stairs from the top floor apartment. Her brown hair was pulled into a messy ponytail, and she carried a little blonde girl in her arms.

"Hi! You must be Olivia!" she greeted me happily. "I'm Amy, and this is my daughter, Sadie."

"It's so nice to meet you," I said, smiling and shaking her free hand. "Thank you so much for seeing me on such short notice."

"It's no problem at all! We live in the upstairs apartment, so we're here anyway. You're also the first person to inquire who isn't a creepy, middle-aged man," she laughed. "It's just the two of us, so I really wanted it to be a woman downstairs. Ready to take a look around?"

The apartment was perfect. It had a bedroom, a small kitchen and dining area, and a living room with glass doors leading to the backyard and a small patio. The lawn sloped down to the shore of the inlet and had a gorgeous view across the fields of marsh. It seemed too good to be true, and I couldn't believe how lucky I was to have found this place. I could easily see myself there.

I liked Amy and Sadie immediately. Amy was incredibly friendly, laid-back and easy to talk to. She was a single mother raising a four-year old daughter, so I already had an enormous amount of respect for her. I knew firsthand just how hard it was to be a single parent, but it was obvious that she was a great mom. Sadie was sweet and absolutely adorable. It seemed impossible not to smile around her. Although the two apartments in the house were separate, it would be nice to be around Amy and Sadie, and I hoped that I would get to know them better.

The downstairs apartment was empty, so thankfully I could move in right away. I signed the lease and wrote Amy a check, eager to get settled in. She helped me unload the few bags that I had with me, and after telling me to stop by for a glass of wine sometime, she left me to unpack my things and adjust to my new home.

I stared down my opponent, taking time to study him carefully and form a plan of attack. We stood across from each other inside a circle drawn in chalk on the cold cement of the basement floor, surrounded by dozens of people shouting last minute bets before the fight started. The air was musty, tinged with sweat, and buzzing with adrenaline, but I blocked everything out and zeroed in on the man who would try to beat the shit out of me as soon as the bell rang. He had a deadly expression on his face, but he couldn't intimidate me. I had already won the fight; he just didn't know it yet.

My lips curled up into a smile. He would find out soon.

"What are you smiling at, you fucking pussy?" he goaded. "You're not even a Marine anymore. You ain't shit, Porter. I almost feel bad that they put me up against your sorry, has-been, disabled, ex-Marine ass."

My smile only got wider. I couldn't wait to teach this prick a lesson. There was no such thing as an "ex-Marine." Once a Marine, always a Marine. The fact that I was no longer considered "fit" for active duty didn't change that. It pissed me off that pieces of shit like him didn't understand that. If it weren't for the partial hearing loss in my left ear, or "acoustic trauma" as the doctors referred to it, I would still be overseas with the rest of my unit. Everything in me wanted to be out there fighting for my country alongside them. But I was stuck here, honorably discharged and forced to retire before the age of thirty.

My body still hummed with the energy and lethal power of a

Marine. My brain still functioned and strategized like a Marine. The only way to take the edge off was by beating the shit out of other guys, which is why I participated in "underground" fighting. It was strictly other guys in the military – some who had been discharged for whatever reason, and others who weren't on active duty – but never any outsiders. Outsiders couldn't be trusted, and keeping it secret was crucial because any active military would be kicked out immediately if they were caught fighting. Sure, there was a lot of shit talking and rivalries between the different branches of the armed forces, but there was also a bond of trust. We were all warriors. Fighters.

We got together every couple of weeks and some people fought while others would just watch and place bets. In the end, we were all looking for the same thing: a way to take the edge off so we could function in our "normal" lives. No one ever got seriously injured. There was always someone assigned to monitor the fight and ensure that it didn't get out of hand. There was an element of structure to the whole thing that set it apart from the average bar fight and kicked the intensity up a notch or two.

Reece—the guy who was in charge and organized all the fights— would send out a mass text message when there was an upcoming fight to let us know where and when to show up. With both the Parris Island Military Base and the Citadel nearby, there was never a shortage of fighters or spectators. The locations rotated between different basements, garages and warehouses in the area, usually every couple of weeks or so. Reece took bets on the winners, and it was crazy how much money people were willing to throw down for one fight. I wasn't in it for the cash, but it sure as hell didn't hurt that I made a nice chunk of change every time I won. Which was often.

As barbaric as the whole thing sounded, it provided an outlet for those who needed it and was done in a controlled environment that made it safer for everyone. Before I found this group, the rage was practically eating me alive, and I was picking fights with random strangers in order to get my frustration out. It was better for everyone if my opponents were willing volunteers. Not to mention, it made for a much better fight when I was going up against someone who had the same kind of training that I did.

It was also one hell of a rush.

Some people had counseling or medication, but I had this. This was my fucking therapy. My momentary dose of freedom. The relief was fleeting, and I wasn't stupid enough to believe it was a cure, but it was all I had.

The bell rang, signaling the start of the fight. I watched as my opponent lunged forward, wasting no time before coming at me full force.

That was his first mistake.

I never struck first. Instead, I watched and analyzed my opponent. I examined their technique and looked for their weaknesses. Then, I waited for them to tire, and I used those weaknesses against them. I fought smart and efficiently because that's what I'd been trained to do. I let them think that they had the advantage, and then I took them down.

My opponent landed a few decent punches. A pair of body shots to my ribs and a hard right hook to my face that split the skin and started bleeding. He was strong, there was no doubt about that, but he was already running out of energy.

His breathing got heavier, and I went in for the kill. As he came at me with another hit to the side of my head, I ducked, throwing him off balance and making him stumble slightly. Before he could completely regain his balance, I had already landed a solid blow to his side and an uppercut to his jaw that sent him tumbling backwards. He flung a sluggish punch that I dodged easily and countered with a powerful shot to his ribs.

The fight was as good as over.

I threw a vicious right hook that landed on his cheek and propelled him into the crowd before he dropped to the floor, not moving. The ref slammed the ground three times, declaring a knockout, and half the crowd began to cheer while the other half groaned.

"That's the match, folks!" Reece yelled over the megaphone. "Your winner, and still undefeated champ, is Dex Porter!" He raised my arm above my head and slapped a pile of cash in my other hand.

Piece of cake.

chapter two

Olivia

I rolled over in my new bed, wide awake and unable to fall back to sleep even though it was barely six o'clock in the morning. It probably had something to do with the fact that I'd gone to bed before the sun even had a chance to set last night.

All the driving—and not to mention the emotional turmoil—of the past couple of days had left me beyond exhausted. I managed to unload and unpack everything from my car and had put my sparse collection of clothing away in the dresser drawers and closet. I was beyond thankful for the fact that Amy had the apartment nicely furnished with everything I needed, including towels and bed linens, so I didn't have to buy any household items. After taking a nice long shower, I'd fallen asleep immediately, without even bothering to eat dinner. Not that I had any food anyway.

Now my stomach was growling for breakfast... and coffee. A trip to the grocery store was definitely on the agenda for today.

After brushing my teeth and running my fingers through my

messy blonde hair, I threw on a loose V-neck tee and a pair of short denim cut-offs that I hadn't seen since my high school days. It was a beautiful sunny morning and on my way out the door, I grabbed my camera so I could snap a few pictures while I was out.

The camera had been buried among the other stuff in our storage unit, and I couldn't bear to leave it there any longer. My mom had always loved taking pictures. There were probably about a million photographs of me growing up because she almost always had a camera in her hand. Never one of those cheap, digital things, but an actual film camera that required more than just pointing and clicking a button. When I was old enough, she showed me how to use it and taught me all about lighting, exposure, and all the different elements that went into taking a picture. It wasn't long before I felt at home behind the camera and was addicted to experiencing life through the lens and capturing the beauty of everything around me.

For my eighteenth birthday, my mom saved up for months to buy me a Nikon FM-10, an expensive film camera that she'd caught me eying at the store one day. It was the best gift I'd ever gotten and the fact that she worked so hard to get it for me meant more than anything. When she died a few weeks later, it was too painful a reminder to use it, so I'd boxed it up and put it in storage.

I was glad that I'd decided to bring it down here. I missed taking photographs. Being behind the camera granted a sense of control; choosing how to capture an image and how it would be perceived, and freezing a particular moment in time the way I wanted it to be remembered. I'd never had any control in my own life, but when I was behind the camera, I could control what I wanted to portray. Besides, South Carolina was far too beautiful a place not to take pictures.

I grabbed a coffee and a bagel from a café I found nearby and drove down to the Folly Beach Pier to sit on the quiet beach and eat. It was still early, and there was nobody else around, giving the beach a sense of stillness and calm that only occurs before the chaos of a new day rushes in.

I plopped down on the sandy beach and watched as the seagulls dove around the pier, hunting for scraps that yesterday's fishermen had left behind. Small waves rolled in and lapped up on the shore, splashing against the large wooden pillars of the pier before fading back into the ocean. Houses lined the beach as far as I could see, but with the summer season still several weeks away, they sat empty and vacant. Everything was so peaceful. I'd only ever been here during busy vacation weeks, and I was glad to experience it this way.

I began snapping a few pictures, reacquainting myself with the camera and looking around through the viewfinder. I noticed movement down the beach and zoomed in on it, turning the dial to bring the image into focus.

It was a man jogging along the beach in my direction. He was shirtless, and the closer he got, the harder it was to look away. His muscular torso glistened in a thin sheen of sweat, like he'd been running for a long time, though he didn't seem to be tiring. His stomach rippled in a defined six-pack, trailing to a distinct inward cut of his hips that disappeared into his mesh shorts and had me practically salivating when I thought about where it led.

He slowed his pace a couple hundred feet away from where I was sitting and stopped running, turning to face the water. I couldn't help but admire the sleek, toned muscles of his back that sloped to what I could imagine was an amazing backside hidden beneath those shorts. His body was marked with several tattoos – one on his back across his shoulder blades, another along his forearm, and one on his bicep. I couldn't make out what they were, but the black ink stood out against his sleek, lightly tanned skin.

For a while he just stood there, not moving, and I wondered what he could be thinking about as he gazed out over the open ocean. He seemed... lost. I snapped a couple of pictures, unable to resist capturing the moment.

He turned around suddenly, his eyes meeting mine through the lens. I flushed and lowered the camera, embarrassed to have been caught not only staring but taking pictures of him. It was easy to forget that I wasn't invisible when I was behind the camera.

I turned and began taking pictures in the other direction, trying to brush off the awkward moment, but I could feel him approaching me. I glanced over at him, and I could have sworn I felt my heart skip a beat. I'd been too distracted by his body to notice his face before, but now that I saw it... wow.

He had short brown hair and handsome, chiseled features. His sturdy jaw line was brushed with light stubble, and there was a slight dimple on his chin. His eyes were dark and deep, and I couldn't look away. I noticed some bruising over his ribs and a small cut above his eyebrow, telltale signs that he'd been in a fight recently. Somehow it made him look rough and sexy, and a little bit dangerous. Bottom line: he was unbelievably gorgeous.

Then... he opened his mouth.

"What's up, baby? You see something you like?" His lips morphed into a cocky grin as he sat down next to me.

I inched away from him, immediately turned off by his arrogance, and pretended to look around. "Nope, I don't think so."

"You sure about that?" he smirked. "Cause you sure seemed interested, not that I mind. In fact, I'd be more than happy to recreate whatever fantasy was playing through your head while you were gawking at me. In fact, I've got some free time right now..."

"Yuck." I stood up and brushed the sand off me. "Somebody's a little full of himself, don't you think?"

"So, that's a no then?"

"Actually, that's a hell no."

He grinned, his eyes dancing in amusement. "Suit yourself, sweetheart. I'm around if you change your mind."

"Don't worry, *sweetheart…* I won't." I heard him laugh as I walked away, but I didn't bother looking back. What a typical, asshole guy. He was attractive enough that he probably never even had to put any effort into getting girls, and therefore never bothered to have a decent personality or act like a civilized human being.

Ugh, I hated guys like that. They thought they were God's gift to woman, and we should consider ourselves lucky to get a chance to be with them. No thanks.

It was the perfect reminder of why I'd sworn off men.

I turned on the shower, enjoying the blast of cold water on my overheated skin before it finally warmed up. I'd run farther than usual that morning in an attempt to ease some of the tension that was radiating throughout my body. Normally the endorphins helped. Not nearly as much as fighting did, but it was the next best thing. Today, though, it just wasn't cutting it.

My morning run was one of the only times that I actually felt at peace. It was quiet, and I didn't have to deal with people… at least, not usually. Today was different, though, and my unexpected encounter with the girl near the pier was the best part of my day so far. I hadn't even gotten her name, but I found myself thinking about her during the run back to my house.

No doubt she was attractive. In fact, she was fucking sexy. But it was her feisty "I hate men" attitude that really grabbed my attention. I could tell she was attracted to me, and while most women couldn't resist me when I turned on the charm, she wasn't having any of it.

So, why the hell was I still thinking about her? When a chick gave me the brush-off—which frankly wasn't very often—she was instantly forgotten, and I was on to the next one. Yet, my thoughts kept drifting back to the girl from the beach. Her long blonde hair... gorgeous blue eyes... full lips... long legs... perfect, tight curves...

My dick immediately started getting hard at the thought of her, reminding me of another way to relieve my tension. I reached down, grabbing my firm length and slowly stroking it up and down. I thought about those plump lips wrapping around my cock, moving my hand faster as I pictured her kneeling in front of me and taking me into her hot mouth, sucking me hard and deep while she looked up at me with those big, blue eyes. I began pumping faster and within minutes I came. Hard.

I stood under the stream of the shower and braced myself against the tile wall, catching my breath and calming myself down. I couldn't remember the last time that I jerked off to a complete stranger, and I sure as hell couldn't remember anyone having this kind of impression on me. What the hell had gotten into me?

I really needed to get laid.

Later that morning, I went into the small auto repair shop where I worked as a mechanic. It wasn't what I'd planned to be doing with my life at this point, but I liked working on cars. There was something therapeutic about it that calmed me down and got me out of my own head. Engines were simple and straightforward. When something was wrong, the problem could be diagnosed and fixed. No matter how complicated or messed up it was, the broken components could be repaired or replaced, and the engine could be put back together again. Good as new.

If only life were that simple.

The shop was owned by my buddy, Nate, who I'd known since high school. He inherited the business from his dad and devoted most of his time to working on cars. I'd devoted *my* life to the Marines, but when I was forced to retire last year and had nothing else to do, Nate had given me a job.

It was still early in the morning, but when I walked into the garage, he was already waist deep under the engine of an old Ford Mustang, one of his pet projects that he was always tinkering with.

"Hey, man," I greeted him. "Don't you ever sleep?"

"I'm avoiding the house," he said, rolling out from under the car and wiping his greasy hands on a rag. "I ended it with that girl Kelly I was seeing, and now she won't leave me alone."

"What are you, scared of this girl? Tell her to get lost."

"She's a little… unpredictable. I figured I'd give her some time to cool off."

"You mean she's bat-shit crazy," I corrected him. "I'm surprised you stayed with her as long as you did. Although… the crazy ones are usually pretty wild in bed, so I get it."

"You're such a dog," he said, shaking his head at me. "Kelly and I didn't click, that's all. I was trying to force something that wasn't there."

While I preferred things simple and uncomplicated with no

strings attached, Nate was the type who wanted to settle down and shit. "Whatever. I'm just glad you're single again," I told him. "I've been stuck without a wingman for over a month while you 'experimented' with a relationship. It's seriously affecting my game. Last weekend, I had a hot chick on the hook, all ready to go, but she wouldn't leave the bar without her damn friend."

"So you had to go home all alone, eh?"

"Hell no, I took them both home," I grinned wickedly. "Turned out to be a pretty great night, actually, but you're missing the point."

He laughed. "Oh, you poor thing... and I'm supposed to feel sorry for you, why?"

"Dude, it's not easy handling two girls at the same time. There's twice as much ground to cover! Do the math... it's a lot of work. I've only got two hands and although my dick is incredibly efficient, I still only have one."

"Yeah, until it falls off. Considering all those dirty skanks you go home with, I'm surprised it hasn't shriveled up and died already."

"Are you kidding?" I said, pulling on my coveralls. "I love my dick way too much to let that happen. I'm always careful. In fact, careful is my middle name. I'm clean as a whistle over here, don't you worry."

Nate poured himself a cup of coffee from the dusty, old machine on the work bench. "Okay, but I still think you need to get yourself a girlfriend. Not one of those dumb, bar sluts that you seem to love so much, but a nice girl that you can actually have a conversation with."

My mind automatically drifted back to the girl from this morning. "Thanks, but no thanks," I said, pushing those thoughts aside. "I'm not built for monogamy. Why be with one woman when you could be with lots of different woman... sometimes at the same time? Relationships are nothing but a headache."

"Okay, Dex," he chuckled. "But one of these days, you're gonna eat your words."

He had no idea how wrong he was. Even if I wanted to be in a relationship, which I really didn't, I couldn't subject someone to being with *me*. I was in no shape to be close with anyone that way, and I'd learned a while back that I was not someone who could be relied upon. Keeping women at arm's length was as much for their benefit as it was for mine. After everything I'd done, I didn't deserve anyone who was worth having, and I sure as hell didn't deserve to be happy. All I would do is fuck it up like I'd managed to do with everything else I cared about.

It was better not to care. To be numb. Sure, I used women, but they used me too. It wasn't like they gave a shit about me. They wanted the same thing that I did. To chase away the pain. To forget.

Even if it was only for a little while.

chapter three

Olivia

Once I'd stopped at the grocery store and stocked up on food, there was only one thing left for me to do. Get a job.

I had a little bit of savings, but it wasn't going to get me very far. After paying for first month's rent and security on the apartment, nearly half of it was already gone. Most of my money had gone toward paying for college, which wasn't cheap. I'd been lucky enough to get in with a scholarship, but it only covered a portion of the cost. It was never a problem when I was with Steven because he always insisted on paying for everything. Not having to shell out money for rent, food and utilities had allowed me to pay off most of what I owed, but unfortunately, it hadn't left much in my savings.

I used to think it was sweet and generous that Steven had insisted on taking care of me, I'd come to realize that it was just another way to make me reliant upon him. As long as I needed him, I wouldn't leave. With Steven, it was always about control. Controlling the way I dressed, the way I acted, and even where I worked. He'd managed to disguise it as love, but now that I saw it for what it was, I would never make that mistake again.

People were unreliable. They would always let you down, if you let them. From now on, the only person I would depend on was me.

However, the first step to independence was getting a job, so I scoured the classifieds for openings. There wasn't much to choose from but at this point, I wasn't picky. I would do almost anything as long as it paid the bills.

I struck out with the first couple phone calls, as the positions had already been filled, but eventually got lucky with the Seaside Bar & Grille. It was right on Folly Beach, and they were looking for a waitress and bartender. I'd never worked as a bartender, but since I waited tables throughout high school, they told me to come in and apply with the manager.

I parked in the small gravel lot behind the restaurant and went inside. It had a great beachy, rustic feel with driftwood and surfboards lining the walls. There was a big bar at the center, surrounded by tables and chairs, and a small area sectioned off for a band. One wall was completely open and led to an outside dining area that overlooked the water. It was before noon, so the place was empty aside from a couple of staff members getting ready for the lunch crowd.

"Can I help you with something?" A friendly woman who looked to be about thirty or so approached when she saw me standing awkwardly near the entrance.

"I called earlier about the job opening," I said. "I'm supposed to meet with the manager."

"That would be me. I'm Sarah." She extended her hand to shake mine. "You must be Olivia."

"Yes, thank you so much for meeting with me."

"No problem. You said you had some waitressing experience?"

"I waited tables at a diner for about four years. It's been a while, but I'm sure I can pick it up quickly."

"Oh, it'll all come back. It's like riding a bike," she smiled. "So, we serve lunch and dinner, and then after the dinner rush, we clear out all the tables and usually have live music or a DJ for the night crowd. The position I have open is mainly for a waitress during the lunch and dinner shifts, but we may end up putting you behind the bar a couple nights a week. We'll have someone show you the ropes, of course, since you've never bartended before, but it's pretty straightforward. Think you'd be up for that?"

"Absolutely. It sounds great." If it meant she was giving me a job, I would do whatever she wanted me to.

"Terrific! The job is only part-time for right now, but once the season hits and we get busy, you'll be able to have as many hours as you want."

"That's fine, I'll take whatever you can offer me." It wasn't ideal, but I could find another part-time job in the meantime. "When can I start?"

"How about Friday night?" Sarah asked. "Come in around four, and I'll put you on the dinner shift so Melanie can train you. Then, if you're up for it, you can stay and get some experience behind the bar, scope the place out and see how everything works."

"Perfect. I'll be here."

After leaving the Seaside, I decided to drive into Charleston to see if I could find another job. I wanted to work as much as possible so I could start saving up some money. Besides, it wasn't as though I had anything better to do. If I wasn't working, I would be hanging around the house by myself, and that was just sad.

I started on Market Street, in the French Quarter, nearby all the various street vendors, and then made my way onto King Street, where all of the upscale stores were. After stopping in numerous swanky retail shops and even a movie theater, none of which were hiring, I decided to call it a day.

Not wanting to head home yet, I opted to walk along the water and explore the city for a while. I checked out Rainbow Row, the famous pastel-colored homes on East Bay Street, and the pineapple fountain at Waterfront Park. Then, after grabbing an Italian ice from one of the street vendors, I found myself near the entrance to the South Carolina Aquarium on Charleston Harbor.

I was probably one of the only people over the age of twelve who still loved going to the aquarium, but I couldn't help it. I'd always loved everything about the ocean. It was vast, open and endless. I was fascinated by how many amazing creatures were hiding beneath the surface. It reminded me of how much more there was out there.

Once I paid the admission, I began at the big ocean tank and looked at all the fish, sea turtles and other cool creatures. There was something relaxing about standing in the dark hallway under the blue glow of the huge tank, watching all the fish swim past in an endless circle. It was hypnotizing, and it never failed to calm me.

I was watching an adorable sea turtle swimming around the reef directly behind the glass when I heard a voice from behind me.

"You like the sea turtles?"

I turned and saw an older man wearing a polo shirt with the aquarium's logo on it and a nametag that read, "Frank", meaning he obviously worked there. "Yes," I smiled. "I love them."

"Have you been down to the Sea Turtle Hospital?" he asked.

I shook my head. "What's that?"

"We have one of the best facilities on the east coast. They bring sick, injured or stranded sea turtles here, and we rehabilitate them until they are healthy enough to be released back into the wild."

"That sounds amazing."

"It really is. You want me to give you the tour?"

"I'd love that," I said, nodding my head like an eager kindergartener. "Are you sure you don't mind?"

"Not at all," Frank said. "We don't normally do public tours on Wednesdays, but it's quiet, and I'd hate to deny a fellow sea turtle lover the opportunity to see it."

He led me downstairs to where the rescue facility was, chatting along the way. He told me that he'd been working at the aquarium for more than ten years and loved it, even though he'd never had any interest in marine life before starting there. After retiring from a stressful corporate job, he'd been looking for something different. Like me, he had been drawn to the place. I explained how I'd just moved into town and had no idea what I was doing. He was really easy to talk to, and I adored him immediately.

Frank showed me around the facility and introduced me to some of the "patients" of the hospital. The place was spectacular, and I couldn't believe that all of this was sitting beneath the aquarium and I hadn't ever known.

"This here is Edisto," Frank said, gesturing to one of the tanks. "He's a Loggerhead that they rescued off Edisto Beach, hence the name."

"What happened to him?" He was missing one of his front flippers, making it difficult for him to swim around.

"He was badly tangled up in some fishing line. Unfortunately, it happens a lot. His was pretty bad and the damage to his flipper was too severe, so they had to amputate it."

"Is he going to be okay?" I asked. "Will he ever get released?" I couldn't imagine how he would be able to survive in the ocean, seeing as how he could barely swim.

"Oh yeah, he'll be fine," Frank said. "You'd be surprised at how well they are able to recover and adapt, with the right treatment. Pretty soon he'll be swimming around that tank like a pro. Ain't that right, Eddie?"

I smiled with relief. "It must be incredible to work here and get to be a part of this."

"You know… they have an opening down here for an intern-type position in the mornings. The pay isn't much, and day starts pretty early. It's certainly nothing glamorous – mostly cleaning and helping with tours – but there's also a lot of assisting the veterinarians. Usually the spots are snatched up by people studying over at the local college, but this year we've had trouble finding anyone. If you're interested, I could speak to the program director…"

"Yes!" I practically shouted, jumping forward and throwing my arms around a surprised Frank. "That would be perfect!"

Frank chuckled, returning my hug. "Don't get too excited now, I haven't gotten you the job *yet*."

But of course, he did end up getting me the job.

It was Friday night, and after two days of hassling Nate, he had finally agreed to come out with me. I was desperate to unwind, and since I didn't have any fights coming up, I would have to settle for booze and sex. That usually did the trick, and now that I had my wingman back, it would be much easier to accomplish.

We decided to stay in Folly Beach because my place was only a couple blocks from the bar, and we wouldn't have to drive. There were a couple of spots that I normally frequented, but the Seaside seemed to have the best food and the most decent music. Also, that's where all the women seemed to flock. So naturally, that's where we ended up.

The hostess seated us right away, openly flirting with us and flipping her hair around. She was cute enough, but since she worked there, I wouldn't touch her. I would never shit where I ate, so to speak. This was one of my favorite spots, and the last thing I needed was an ex-one-night-stand making things awkward and preventing me from coming back. There were more than enough college girls and vacationers coming in on the weekends, so I stayed away from the locals.

Our waitress, Melanie, who I knew fairly well from being a regular, came over to take our order.

"Hey, Dex," she said, pulling out her pad and paper. "Let me guess, a shot of whiskey and a Bud Light?"

"You got it," I said, "and this guy will have the same thing." I knew Nate well enough to know he probably only wanted a beer, but tonight was about having fun and letting loose. Even if I had to make him do it.

"Okay, I'll be back in a minute with those, and then I'll take your dinner order."

"Thanks, Mel, you're the best."

After we ordered two burgers, I held up my shot glass and made Nate do the same. "To finally getting your freedom back!" I toasted, clinking my glass against his and letting the warm, amber liquid slide down my throat. It pooled it my stomach, heating my insides and calming me almost immediately.

There was a new bartender working behind the bar, and I did a double take when I realized it was the gorgeous girl from the beach the other day. She had her back to me, but I knew that perfect ass and blonde ponytail belonged to her.

She spun around, and when her eyes met mine there was a flicker of recognition in them. Her gaze lingered on me for a moment before she finally got back to the order she was taking. It seemed that she was a little flustered, and I wondered if it was because of me or if she was simply overwhelmed with the job. I'd never seen her here before, so she had to be new. Part of me was a little disappointed that she lived around here. I didn't want to break my rule about hooking up with locals, but I also couldn't help but be excited at the prospect of seeing her regularly.

While Nate and I ate, I continued to watch her as she moved around behind the bar and served customers. Every once in a while I caught her sneaking a glance at me, causing her to blush and quickly look away. She was clearly trying to ignore me and yet, she couldn't help but look over here. I liked the fact that she was seeking me out. It kind of turned me on to think that she was watching me, too.

After we paid our bill, we got up from the table and relocated to the bar. More people were flooding in, and the staff was starting to move the tables out of the way to make room for the bar crowd. Nate went to use the bathroom, and I plopped myself down on an open bar stool in front of where blondie was working.

"So, we meet again," I said when her eyes settled on mine.

"So we do," she replied elusively. "What can I get for you?"

Apparently, she wasn't interested in small talk, which didn't come as a surprise considering her stand-offish attitude toward me on the beach. Still, she'd obviously been noticing me. All the coy glances in my direction told me that she was intrigued, and yet when I sat down in front of her she acted like she wanted nothing to do with me. This girl was a total mystery.

"Two shots of Jameson," I finally said.

She fumbled with the shot glasses, knocking one over as she placed them on the counter. I reached out to pick it up at the same time she did, causing my hand to brush against hers.

"Thanks," she mumbled, embarrassed.

"First day?"

"Yeah. I've waitressed but the bartending thing is new to me." She managed to pour the two shots without further incident. "I'm still getting the hang of it."

"Looks to me like you're doing just fine," I winked, letting my eyes rake over her body. She responded by rolling her eyes and moving on to another customer.

By the time I was ready to order another drink, Nate had returned, and a couple of girls had already approached us. They were in town for a bachelorette party and were already fairly drunk. The redhead—I think her name was Bridget—was hanging off my arm and taking advantage of every possible opportunity to touch me or press herself against me. I probably could've taken her home right then, but I wasn't quite ready to leave yet.

I edged up to the bar and caught blondie's attention. "Hey, beautiful," I said, giving her my most charming smile. "Can I have two more, please?"

"You certainly don't waste any time." Her eyes moved to the redhead who was clinging to me, and I had a feeling she wasn't talking about the drinks.

"Can't seem to keep them away." I leaned across the bar and whispered in her ear. "But if you want to get in on this action, all you have to do is say the word, sweetheart."

"Asshole," she scoffed, pushing my shots toward me.

"Yup, that's me." I didn't bother disagreeing with her. It was the truth, after all, but my resolve was faltering. Even though I knew she was right, it stung more than I thought it would to hear it drop from those pretty lips. I threw down some money for the drinks, plus a generous tip, but she had already moved on to help the next person.

I turned to the redhead, pulling her against me suggestively. "Are you ready to get out of here?"

"Absolutely," she purred, trailing her finger along the waistband of my jeans.

"Good, let's go to your place. Lead the way."

My night-vision goggles illuminate the desert landscape in a soft green glow, and the headlights of the Humvee cast odd shadows along the edges of the desolate dirt road. We almost always travel at night, so this is the Iraq that we're used to. The cloak of darkness offers a thin veil of protection that we don't have under the blazing sun. The night air seems cool, despite the fact that it's almost one hundred degrees and the scorching heat from earlier in the day radiates from the sand.

Cramped inside the armored vehicles and drenched in sweat, we pray for the slightest breeze that we know will never come. My muscles are tense from the burden of wearing my heavy armor for days on end, but it's far better than the alternative of being vulnerable and unprotected. Often times, our protective gear is the difference between life and death.

I can see the small village in the distance, only a few hundred yards away, and I'm anxious to get there because we'll finally have a chance to rest. The Humvee navigates over the rough terrain and with each rock and pothole that we hit, the rattle of grenades, bullets and weaponry fills the small space.

It's a comforting sound, in a way... a constant reassurance of the firepower that we're armed with in case of an attack.

I look through the dirty bulletproof window, scanning the area ahead of us and to our flank, searching for anything out of the ordinary. No one has traveled this route in several weeks, giving insurgents plenty of time to camouflage roadside bombs along our path. Spotting something abnormal ahead of time gives us a greater chance of survival.

These roads have an eerie feeling and at night, in these desolate areas, there aren't always clues or signs of trouble ahead. All you have is your gut telling you that something's not right, and right now my gut is screaming at me that something is wrong.

Before I have a chance to stop the convoy, there's a blinding flash and then a deafening sound as our Humvee lurches into the air.

I was jolted awake by my own thundering heartbeat. Covered in a cold sweat, I glanced around at my surroundings and found that I was lying in my bed, safe at home. I tried to steady my breathing and regain my bearings, reminding myself of where I was and how I got there.

As soon as the redhead and I were, well... finished... I'd made an excuse to leave and walked myself back home where I'd eventually fallen asleep. I didn't do relationships, and I didn't stick around for breakfast. Never anything more than a quick fuck.

Normally a night of drinking and sex led to a peaceful night's sleep, free from the nightmares that had been plaguing me since I returned home from Iraq. But for some reason, tonight they found me.

It was always bits and pieces of the same dream. Parts of a night that I couldn't escape. Almost every time I fell asleep I had to relive it—the sights, the sounds, the smells—it was as real as the night it happened.

The sun was only just beginning to rise, but I knew I wouldn't be able to go back to sleep. Once my heart had slowed to a somewhat-normal rhythm, I got out of bed and dressed to go for a run.

In the light of day, I could hide from my ghosts, but the reprieve was only temporary. As soon as I drifted to sleep, they would chase me down again.

chapter four

Olivia

I let myself sleep in after my long night at the bar. I'd waitressed during the dinner shift, which hadn't been as bad as I thought it would be. Sarah had been right about it all coming back, and Melanie, the waitress who'd been assigned to train me, had been friendly and extremely helpful. After a while, she realized that I didn't need much training, and she threw me behind the bar to learn the ropes.

It was easy at first. The bar was slow during dinner and mostly consisted of making drink orders for the waitresses; however, once the tables were cleared and the place went from "restaurant" to "bar", it got a little hectic. It took me a while to get the hang of things and find my rhythm, but once I did, it went smoother than I thought it would.

The Seaside had a great atmosphere, and everyone was really welcoming and fun to be around. Staying busy meant the night flew by, and I went home with a nice stack of tips. All in all, I liked working there.

Of course, working at the bar also meant that I would have no choice but to deal with idiots and assholes on a daily basis, like the jerk from the beach. Melanie told me that he was a regular who never went home from the bar alone and never with the same girl twice. None of that came as a shock to me. In fact, it only confirmed my assumptions about him. Melanie also mentioned that he typically steered clear of the girls who worked there, and she was shocked to see him direct his "attention" toward me. Whatever. I wasn't about to analyze the situation. I had no idea what kind of game he was playing, but I did know that was all it was… and I didn't want any part of it.

I was meeting my old roommate and friend, Nora Montgomery, for lunch, and I couldn't wait to finally see her. Of course, I'd called her while I was on my way down south, but she was a songwriter and had been in Nashville recording a new song. She'd only come back last night. I hadn't had a chance to fill her in on my whole situation. I knew she was eager to catch up and find out why I'd all of a sudden ditched my fiancé and my life in New York in order to move to a place that I'd only visited a couple of times. We certainly had a lot to talk about. With all the sudden changes that had occurred in my life, I was glad to have one relationship that I could count on.

Nora and her boyfriend, Jake, were living in her grandmother's house in Charleston. It was the house we'd stayed in when we came down here during our college breaks, and I couldn't imagine a more wonderful place to live. It was on Bay Street, right downtown, and was one of those great historic houses with big white columns and a front porch complete with rocking chairs. It looked like something out of a magazine.

As soon as I stepped out of my car, Nora came barreling down the front steps, her long brown hair flowing behind her as she threw her arms around me in a hug.

"Liv!" she cried out happily. "I can't believe you're here!"

"You have no idea how happy I am to see you!" I said, giving her a squeeze before releasing her and following her toward the house. "How are you?"

I had missed this girl. She was truly the sweetest and most genuine person I'd ever met, just as beautiful on the inside as she was on the outside. It was such a relief to see her, and I could feel my eyes welling with tears. I didn't realize until now just how desperate I was to have someone familiar to talk to.

"Never been better," she smiled. "But right now, it's your turn to spill. What the heck happened?"

Nora ushered me up the steps to the front porch, and we settled into the rocking chairs. I filled her in on the whole story, from beginning to end, while she listened with rapt attention. Her face filled with rage when I got to the part about catching Steven with another woman.

"Ugh! I always knew he was a slimeball. I *knew* it!" she when I was finished. "He got his claws into you early, like he knew that you were too good for him and he had to make sure no one else ever had a chance. Then, he was always dictating what you should wear and what classes you should take… God, I *hate* that guy!"

I couldn't help but smile at how caring she was. I'd always known that she wasn't a huge fan of Steven, but she kept it to herself because I told her that I was happy. I should have known that someone like Nora, who never disliked anyone without good reason, was right about him.

"You know what?" Nora continued. "I'm glad you're done with him. He'll get what's coming to him, and now you can finally find someone who really deserves you and treats you right. As hard as it is, you're so much better off!"

"I know," I nodded. "It didn't take me long to realize that I wasn't truly happy with him and with my life there. I never let myself admit it though, because I was too scared to start over. Now that I'm here… I'm actually excited for a new beginning. I can do whatever I want now, without worrying about accommodating someone else or disappointing them. My life is finally about *me*."

"I'm so proud of you, Liv," she said, squeezing my hand. "You're the strongest, bravest person I've ever known. There's no doubt in my mind that you will be just fine."

"Thanks, but I'm hardly brave—" I abruptly stopped talking when I caught the glimmer off of Nora's left hand. "Holy shit!" I grabbed her hand and held up the stunning diamond ring to inspect it. "You let me go on and on about that idiot Steven Chambers and didn't even tell me you're *engaged?*"

Nora grinned. "I was going to tell you! I was just waiting for the right time…"

"Details, now!" I squealed, barely able to contain my excitement. I was beyond thrilled for my friend. No one deserved happiness more than Nora.

She and Jake had been high school sweethearts. Nora's dad had never approved of them together, and orchestrated their breakup before Nora left for NYU. She nursed her broken heart all through college; never getting involved with anyone else and avoiding going back home where she would see him. After we graduated, she finally returned home to Beaufort, and it was clear that neither of them had ever moved on. When the truth about their breakup finally came out, they picked up where they'd left off in high school and had been living together happily ever since. Once Nora worked things out with her father, she was finally able to pursue her dream of being a songwriter. Now she was going to Nashville once a month to record her songs, and several had already been picked up by various artists. Jake had proposed to her last week before they left for the trip. It was easy to see just how happy she was. I hadn't met him yet, but considering all the great stuff that Nora had told me about him, I knew I would like him.

The Nora who was sitting next to me now was an entirely different person than the one I'd lived with for four years of school. She'd always been wonderful, but there had been a veil of sadness below the surface. Despite how well she hid it, it lingered underneath the smiles and the laughter. There wasn't even the slightest hint of it now. Everything about her radiated happiness, and she was practically glowing.

When she was finished telling me all the romantic details of the proposal, an old truck pulled into the driveway. That truck had definitely seen better days, and it certainly didn't fit in with the elegant surroundings here. But the way Nora's face lit up when she saw it, I might have thought it was the Publishers' Clearing House, arriving with a check for five million dollars.

"Oh, good! Jake's home," Nora said excitedly. "I was worried you wouldn't get a chance to meet him!"

Jake strolled up the stairs wearing the same happy smile as Nora. His eyes never left hers. If I didn't know better, I would have thought they'd been apart for weeks rather than mere hours. If they weren't so adorable, I would probably be nauseated by how in love they were.

"Hey, baby," Jake said, leaning down to greet Nora with a kiss. Then he turned to me with a smile and surprised me with a hug rather than a handshake. "You must be Olivia," he said. "Nora hasn't stopped talking about you since she heard you were moving here. It's good to finally meet you."

"You too," I smiled, liking him already. I turned Nora and said,

"Well, now it all makes sense… I wouldn't have been interested in any of the guys from school either if I had this waiting for me at home!"

They both laughed, and we all went inside the house to eat lunch. For the first time since arriving in Charleston, I didn't feel completely alone.

When I returned home, I saw Sadie in the yard with a guy I didn't recognize. The two of them were sitting in the grass on a checkered blanket having a picnic together. Amy hadn't mentioned a boyfriend, and it didn't sound like Sadie's dad was in the picture, but I wondered if it maybe that was him. As soon as she saw me, Sadie came running over.

"Oleeva!"

She still hadn't quite gotten the hang of my name yet and I couldn't help but smile. "What's up, girlie?"

"Me and Dee are having a tea party." She took my hand and dragged me over to where she was playing. "Will you come play with us?"

The guy she was with, "Dee," turned around when we approached, and my jaw dropped to the grass. There, holding a tiny pink teacup in his enormous hand, was the jerk from the beach. And the bar. His lips turned up in a smile when he saw me.

"This is my Uncle Dee," Sadie announced, patting him on the back affectionately.

He flashed me a cocky grin. "Well, isn't this a surprise. You must be my sister's new neighbor… Olivia, right?"

"Yeah," I choked out, still confused. "So, Dee… you're Amy's brother?"

"Actually we're twins, but I'm a whole three minutes older," he jokingly pointed out. "And it's Dex. Dex Porter."

"Olivia Mason." I shook his extended hand, in what was easily the most polite exchange we'd had so far.

"Are you joining in our tea party festivities?" Dex asked, gesturing to the blanket and tea set that he and Sadie had set up.

"Yes!" Sadie said, jumping up and down.

"Well, I can't say no to that," I smiled, sitting down while Sadie poured me a cup of "tea."

There was something about seeing a tough guy like Dex playing tea party with his little niece that made my heart melt. I knew it was probably an act, but I still couldn't help wondering if there was more to him than the crude jackass I'd previously encountered. Anyone who acted as sweet as he did with Sadie couldn't be all bad, right?

"It's good to know that there's at least one girl in the world who can hold your attention," I teased Dex while Sadie was busy handing out fake cucumber sandwiches.

"That's because she's my special girl. Ain't that right, Sadie?" Dex smiled the first genuine smile I'd ever seen, and I couldn't help but return it.

"Right!" Sadie giggled.

Just when you think you have someone all figured out, they turn around and surprise you.

Dex

Olivia. Of course, she had a beautiful name too. I couldn't believe that she had actually agreed to play tea party with us, and I was strangely excited about it. Sure, she was only doing it for Sadie, but it was good to know that I didn't repulse her so much that she couldn't stand to be near me. I made a mental note to buy my niece a new doll or an ice cream cone to reward her for getting Olivia to stay.

"More tea?" Sadie held up her pink plastic teapot to Olivia.

"Oh, yes please!" Olivia said, holding out her cup. "This tea is delicious, Sadie. I'm so glad you invited me to your party."

"Now we're friends, so you come to all my parties!" Sadie exclaimed.

"What about me, Sadie girl?" I said. "Am I invited to all your parties?"

"Umm… yes! Except when it's girls only, then no boys allowed. Not even you, Dee."

"Fair enough." I locked eyes with Olivia, holding her gaze until her cheeks flushed pink and she looked away. I liked making her blush—it was so unexpected coming from her. She seemed like such a tough girl, with her witty comebacks and confident take-no-prisoners attitude. Then there were times when she seemed almost shy. She was really sweet with Sadie, too. Kind of adorable, actually. I was a total sucker when it came to my niece, and anyone who made her smile and laugh the way that Olivia did automatically had my stamp of approval. She didn't pay much attention to me, but at one point when I was sipping my "tea"—which was really just a glass of fresh South

Carolina air—I was pretty sure I saw a smile directed at me. It vanished almost as quickly as it appeared, but I was glad that I could get a reaction from her that wasn't disgust.

I felt bad about the way I'd treated her during the first couple of times I saw her. The truth was, I didn't know how else to interact with women. Except for my sister, my mom, or Sadie. All other women were kept at arms-length because I didn't want to get close to them, or have them get close to me. Unless it was in the physical sense, of course. That was the extent of my female relationships. Anyone other than family or a one-nighter existed in a gray area that I didn't know how to navigate.

Now that I knew Olivia was Amy's neighbor, any hopes I might have had about her falling into the one-nighter category were long gone. Chances were that I was going to be seeing her a lot and spending time with her, which meant I could never get involved with her in the way that I wanted. I needed to figure out a way to be friends with her and put my obvious attraction aside. It was time for me to find my way around the gray area.

Every once in a while, I would catch Olivia looking at me. Not in a dreamy or admiring kind of way, it was more like she was studying me. Trying to solve a puzzle. I wasn't used to women looking at me like that. In my experience, all women looked at me the same way—like they expected or wanted something from me. None of them gave a damn about anything beneath the surface. Normally I liked to keep it that way, but Olivia… she looked at me like she wanted to get to know me, and a part of me wanted her to. That thought terrified me. If things were different, maybe she could. They weren't, though. If Olivia caught a glimpse of what was beneath the surface, it would only send her running.

Something beeped in Olivia's pocket, and she pulled out her cell phone and glanced at it.

"Yikes! It's already four o'clock. I have to get to work." She stood and ruffled Sadie's pigtails affectionately. "Let's do it again soon, okay?"

"Okay!" Sadie beamed up at her.

"See you guys later," she said, glancing quickly at me before turning toward her car.

I started packing up Sadie's tea set and was folding the blanket when I heard the familiar whine of an engine straining to start, followed by an aggravated voice.

"Ugh! Stupid piece of junk!"

I walked over to where Olivia was trying—and failing—to start her car. "What's wrong?"

"This stupid dinosaur of a car has apparently chosen this moment to curl up and die," she huffed, continuing to turn the key and further aggravate the engine.

"Well, I'm a mechanic. So, it's your lucky day," I said, stepping closer. "Mind if I take a look?"

"Be my guest," she said, popping the hood. "Although knowing my luck, it's probably beyond repair."

I examined the engine, and it didn't take long for me to figure out that the problem was a faulty ignition switch. "It's an easy fix," I assured her. "Amy will be back any minute to stay with Sadie, so how 'bout I give you a lift to work, then I'll swing by the garage and grab the part I need. She'll be good as new by the time you get home."

"Oh no, you don't have to do that," she said. "I can walk, it's not that far to the Seaside."

"No way am I going to let you walk. Come on, I thought we were finally becoming friends. This is what friends do."

"Hmm… I don't know about friends. That might be pushing it," she teased.

"Okay," I laughed. "Well then how 'bout you let me do it to make up for being such a dick to you before? Then we can call it even. I promise I don't have any ulterior motives other than friendship. What do you say?"

"Okay, fine," she conceded with a smile. "Thank you."

When Amy pulled into the driveway a couple of minutes later, Olivia and I climbed into my truck to make the short drive to the Seaside. Truthfully, I probably could've gotten her car going right then, but I was selfish and wanted a few minutes alone with her.

"Do you want me to swing by and pick you up when your shift is over?" I offered when we pulled into the restaurant parking lot.

"That's alright, I can catch a ride with one of the other waitresses." She stepped out of the truck and looked up at me with those gorgeous eyes of hers. "But thank you for all your help, Dex. I really appreciate it."

"Any time." I watched her walk across the parking lot, fixated on her smooth stride and the gentle sway of her hips as she moved. It wasn't until she disappeared inside that I finally tore my eyes away and drove off.

I ended up grabbing a few extra parts when I stopped by the shop. I only needed the new ignition switch to get the car running, but some of the other engine components were really old and worn so I figured I might as well replace them now and save Olivia a trip to the mechanic later on.

I couldn't remember the last time I had the desire to help a woman out and expect nothing in return. Okay, well maybe not nothing. I wanted to get to know her. She had so many different sides—feisty, sweet, shy, and funny—I wanted to know more. There was something about her that drew me in, and I didn't understand why. We couldn't be anything more than friends, yet I still wanted to be around her.

As I was finishing up the repairs on her car, Amy came down from her apartment with a beer in her hand. She was smirking in the way that warned me she was about to give me crap about something.

"Got a little crush on my new neighbor, Dex?" she teased, handing me the beer.

"Yeah, right…" I said, taking a long pull from the beer and swallowing. "You know I don't do the girlfriend thing. I'm just trying to be a Good Samaritan over here."

"I wouldn't blame you if you were interested in her. She seems really great, and in case you haven't noticed, she's drop dead gorgeous."

Oh, I had definitely noticed.

I shrugged. "She doesn't seem like the one-night-stand type, and that's all I'm good for."

"That's a load of crap, and you know it," Amy said, narrowing her eyes at me. "I wish you would let other people in, Dex. It's impossible not to love you when you do. You don't need to isolate yourself so much. You deserve to be happy."

It wasn't the first time we'd had a conversation like this. My sister knew me better than almost anyone else, she still didn't know everything. I deserved a lot of things, but happiness was definitely not one of them.

chapter five

Olivia

It was a busy night at the restaurant and before I knew it, my shift was over. I'd barely even looked up in five straight hours and was downright exhausted. All I wanted to do was take a shower and climb into bed. Unfortunately, the only waitress I felt comfortable enough to ask for a ride home was Melanie, and since she was staying late to work behind the bar, it looked like I would be walking.

I could have asked one of the other waitresses, but I'd barely been working there a week, and I didn't want to make a bad impression or put anyone out. I needed to take care of myself. It was bad enough that I had agreed to let Dex fix my car for me. I didn't need any more favors. Besides, it wasn't that long of a walk and it was a beautiful night.

I was on my way out the door when the hostess called out to me, stopping me in my tracks.

"Wait up, Olivia! Dex came by earlier to drop these off for you," she said, pressing my car keys into the palm of my hand. "You were really busy so he didn't want to bother you, but he asked me to make sure you got them."

"He did?" I said skeptically, examining the keys. "Um, thanks."

"No problem, see you later!" she said, returning to her post at the hostess stand.

I didn't fully understand why Dex had come all the way down here to bring me my keys until I walked outside and spotted my car in the parking lot. He couldn't have fixed it already… could he?

Climbing into the driver's seat, I pushed the key into the ignition and turned it cautiously. Sure enough, the engine hummed to life, sounding better than I'd ever heard it. I slumped back in disbelief. Dex had not only brought my car back from the dead, but he'd also gone to the trouble of bringing it here for me so that I would be able to get home. I couldn't believe it.

There was a piece of paper folded in half and propped up on the dashboard with my name was scribbled across the front in messy handwriting. When I opened it and read the note inside, I couldn't help but smile.

Are we friends yet? - D

Apparently, Dex *was* capable of being a nice guy. Maybe we could be friends after all. Just because I'd sworn off men didn't mean I couldn't be friends with one… even one as dangerously sexy as Dex Porter. It was possible for men and women to be friends without it turning into more, and Dex seemed like the type of guy who kept his friends and his "hookups" separate. Besides, I was in no position to be turning down friends of any kind.

I got the distinct feeling that there was more to him than met the eye. One minute he was this rude, arrogant player, and the next he was a sweet, devoted uncle who played tea party with his niece and went out of his way to help me. He was a total enigma. I was curious to find out which side of him was the real Dex and which was just an act.

The next morning was my first day of work at the aquarium and I was full of nervous energy. I'd never done anything like this before and was terrified that I would do something wrong or mess up. Part of me hoped that my job would be limited to basic tasks like cleaning the tanks and mopping the floors. It might be boring but at least it was something that I knew how to handle.

It was barely six o'clock when I walked through the doors of the rescue center, but I was met with a flurry of activity. There were half a dozen people crowded around one of the examination tables, and I wondered what all the excitement was about. One of them had on a shirt with the logo for the Department of Natural Resources, and I remembered Frank telling me that they were the ones who rescued the turtles and brought them in for treatment. Liz, the director of the program, saw me cowering in the doorway and ushered me over.

"Good morning, Olivia!" she said enthusiastically. "It looks like your first day is going to be an exciting one."

"What's going on?" I asked, peering around the crowd of people to try and catch a glimpse of what all the fuss was about.

"The rescue team just brought in a Loggerhead turtle that some fishermen found floating near Myrtle Beach. They arrived with her about thirty minutes ago, so we are going to have to do a full examination and assessment so we can figure out how to treat her. I hope you're ready to get to work!"

"Absolutely," I said, doing my best to keep my nerves under wrap. "I, uh… don't have much experience with this kind of thing, but if you tell me what you need me to do, I promise I'll do my best and try not to mess anything up."

"Don't worry," Liz smiled. "There's really no experience necessary for what you'll be doing. You're just going to be on hand to assist the vet, so as long as you follow their instructions, I promise you'll be just fine." She handed me a blue polo shirt with the rescue program logo on it. "Now go put this on, grab some rubber gloves, and then, we'll go meet this turtle."

I breathed a sigh of relief, feeling a whole lot better about what I was there to do. Wearing the staff uniform, I looked every bit the part of someone who knew what they were doing, and I was excited to get started.

The turtle they brought was a small female. She was covered in barnacles and lesions, and according to the vet, had a very low heart rate. I watched intently as they hooked her up to an IV that would administer fluids of antibiotics, vitamins and other medications and drew a small amount of blood for testing. They showed me how to clean and treat the wounds, which I did carefully and methodically until every lesion had been taken care of.

The turtle looked so sad and helpless on the metal table, tubes coming out of her from every direction. My heart ached for the poor thing and I wanted to do more to help. "What happens now?" I asked Liz.

"Now we wait until the tests come back," she explained. "We should have the results by later today, and once we know what's wrong with her, then we have a better idea of how to treat her."

"Are you sure there isn't anything else we can do?"

"You did a terrific job today." She gave my arm a reassuring squeeze. "The only thing left to do is give her a name. Will you pick one out for her?"

I thought about it for a couple of minutes and smiled. "How about Myrtle?"

"Myrtle the Turtle," Liz laughed. "I love it! I have a feeling you're going to fit right in."

I came home from the aquarium around noon, already sweating through my new shirt from the heat, and saw Amy loading up her car while Sadie ran around in her swim suit, complete with bright yellow water wings.

"Hey!" Amy greeted me. "I was hoping you'd be back before we left. We're heading to the beach. Want to join us?"

"I'd love to!" I was done with work for the day and a relaxing afternoon on the beach sounded absolutely perfect. I was eager to spend time with Amy and Sadie, too. I'd been so busy that I'd barely seen them for more than a few minutes here and there. "I'll go change. Just give me ten minutes."

I hurried inside and began digging through my clothes to try and find a bathing suit. I finally found one and when I held it up to look at it, I wondered if maybe the beach was a bad idea.

The bathing suit, like the rest of the clothes I'd brought with me, was from when I was a teenager and there wasn't much to it. It was a red string bikini, and though I wouldn't have hesitated to wear it when I was eighteen, it wasn't exactly something that I would have picked out now.

Throwing it on, I examined myself in the mirror. It wasn't exactly modest, and my cleavage was most definitely on display, but it wasn't as bad as I thought it would be. It was only going to be us girls anyway, and I'm sure they didn't care what I was wearing. Shrugging, I threw my denim shorts and a tee shirt on over it and met them outside.

Nate and I navigated our way through the groups of people on the beach until we caught site of Amy's colorful beach umbrella. I was surprised to see a third towel laid out next to theirs and I wondered who else was with them. My question was answered when Olivia stepped out of the ocean, and I practically choked on my own goddamn tongue.

She was dripping wet from swimming and her skimpy red bikini displayed every soft curve and flawless inch of her body. I couldn't peel my eyes away from her. It seemed like she was moving in slow motion. Naturally, I'd thought about what she looked like naked—I'm a guy, after all—but seeing her now, she put my imagination to shame. She was fucking perfect.

Friends, I reminded myself. *Just friends.*

Amy waved to us, and when Olivia finally looked our way, I could see the surprised look on her face. She definitely hadn't been expecting us.

"Olivia, this is Nate," Amy said, making introductions. "Nate, this is my new neighbor, Olivia. She just moved into town."

"Nice to meet you," Olivia said. "Thanks for letting me crash your beach day."

"The more the merrier!" Nate said, dropping our huge cooler

into the sand. "We brought enough food and beer for a small army, so I hope you're hungry."

Nate and Amy started unpacking the food, leaving Olivia and me standing there awkwardly.

"Hey," she said with a tentative smile. "Thank you so much for helping me with my car... you totally went out of your way for me, and I really appreciate it."

"Anytime. That's what friends do. Wait... we are friends now, right? Or do I have to hang around and wait for another mechanical emergency?"

"That won't be necessary," she laughed, and I loved the way it sounded when it was directed at me. "I think you've done more than enough to earn the 'friend' title."

As I was struggling to stay focused on her face and not at her amazing tits propped up in that sexy bikini, I noticed her eyes scanning over my shirtless torso. She bit her bottom lip, and my skin burned under her intense scrutiny. She was totally checking me out.

I could tell she was attracted to me. I wondered why she was so determined to keep her distance. Her eyes shifted up and met mine, her cheeks blushing pink when I caught her staring. She was cute when she was embarrassed. I decided that the gentlemanly thing to do would be to let her know I was checking her out, too. It was only fair.

"Nice suit," I grinned, keeping my tone as even as possible.

"It was all I had!" Her blush deepened and she crossed her arms in an attempt to cover herself, which only pushed her breasts up even more for my viewing pleasure. "I wasn't expecting such a crowd, and I didn't have time to stop and buy a new one..."

"Oh, I'm not complaining..." I said, letting my eyes wander from her head to her toes. "Trust me."

"Dex!" She smacked me playfully on the shoulder. "If we're

going to be friends, then you can't look at me like that."

"What!" I feigned innocence. "I'm just a *friend* admiring my *friend's* well-toned physique... nothing wrong with that."

"Okay, *friend*... just keep your eyes to yourself from now on," she laughed, turning to walk away.

"I will if you will. You know, I'm not a piece of meat, Olivia!" I called after her loudly, causing her to shoot me an adorably sassy look over her shoulder.

"More seashells!" Sadie demanded. "And a moat!"

Sadie and I were building sandcastles a little way down the beach from where Amy and Olivia were lounging on their towels. Nate had tried to help, but his skills hadn't been up to Sadie's standards, so she'd kicked him off the project. Now he was sitting next to us drinking a beer.

"Okay, boss," I told Sadie. "Why don't you go find some seashells, and I'll work on the moat?"

"Mmmkay!"

While I worked on digging a moat around the sandcastles, I saw a couple of girls walking in our direction. They looked like typical college girls, with their teeny-bikinis, fake tans and oversize sunglasses. It was normal for college students to flock down to the beach on the weekend, and it was easy to distinguish them from the rest of the crowd.

"Cute sandcastle," one of the girls said, stopping next to us.

"Thanks," I deadpanned, not bothering to look up at them.

"Looks like you're really good with your hands," she continued, smirking at her friend as if she was so proud of herself for coming up with such a clever line. "Maybe we could… help you out somehow?"

Considering the way she was shamelessly eye-fucking me, this girl was ready to drop her panties for me right there in front of the whole beach, my niece included. Unfortunately for her, I didn't go for this shit. At least, not around Sadie.

"We're all set." I dismissed them coldly and focused my attention on Sadie, who had returned with a bucket full of shells.

"Whatever," the girl said, flipping her hair and stomping off with her friend.

Nate laughed. "Wow, Dex, I think that's the first time I've ever seen you turn down a willing female."

"Way too easy," I said. "This place is flooded with easy college chicks looking for a good time. They'll give it up to anyone with a six-pack." It was true. Normally I was willing to provide them with a good time, but I wasn't feeling it.

"It's not just the girls…" Nate said with a frown, gesturing to Amy and Olivia. They'd been joined by a couple of meathead frat boys who were standing over their beach chairs, looking down at them with cheesy smiles plastered on their faces, clearly trying to flirt with them. "Who are those assholes?" He looked over at Sadie and corrected himself. "Uh… I mean those guys."

"I don't know. Who cares?" I shrugged casually, while simultaneously fighting the urge to run over there and show those idiots that they were barking up the wrong damn tree. Of course it bothered me, but I didn't know why Nate was worried about it. Did he have a thing for Olivia? The idea of that bothered me even more than Douchebag #1 and Douchebag#2 over there chatting them up.

"Sure you don't care. That's why you keep glancing that way with a murderous look in your eye like you want to kick someone's ass." He glanced at Sadie. "Uh, I mean butt."

I shook my head at him. At this rate, Sadie was going to be using curse words by age five.

"Why don't you ask Olivia out?" Nate said.

"Because, we're just friends," I explained. "Amy's the one I'm worried about. She has a tendency to attract assholes." That part was true. Amy had always managed to end up with idiots, the biggest one of all being the guy who got her pregnant and then ran off before Sadie was even born. Naturally, I found him and beat the shit out of him, but it didn't come close to making up for what he did.

Nate was watching Amy, his eyebrows furrowed and his expression conflicted. "I'm going to grab another beer. Want one?"

"Nah, I'm good." I watched as Nate walked over to where they were gathered, immediately scaring off the two goons who were flirting with them. As soon as they were gone, I relaxed and got back to digging a moat for Sadie's castle.

chapter six

Olivia

I couldn't help but laugh at the macho-man expression on Nate's face when he stalked over to scare off the two guys who were trying to flirt with Amy and me. It worked, though, and I was grateful to him for getting rid of them for us. They were totally harmless but didn't seem to sense our disinterest. They kept chatting about sports and college exams while Amy and I looked back and forth at each other like, *how do we make them leave?!*

There was something. . .tender. . .about the way that Nate looked at Amy, and I wondered if there were anything going on between them. He had his eyes glued to her the whole time the guys were talking to us, and I noticed that Amy kept glancing in his direction. It certainly seemed like there was history there.

"No, there's nothing going on with Nate and me," Amy said when I asked her about it. "He's just protective because I'm Dex's sister. I used to think that there might be something more between us, but then he was dating someone else, and nothing ever happened."

"Was?" I asked. "So, they're not together anymore?"

"No, Dex mentioned that they broke up a couple weeks ago."

"Well, maybe now something will happen with you two."

"I don't think so," she sighed. "Nate is really sweet and funny—and cute—but we'll never be more than friends. He and Dex are so close that he probably just thinks of me as a sister."

"Those looks definitely didn't seem brotherly," I pointed out. "But if not Nate, is there anyone else? I don't suppose those two chumps from earlier are your type?"

"Definitely not!" she laughed. "My 'relationships'—if you can even call them that—typically only last a couple of dates. As soon as the guy figures out that I have a kid, they tend to bolt." She shrugged, brushing it off even though it was obviously hard for her.

"What about Sadie's dad?" I asked tentatively. "Is he around at all?"

"Nope, he was out of the picture before she was born. I met him in college, and we'd only been dating for a few months when I found out I was pregnant. He totally freaked out, said he couldn't handle it, and that was it. Haven't heard from him since, which is fine by me. We're better off without him."

I couldn't help but draw comparisons between my mom and Amy. They'd both been deserted by the father of their children and left to be a single mother. I knew how hard it was, and I respected Amy tremendously for it.

"What about you?" Amy said, steering the conversation towards me. "Is there anyone in your life?"

"Not anymore," I said. "I moved down here after I caught my fiancé cheating on me."

"Wow. Men are scum," she said simply.

"Yes, they are! Which is exactly why I've sworn them off. They bring nothing but trouble."

"So, I guess it's pointless to try to get you together with my brother, then?"

I laughed. "Hate to break it to you, but Dex and I will only ever be friends." I glanced briefly in his direction, resisting the urge to stare. "Besides, he doesn't seem like someone who's interested in any relationship that lasts longer than twelve hours... no offense."

"None taken," she replied. "Believe it or not, he wasn't always like this. In high school, he was so focused on joining the Marines that he didn't really have time for anything else. He enlisted right after he graduated, started boot camp, and went overseas to Iraq. He was... different... when he came back. Iraq changed him."

"How so?" I'd seen Dex's tattoos but never put it together that he had been in the military.

"He's just... darker, in a way, and more withdrawn than he used to be. Dex was always the life of the party, you know? Sweet and funny, the kind of person who got along with everyone and who everyone loved to be around." She glanced over at him, watching him and Sadie play together in the sand. "In a lot of ways he still is, but then there are times when he's so tense and gets so angry that he distances himself from everyone."

I'd see glimpses of that pain and darkness in him; brief flashes of anger behind his soft brown eyes and cocky smile. He hid it well, though, and I wondered if that was why he sometimes acted the way that he did.

"He devoted his life to being a Marine," Amy continued. "It was all he ever wanted. Despite everything he went through in Iraq, I know that he would still be over there if he could."

"Why can't he?"

"He lost partial hearing in one ear when an IED exploded right near him. It left him with a pretty bad head injury, too, but Dex still managed to reach three men from his unit and pull them to safety." A faint, proud smile touched her lips. "He saved their lives. Earned a Silver Star, one of the highest awards you can get. Unfortunately, he couldn't continue to serve with the damage to his hearing, so he was honorably discharged."

"Wow." I was at a total loss for words. Learning about his past made me see him in a whole new light. What he'd done, and what he'd been through… it was incredible.

"He doesn't talk about it, though. We only know what was written in the official report, which didn't tell us much. We have no idea what else happened out there, or what he had to live through. We've tried—my parents and I—to get him to open up, but he plays it off like he's fine. He's not big on letting people in, and I worry that if he keeps it all inside, it will eventually destroy him."

We sat there in silence for a few minutes until Nate came back over and started chatting with Amy. Reaching into my beach bag, I pulled out my camera and began taking a few pictures. I found myself drifting towards Dex and Sadie, snapping photos of them laughing and digging in the sand at the edge of the water.

I couldn't help but examine Dex through the viewfinder. I zoomed in on his muscular back, taking particular notice of the tattoo that spanned his shoulders. Etched proudly in black, bold lettering were the words "SEMPER FIDELIS." The design traced on his forearm led to another prominent tattoo emblazoned on his bicep, with the Eagle, Globe and Anchor that symbolizes the Marine Corps. I'd seen his tattoos before, when I saw him running on the beach, but I hadn't looked closely or given much thought to it. It made sense now, though. Dex was a proud Marine.

When Sadie ran back to Amy, Dex came over and dropped down

in the sand next to me, sitting close but leaving enough space between us so we weren't touching.

"What happened to the herd of floozies that were following you around?" I teased him with a smile.

"Hopefully long gone," he muttered with annoyance. "I try to keep that shit away from Sadie. I don't want her to ever think badly of me, and I definitely don't want her to be around girls like that. No fucking way will I let her end up like one of them, with no self-respect and willing to spread her legs for anyone who gives her the slightest bit of attention."

"Obviously, I don't know you very well..." That was becoming increasingly evident. "... But one thing I do know is that Sadie thinks the world of you. It's easy to see how much she loves you and admires you." I shifted slightly, lessening the space between us. "I'm probably not the greatest influence, either, but I promise to be on my best behavior around her... and you definitely don't have to worry about me whoring it up!"

Dex turned to face me, his expression serious as his eyes dropped to mine. "She would be lucky to end up like you, Olivia."

His arm was brushing against me, warming my skin where we touched and sending flutters into my stomach. "How do you know that?" I asked quietly, keeping my eyes locked on his. "You don't even know me."

"I think I'm a pretty good judge of character," he said. "But you're right, I don't know you. I'd like to, though, and since we're friends now, you're required to tell me a little bit about yourself."

"What do you want to know?"

"For starters, how did you end up in Charleston?" he asked.

"I needed a fresh start," I said, without going into detail. "I came here with my friend a couple of times and always thought it would be a great place to live. So, here I am." I knew it wasn't much of an answer, but I wasn't quite ready to spill all the details. "What about you? Have you always lived here?"

"Born and raised," he answered. "Now, that wasn't so hard, was it? I feel like we're better friends already." He nudged me playfully, closing the remaining space between us. "From now on, whenever we see each other, we both reveal something new about ourselves. Deal?"

"Deal," I smiled.

We didn't leave the beach until early evening, staying long after most of the crowd had scattered. The day had turned out much better than I expected, and I'd be lying if I said that Olivia had nothing to do with it.

There was something about her that both captivated me and made me feel comfortable. There were no expectations or judgments with her, and it put me at ease. There had been a couple times during the day when I caught myself nearly revealing too much and letting my guard down. That never happened. Most of the time, I was trying to keep people from getting to know me, but for some reason with Olivia, I found myself *wanting* her to know me.

I wasn't sure how I felt about that.

What I did know was that I wasn't ready for the day to end.

"Anyone want to go grab some dinner?" I asked. "Maybe a drink?"

"Yeah, sounds good," Nate said.

"I'd love to but I have to get Sadie home," Amy replied. "Rain check!"

I looked at anxiously at Olivia, waiting for her answer even though she was probably going to say no. She didn't seem like the type who would want to go hang out at the bar with two guys.

"Sounds like fun," she said. "Count me in."

"Really?" I asked, taken by surprise.

"Sure," she said. "But I don't have my car with me, so one of you guys is going to have to give me a lift home."

"That can certainly be arranged," I told her, unable to contain my smile. This girl continued to astound me. It seemed like she always did the exact opposite of what I thought she would do, and it kept me on my toes. I was used to women being predictable, and Olivia was anything but.

I didn't think that Olivia would want to go to the Seaside on her day off, so we went to another place nearby instead. We sat down at the bar, and by the time our food arrived, we were already a couple drinks in and feeling pretty damn good.

After making a quick trip to the bathroom, I returned to find some random guy perched in my seat, talking to Olivia. He was leaning in way too close, flirting with her while she was trying to distance herself from him as much as possible. She looked uncomfortable, and based on the way he was swaying on the bar stool, he was already wasted. Nate was sitting on the other side, engrossed in a conversation with the guy next to him and completely oblivious to what was going on.

The second the drunk guy rested his disgusting hand on Olivia's thigh, I was in motion. The anger that I tried so hard to keep in check pulsed through me as I made my way across the bar to where they were seated.

"Move. Now," I demanded, coming to a halt inches away from him.

"Chill out, man. We're having a conversation," he slurred, still not moving his hand or getting up from the stool.

I edged closer, hands fisting at my sides as I glared down at him. "If you don't get your drunk ass out of that seat and move your fucking hand, I will rip it the fuck off," I snarled through gritted teeth.

"Jeez, calm down." He put both his hands up defensively, finally stumbling out of the seat and away from Olivia. "I'm outta here."

Relief spread across Olivia's face, and I returned to my seat, immediately tossing back the rest of my drink in an attempt to calm myself down.

"Thanks," she muttered. "I never know how to deal with guys like that. It's easier when I'm on the other side of the bar."

"Slimy drunk guys aren't your type, eh?" I gestured to the bartender for a refill. "And neither are college frat boys… sounds like you're awfully picky when it comes to the male sex," I joked, letting the alcohol soothe the anger buzzing underneath my skin.

"Not picky, just not interested," she clarified. "I've sworn of all men in general."

"Interesting," I said, studying her. "I'm not picking up a lesbo vibe from you, so who's the asshole who made you decide to do that? Ex-boyfriend?"

"Ex-fiancé, actually."

So Olivia had been engaged. It made sense, considering her apparent lack of interest in the opposite sex and why she worked so hard to pretend that she wasn't attracted to me, even though I knew she was. She didn't *want* to be attracted to me, or anyone. Obviously the breakup was still fresh, and I couldn't help wondering what had happened to leave her so jaded. It was clear that she didn't want to talk about it, though, so I didn't push it.

"Well, whoever he is, he sounds like a fuckin' dick."

"Pretty much," she giggled, sipping on her drink. I didn't know if it was the alcohol, or if she were just having a good time, but she actually seemed to be loosening up around me.

"You don't seem like the random hookup type, so how are you going to fulfill your... you know... needs?" My verbal filter had disappeared along with my third drink. I was playing with fire, but I couldn't seem to help myself. "And don't pretend that women can live without sex, because I'm not buying it. I know you chicks get horny, too."

"You certainly get right to the point, don't you?" Olivia laughed, her cheeks reddening. "Well, you know what they say... self-love is the best love." She winked.

I choked on my drink and nearly fell out of my damn seat. "Holy shit," I sputtered. "I think you might be the best friend I've ever had!"

Still howling with laughter, Olivia raised her glass. "To friendship!"

"Cheers." I clinked my glass against hers, still stunned. Friend or not, when the words "self-love" poured out of those perfect lips, my cock immediately stirred to life. Just the thought of Olivia touching herself, writhing and moaning as her fingers worked frantically to find release...

Fuck. Now I was hard.

Leaning toward her, I tilted my head and watched her eyes go wide as I moved intimately close. My warm breath tickled her ear as I whispered, "If you actually think that's better than the real thing, then your guy wasn't doing it right."

I heard her sharp intake of breath and felt a shudder run through her before I settled back in my seat. She jumped off her stool, mumbling something about needing to pee, before bolting in the direction of the restroom. I smiled in satisfaction at the realization that I might affect her as much as she affected me. I almost didn't notice when someone approached me and sat down in Olivia's empty seat.

"Hi, there," the women said, crossing her legs and making her already short dress ride up even more. Her lips turned up in a pleased smile as she locked her eyes on me and sipped from her straw suggestively. "Is this seat taken?"

"Uh, yeah," I said, gesturing toward the bathroom. "She'll be right—"

"It's all yours," Olivia cut in, appearing out of nowhere. "I was just leaving anyway." She offered the woman a warm smile and reached for her purse from on top of the bar.

"You're leaving?" I was confused. I didn't want her to think she had to leave. Was she upset? It's not like I asked this chick to sit down next to me, and I was happy to tell her to take a hike.

"I have to work early tomorrow morning so I should really get home," Olivia shrugged, throwing down some cash to pay for her drinks.

"Okay, I'll give you a ride home." I started to get up but Olivia stopped me.

"No, really, it's totally fine. Don't let me interrupt your night." She made a subtle gesture toward the woman seated next to me and flashed me a knowing smile. "Thanks for including me today. I had a great time. See you soon."

Before I could insist on driving her home, Nate magically reappeared and offered to take her. I struggled to come up with something to say to change her mind, but they were already walking out the door.

Discouraged, I slumped back in my seat. I felt like I was finally getting through to Olivia, but then she went and basically pushed me toward someone else. After that heated moment between us, I thought she might be at least a little bothered by it, but she didn't seem to care at all. Now she was riding home with Nate.

Fucking perfect.

What the fuck was I doing, anyway? I knew that Olivia and I could never be more than friends and yet I kept pushing for... what? I had to get my head on straight. Nothing was going to happen with her. Nothing *could* happen with her.

The girl next to me, on the other hand...

Within twenty minutes, she was sitting so close that more of her was on me than was in her seat. She pushed her chest out, begging me to look, while her hand continued to inch further up my thigh. If we didn't get out of here soon, I was pretty sure that she would end up rubbing my cock right here at the bar.

"Wanna go back to my place?" she hummed, her fingers wandering closer and closer to my junk while her leg slid against mine.

It should have been an easy answer, but I hesitated. She was attractive and would obviously be an easy fuck. I just couldn't get into it.

"It sure seems like you want to..." Her eyes shifted to the massive hard-on in my shorts.

My dick was definitely into it. But was I?

"I have a better idea." I stood up, adjusted myself, and towed her into the narrow hallway where the restrooms were. Checking to see that the coast was clear, I opened the door and pulled her inside with me. "Why wait?"

As soon as the door was closed and I clicked the lock into place, she was plastered against me, rubbing her willing body along the length of mine and plunging her tongue into my mouth. I let her kiss me for a few seconds before guiding her hand south. Taking the hint, she began stroking me through my shorts while I popped the button and lowered the zipper.

She dropped to her knees, a pleased smile curling at her lips when I pulled out my cock and offered it to her. She took it greedily, wrapping her lips around it and drawing it into her mouth. I let my hands drop to her hair, guiding her mouth and plunging myself deeper and deeper.

I closed my eyes and let my head fall back as she continued to suck, bringing me closer and closer to release. She moaned in pleasure, which I never understood because I wasn't even touching her, but the vibrations of her mouth felt good so I didn't give a shit. She knew exactly what she was doing, and I doubted that this was her first bathroom blowjob.

She began sucking more furiously, and I knew she expected me to finish. I should have been close, but I wasn't. My mind began to drift. As soon as my thoughts wandered to Olivia lying in bed, touching her perfect pussy as she cried out in pleasure, my cock began to jerk, and I exploded with a heavy groan.

chapter seven

Olivia

"You and Dex Porter, huh?" Melanie asked, waggling her eyebrows at me suggestively while we set tables for the dinner rush. "What's going on there?"

"Nothing's going on!" I insisted, unable to hide my frustration. "We're just friends. That's it."

"Are you sure about that? Dex isn't the type of guy to be *just* friends with a girl. Aside from the ones that he humps and dumps, the only girl I've ever seen him with is his sister." All of a sudden, she stopped setting the table and turned, studying me closely. "Now that I think about it, I haven't seen Dex come in here lately for his usual debauchery. In fact, the only time I've seen him in here is when he's with you or you're working."

"Trust me, we're just friends. He's pretty great once you get to know him." It was true. Ever since that day at the beach, we'd been hanging out a lot. At first, I hadn't been sure if a friendship with him was really possible. Especially after our intense moment at the bar when I'd managed to get so wrapped up in him that I hadn't been thinking clearly. It had taken a stern lecture to myself in the mirror of the bathroom and a splash of cold water on my face to get my head back on straight.

Since then, though, the "friend" boundary had been firmly in place. I was glad for that, because I actually had a lot of fun when I was with him. He brought me out of my shell and helped me loosen up.

"Yeah, he's also pretty gorgeous!" Melanie pointed out, unwilling to let it go. "And I hear he's un-freaking-believable in bed. It's no surprise that women clamber to get with him even when they know he doesn't give a damn about them."

Also true. It blew my mind how women were so desperate for a piece of him that they didn't care how he treated them. I used to think that Dex was an asshole for taking advantage of women, but I'd come to realize that they were using him just as much as he was using them.

"I don't understand why you only want to be friends with him," Melanie said. "If I were you, I would be all over that. Maybe you should send him in my direction… what I wouldn't give for one night with Dex Porter. Yum!"

"He's not a carnival ride, Melanie!" I hated the idea of people thinking he was only good for sex, because I got the sense that he thought that about himself sometimes, too. I also couldn't help the twinge of jealousy I felt at the thought of Melanie with Dex. Which was stupid, so I pushed it aside.

"Well, jeez, no need to get defensive, Olivia. I thought ya'll were just friends?"

I sighed in exasperation and got back to work.

Dex

It was Sunday, which meant it was time for our weekly family dinner at my parents' house. Amy, Sadie and I piled into the car and made the short drive across town to the house where we grew up. As usual, my mom and dad were out the door and in the driveway to greet us before we even stepped out of the car.

"You're here!" my mom said cheerfully, welcoming each of us with a hug and a kiss on the cheek. My dad was close behind, squeezing my shoulder affectionately as they led us inside.

Our parents always acted like they hadn't seen us in ages, despite the fact that we never went a week without spending time with them. It was just the way they were. Throughout our whole lives, they never made us feel anything less than loved, cherished and accepted. I knew how lucky we were to have them.

I often felt guilty that, even with parents as great as them, I'd turned out the way I had. They deserved to have a son who was as wonderful as they were, and that definitely wasn't me. I tried to keep them from seeing my dark side and did my best to act cheerful and happy when I was around them. The way that I used to be. But I couldn't always keep up the act, and when that happened I felt like a total disappointment. My parents were terrified when I first told them that I wanted to enlist in the Marines, but they supported me anyway. Through it all, they had been there for me. Now it was me who wasn't really here—a mere shell of the person I'd once been.

"How are you doing, son?" my dad asked. Every week he did the same thing; pulled me aside while my mom and Amy were busy in the kitchen, giving me an opportunity to open up to him. "Have you talked to anyone?"

Like it was that easy. I knew that my dad meant well, but I didn't know what he expected me to do. He certainly didn't want to hear that the only counseling I attended took place inside a chalk circle, and the treatment involved beating the shit out of people.

"Don't need to," I said, forcing a smile. "I'm great, Dad. Really."

He knew me well enough to see through the bullshit, but he never pushed. Instead, he reminded me that he was there for me when I was ready to talk. What he didn't realize was that my problem wasn't about being ready to talk about it… I just wasn't ready for my dad to hear it. I never wanted him to look at me the way I looked at myself in the mirror every day. With disappointment.

"So, who's this Olivia who you all keep talking about?" my mom asked us while we were seated around the dinner table.

"She moved into my downstairs apartment," Amy explained. "We've been spending a lot of time with her lately. She's really great, you'll like her."

"She's super nice," Sadie chimed in between spoonfuls of ice cream. "And pretty!"

"Is that right…?" My mom eyed me curiously, a smile tilting the corners of her mouth.

I gave her a warning look. "Don't even start with me, Mom. I like hanging out with her, but we're just friends. That's it. I don't do relationships."

My parents exchanged a glance that translated to them not believing a word I said.

"You will when the right woman comes along," my dad said. "Mark my words."

We were almost out the door after dinner when my mom waved

something in front of me. "I almost forgot! This came in the mail for you," she said, handing over an envelope addressed to me. "It's from Teddy's parents."

I looked at the return address, written in neat script, and my stomach immediately clenched into knots. I had a pretty good idea of what was written in that letter, and I wasn't sure I was strong enough to read it. I'd failed them. I'd failed Teddy. Opening it would mean facing their disappointment. I deserved to hear what they had to say, but not yet.

Shoving the envelope into my back pocket, I mumbled a quick goodbye to my parents and rushed out of the house.

The dark sky lights up in a fiery blaze, and our Humvee lurches into the air before finally coming to the ground with a deafening crash. Immediately I know that it's a roadside bomb. A pressure-plated IED that detonated when the vehicle in front of us drove over it.

"You okay?" I hear the driver yell to me.

I move my arms and legs carefully, assessing my condition before I answer. "I'm good."

Scrambling out of the vehicle, I carefully approach the bombed Humvee in front of us, which landed in a ditch off to the side of the road. The blast detonated right beneath it, and the damage is far more extensive than what we suffered. I have no idea what I'm going to find when I look inside, and I get no answer when I call out to the occupants.

It's so quiet that I can make out the static of the radio coming from the inside of the truck. A few moments pass, and it feels like an eternity before I hear them say that they're okay. Relief floods through me, and I start helping them climb out safely.

The driver is sitting there so still that if it weren't for his hands, I might think he was dead. His hands are shaking so fucking hard that he can't unscrew the lid of his water bottle to take a sip.

"You're okay?" I clarify.

His eyes shift up to meet mine, but he seems to look right through me. He nods yes. I want to tell him that this still isn't over. That we aren't safe yet and he needs to snap out of it, but all I can focus on are his shaky hands.

We begin to sweep the blast site, searching for any secondary IED's that might be waiting to inflict more hell and destruction upon us unless we find them. We finish clearing the scene and no additional IED's are detected. The entire convoy breathes a sigh of relief.

Then, all of a sudden, a second blast rips through the sky.

The sounds in my head rattled me awake as my heart continued to race. My eyes frantically searched my dark bedroom for signs of a threat, but there was nothing there. The only monsters that existed here were the ones in my fucked-up head.

chapter eight

Olivia

Summer was descending on Charleston. I finally felt like I'd settled into my new life. Although most of my days and nights were spent working either at the Seaside or the aquarium, I took advantage of the time that I had off. I would explore the city or wander around with my camera and take pictures. There was so much beauty to capture; it was a photographer's dream. Everything was new and different from what I was used to, and I enjoyed taking it all in. I loved everything about this beautiful, amazing, magical place. It gave me a feeling of home and comfort that I'd never felt before. It made me wonder why my mom would ever have chosen to leave.

I wasn't as lonely as I expected to be when I first arrived. Sure, there were times when I missed having someone to share my life with, but I was surrounded by so many great people that I didn't find myself alone very often. I was more content than I'd been in a really long time.

Most of my free time was spent with Amy, Dex and Nate... and of course Sadie. We had such fun together, always laughing and having a great time. It was a refreshing change from the uptight lifestyle I'd had with Steven in New York. I was so lucky to have met them, and I knew that they were a huge part of why I was so happy in my new life.

I never thought I would say it, but I even had a great time hanging out with just Dex. It turned out there was a lot more to him than a gorgeous face and perfectly chiseled body. He was goofy, caring, funny, and at times, fiercely protective. Despite the rather bumpy start to our friendship, it never felt weird when it was the two of us alone together. There was still an attraction buzzing beneath the surface, but it didn't affect our friendship. Being around Dex felt surprisingly... natural.

He often came into the restaurant while I was working, and I would spend time chatting with him when I wasn't busy with customers. Many nights we would cook dinner at Amy's house with her and Nate, and spend time playing with Sadie or watching old movies.

As wonderful as Dex was, there was definitely something dark beneath the surface. I saw flashes of it occasionally, as though there were a chink in the armor that he wore to shield that part of himself from everyone. Sometimes it was in his eyes, a dark shadow eclipsing his warm, chocolate irises. Other times, it was in his behavior, his temper igniting into full-blown rage at the slightest provocation. Most of the time, it was a subtle shift, as if he were sinking into himself and disappearing into his own head for several minutes before finally snapping out of it.

I never asked him about it or brought it up when it happened. I worried that it would only make him run away, and I didn't want that. I wanted him to trust me enough to open himself up, but I didn't want to force him. There were still plenty of things that I wasn't ready to share yet, either.

We continued our game of disclosing one new thing about ourselves each time we saw each other, but we stuck to easy things like *"I sing in the shower," (mine)* or *"I own a Backstreet Boys CD," (surprisingly, Dex.)* However, those seemingly insignificant truths were surprisingly revealing, and I felt like I was really getting to know him. I still hadn't told him the details of my breakup with Steven or anything about my family. It wasn't something that I liked to talk about, especially when it came to my family. I didn't want people to feel sorry for me or look at me with pity in their eyes. Whenever I told people about my mother dying or my father abandoning me, they began tiptoeing around me as though I were going to burst into tears every time they got a phone call from their own mom or mentioned family. I didn't want to be treated differently. Especially not by anyone here.

The only time I'd ever been deeply concerned about Dex was when he showed up at the beach one day with a black eye, a split lip and bruises on his ribs. I remembered seeing bruises on him the first time we met, and I worried that he was involved in something dangerous. When I asked him about it, he brushed it off, saying that it was the result of a "casual fight between friends," something he did every once in a while to "let off steam."

What the hell did that even mean?

Dex just laughed, wrapped his arm around my shoulder and told me not to worry about it. I started to protest, but Amy flashed me an understanding smile, suggesting that she'd already tried and failed to talk to him about it. So, I let it go.

I came home from one of my mornings at the aquarium to find Amy and Dex bickering in the driveway. Sometimes they would get into it over the most trivial things, the way that only siblings who really love each other could do. It was pretty amusing, actually. Especially when Dex would try to win an argument by using the fact that he was three minutes older than her, and therefore superior.

"Hey, guys, what's up?" I asked, climbing out of the car.

"I was trying to convince my sister to let me watch Sadie while she's away this weekend," Dex explained with a sideways scowl in her direction. "But apparently, she doesn't trust me enough to do it."

"That's totally not the reason," Amy said, rolling her eyes at him. "All I said was that having her for a whole day and night is a lot, and it might be better for Mom and Dad to do it."

"It's their anniversary, Amy. It's stupid to make them cancel their plans when I'm offering to help. Besides, you and I both know what goes on when they 'celebrate' their anniversary… do you really want to subject poor Sadie to that?" he said with a grimace.

"I don't know…"

"I can handle it, Sis. Sadie and I always have fun together. Don't we, Sadie-girl?" Dex hoisted her up onto his shoulders, making her squeal with laughter.

"The problem is that you have too much fun!" Amy said. "Sadie has you wrapped around her little finger, and you know it. Are you really going to be able to get her to bed on time or discipline her when she acts up?"

"I could help," I chimed in. They'd done so much for me since I'd been here, it was the least I could do. It was also really sweet how badly Dex wanted to help.

"No way, I can't ask you to do that," Amy protested, shaking her head.

"I don't mind at all. It will be fun," I assured her. "I'm not working this weekend, so chances are I'll be hanging around here with them anyway."

Amy finally agreed, making Dex and Sadie jump around the yard in excitement. He really was a terrific uncle, even if sometimes he acted like as much of a kid as she was.

Nate and I were at the gym getting an early workout in when I mentioned that I was watching Sadie while Amy was out of town, and therefore couldn't work at the shop over the weekend. Not that I normally did anyway.

"Where's Amy going?" Nate asked curiously, setting down the dumbbells between sets. "Who's she going with?"

"I don't know, she has some work thing," I said, unsure why he was so interested in my sister's plans.

"How did you end up with babysitting duty… don't your parent's usually take Sadie?"

"It's their anniversary tonight, so I offered."

"That was unusually considerate of you." He eyed me skeptically. "This act of kindness wouldn't have anything to do with the person who just so happens to live right below your sister, would it?"

I took a swig of water from my bottle and ignored his smug grin. "Olivia and I are just friends. You know that."

"Yeah, but in all the time I've known you, I've never once seen you be 'just friends' with a girl. So what's different?"

"I don't know," I shrugged. "Olivia's cool... she's fun, smart... and she's never afraid to say what she's really thinking. She doesn't pretend to give a shit about what I'm saying just so I'll spread her out on the mattress."

"You're not biding your time to eventually get with her?"

Without answering, I went back to lifting weights. I didn't know *what* the hell I was doing. As much as I liked being friends with Olivia, I didn't know how long I could hide my attraction to her. I wanted her.

"Yeah, that's what I thought," Nate smirked.

"I would only find a way to fuck it up if I did get with her, so no, I'm not," I clarified. "She's too good for a cheap fuck, and I don't do more than that."

"Maybe not, but the Dex Porter I know doesn't back down when things get tough... he fights for what he wants."

"Not anymore."

"Ooooh, look at that one!" Sadie said enthusiastically, pointing her tiny finger at one of the fish through the glass.

Olivia and I had decided to take Sadie to the aquarium for the afternoon. She was taking her time to examine everything. At the rate we were going, we'd likely be there all day. I didn't mind, though. Olivia was telling Sadie about the different varieties of fish and other creatures in the huge tank, and Sadie was loving every minute.

I carried her so that she could see better, and Olivia was huddled right next to us as we stood in front of the glass. Glancing to the side,

I saw an elderly woman watching us from a few feet away with an appreciative smile on her face.

"You have a beautiful family," she said, gesturing to Sadie and Olivia who were happily watching the fish and chatting quietly, completely absorbed in what was going on inside the tank.

I gave her a small smile and nodded, not bothering to correct her. Her words tugged at my heart and as I looked at the little girl in my arms and the gorgeous woman nestled at my side, I felt myself wishing that I could have that for real. For once, I wanted normal. I'd never given much thought to having a family. I'd always thought that the better part of my life would be devoted to the Marines, not retired at twenty-five and stumbling through whatever fragment of a life I had left. Having a family wasn't in the cards for me. I couldn't be responsible for anyone else, much less be there to protect them and guide them. I couldn't survive another failure.

A small group of people came up and stood next to us, and I put my free hand on Olivia's hip, gently shifting her in front of me to make room for them. I let my hand rest there, unable to move it even though I knew I should. She was close enough that my chest was scarcely brushing against her back, her magnetic pull drawing me in and charging the blood that pumped through my veins. My thumb found a slice of bare skin at the hem of her shirt and gently skimmed across it, sending a faint shiver through her. I held my breath, waiting for her to pull away from me or push my hand off, but she didn't move. Our bodies hovered as close to each other as possible without touching, connected only at the point where my thumb lingered on her skin. The air between us was thick and crackling with electricity as we stared at the tank in silence, mesmerized by the fluid motion and vibrant colors that passed by.

"Can we go see the turtles now?" Sadie's voice broke the trance, and I dropped my hand, taking a step back.

"Sure," Olivia replied, her voice quivering slightly as she put more space between us. "How would you like to meet Myrtle? She's the coolest and most special turtle in the whole world."

"Yes! I wanna meet Myrtle!" Sadie clapped her hands excitedly, dissolving any tension between us.

After a long day at the aquarium, we were all sufficiently exhausted by the time we got back to Amy's house. We ordered pizza and cozied up on the couch to watch Sadie's favorite movie, *The Little Mermaid.*

"That's a pretty bathing suit," Sadie said, pointing to Ariel on the screen. "Can I get one like that, Dee?"

"Not until you're twenty-one," I replied seriously, ignoring Olivia's eye-roll. "In fact, I'm not sure this movie is appropriate. Those shells she's wearing don't leave much to the imagination."

"Did you just admit to checking out a children's cartoon character?" Olivia asked quietly, peering at me in amusement from the other end of the couch.

"Um, it's hard not to notice," I whispered back. "And while I do appreciate a nice rack, I think that Ariel should be wearing a tasteful one-piece, or maybe a wet suit. This is supposed to be a children's movie!"

Olivia burst out laughing, shaking her head at me. "You're ridiculous."

Halfway through the movie, Olivia and Sadie both fell asleep, cuddled up together on the couch in a way that couldn't possibly be comfortable. Moving carefully so I wouldn't wake them, I picked

Sadie up and carried her into her bedroom, tucking her into bed and placing a kiss on her forehead.

I stood over Olivia and tried to decide whether or not to wake her so she could sleep comfortably in the guest room. I felt bad waking her up, so I cautiously reached underneath her and cradled her small frame in my arms, lifting her up and carrying her into the other bedroom.

Laying her down on the bed, I wondered briefly if I should change her clothes before thinking better of it. I covered her up with the blankets and brushed my hand along her smooth cheek, taking a brief moment to enjoy how perfectly peaceful she looked as she slept. I stood to leave and she grabbed my hand.

"Stay," she muttered sleepily.

I stood frozen in place, debating with myself about whether or not I should do it. There was a good chance I would have a nightmare, and I wasn't ready for Olivia to experience that or for the questions that would go along with it. On the other hand, I didn't want to pass up the chance to sleep next to her. As stupid as my cravings for her were, I couldn't fight them.

Sighing, I moved to the other side of the bed and pulled my shirt off before climbing into the bed and lying next to her. She automatically curled into my side, resting her head on my shoulder and draping her arm over my stomach. I wrapped my arm around her shoulders and pulled her close, breathing in the coconut smell of her shampoo. My skin burned from her soft touch and ached with the tickle of her warm breath. Being this close to her was perfect and comfortable and confusing. I wouldn't let myself worry about what might happen tomorrow or if it would change things between us. I wanted to enjoy it while it lasted.

I avoided sleep for as long as I could, and when I couldn't keep my eyes open any longer, I drifted off to sleep, hoping that no nightmares would find me.

chapter nine

Olivia

The first thing I noticed when I woke up in the morning was the temperature. It was warm. Much warmer than usual.

During the night, I had managed to completely wrap myself around Dex—my head nestled in the nook of his shoulder, my hand splayed across the bare ridges of his stomach, and my leg hitched over his. Mortified, I started to untangle my limbs from his but froze when Dex stirred briefly, his arm tightening around me and pulling me closer.

His touch caused something inside of me to stir, spreading warmth throughout my body, and for a moment I let myself snuggle into him, enjoying the safety and comfort he provided. It had been a really long time since I'd felt that. I considered staying in bed and going back to sleep, but that would mean dealing with the inevitable awkwardness of waking up together. Staying would only blur the lines between us even more, and I wasn't ready to face him just yet.

I'd been having a weak moment when I asked him to stay with

me last night, yielding to my deep-seated desire for closeness. It didn't help that I'd cuddled with him. I don't know what I'd been thinking, and I really hoped that Dex wouldn't give me a hard time about it. I wanted to blame it on the fact that I was used to sleeping next to someone, and it was simply an automatic reaction, but the truth was I hadn't been a cuddly sleeper with Steven. I normally preferred having my space, but being near Dex had a strange effect on me. I found myself gravitating toward him whenever he was around.

I wasn't in denial; I knew that I was attracted to him. I mean, who wouldn't be? But I also knew that I couldn't go there. A simple physical attraction, no matter how strong, was not enough to offset the countless reasons why it was a terrible idea. Unfortunately, it seemed that my body hadn't yet received the memo about us being just friends.

Once I was able to unravel myself from Dex's warmth, I carefully climbed out of bed and went into the kitchen to make some coffee. While it brewed, I sifted through the shelves and pulled out the various ingredients to make pancakes. Sadie woke up a few minutes later and joined me in the kitchen, eager to help out so we could surprise "Uncle Dee" with breakfast.

As we were setting the table and putting the finishing touches on breakfast, a sleepy-looking Dex emerged from the bedroom. He wore jeans with bare feet and was pulling a shirt over his head to cover up his naked torso. My cheeks flamed when he looked at me, and I quickly turned away to pour the coffee, avoiding his eyes.

"What's all this?" Dex said, gesturing to the heaping plates of pancakes, eggs and bacon that were spread out on the table.

"We made breakfast!" Sadie grabbed his hand and pulled him over.

"Wow, you sure did," he replied, sitting down at the table next to her. "It looks delicious."

Once we had devoured the breakfast and nothing was left—thanks to Dex's enormous appetite—I started clearing the table while Sadie relocated to the couch to watch her morning cartoons. As I went into the kitchen to begin cleaning up, Dex came up behind me, and I knew I couldn't avoid him any longer.

"I'm really sorry about last night," I blurted out clumsily. "I swear I didn't mean to get all cuddly like that, I think it was just an automatic reaction to sleeping next to someone… I couldn't help it and I really hope I didn't make things too awkward…"

Dex chuckled. "It's no big deal, Liv. Really. It was actually the best night's sleep I've had in a long time. You're more than welcome to cuddle with me anytime." He flashed me his trademark cocky smile and waggled his eyebrows provocatively, immediately putting me at ease.

I smacked his arm playfully, grateful to him for letting it go without a fuss. From now on I would be more careful, even when I was half asleep.

By noon, the temperature was approaching ninety degrees, and we were desperate for a way to cool off. Since the beach was likely to be swarmed with other people all looking to avoid the heat, Dex suggested that we go to the swimming hole on his parents' property. We would have it entirely to ourselves, and it was better for Sadie because there weren't any waves or currents to worry about.

I'd never seen anything quite like it. It was tucked away in the woods, completely obscured by the surrounding trees. Our own peaceful, private oasis. When Dex mentioned a swimming hole, I'd automatically pictured a small muddy pond, but I couldn't have been more wrong. It was fairly large and the water was clear, cool and refreshing. It was deep in the middle, but with shallows along the shore and a sandy bank where we could spread out our towels and sit down.

Dex carried Sadie on his broad shoulders, taking her into the deeper water where she could jump off his shoulders and swim the short distance over to me. Her cheerful giggles and excitement were contagious, leaving us all with matching megawatt smiles by the time we went back to the shore for a break.

I sat on my towel watching Sadie splash happily in the shallow water while Dex disappeared into the trees. A few minutes later, I heard him yell loudly and observed as he swung from a rope that was attached to a large tree branch, letting go of it at the last second and dropping into the water.

His head popped up a few seconds later, confident grin in place as he strode out of the water to where I was standing.

"Wanna try it, Liv?"

I gave it about a half second's thought before shaking my head. "No, thanks, I think I'd rather keep my feet on solid ground." Mainly because I was scared of heights.

"Oh, come on!" He held out his hand out to me. "You'll love it, I promise. I'll go even go with you, and you know I'll keep you safe."

His words resonated inside me, making me feel protected and cared for. His brown eyes were pleading for me to trust him, bursting with something so caring and genuine that I was defenseless against them.

"Okay," I said, grabbing his hand and pulling myself up. "Let's do this."

After making sure that Sadie was playing safely on the shore, Dex led me to a tree at the edge of the water and gave me a boost onto the first branch, following close behind and showing me where to go.

"You better not look at my ass," I warned.

"Can't make any promises."

We got to the small platform and Dex grabbed a hold of the rope, gripping it tightly above where it was knotted before motioning for me to climb onto his back.

"You're kidding me, right?" I glanced at the hard ground below us that would surely cause at least a few broken bones if we landed there instead of in the water. "What if you can't hold me and we fall before we're supposed to?"

"Don't be ridiculous, Liv. You weigh like a hundred and fifteen pounds soaking wet. Of course I can hold you." He took my hand and pulled me forward. "Now quit being a chicken shit and hop on."

I did as I was told, wrapping my arms and legs around his back so tightly that I was surprised he could still breathe. Even through the fear, my body responded to the feeling of our nearly-naked bodies pressing tightly together, and warmth flooded through me.

"You ready?" he said, craning his neck around to see me.

"Now or never," I nodded, clinging even more firmly against him.

I kept my eyes off the ground and focused on Dex as he drew the rope back and then launched off the platform. We were in the air for less than a second before he released his grip and we plunged into the water with a splash.

It was a total rush. There was something liberating about those seconds of free fall before hitting the surface of the water and cascading beneath it. As pitiful as it sounds, I'd never felt anything like that before because I rarely felt secure enough to drift out of my comfort zone. But Dex... he made me feel safe.

I came up from the water with a huge smile on my face. "Let's do that again."

Dex took me on the rope swing at least a half dozen more times before we finally called it a day. It was nearly time for dinner when we finally piled back into the car and made the short drive to Dex's parent's house. It was their weekly family dinner, and they had invited me along. As nervous as I was to meet them, I was eager see what they were like. They were such a close family, and that was an entirely new concept to me. I'd been close with my mom, of course, but it had only ever been the two of us. I'd never experienced the big, happy family that Dex and Amy seemed to have.

As soon as I walked through the door, the Porters—who insisted that I call them Paul and Emily—greeted me excitedly and made me feel welcome. They were warm and genuine, and I envied the fact that Dex and Amy had grown up in a family with so much love for each other. It was all I'd ever wanted. I hoped that they realized how lucky they were to have that. As I watched them joke around with each other and banter back and forth, I found myself wondering what my life would have been like if my dad had stuck around. Would we have been happy like they were, or would we only have been more miserable?

I hated myself for even thinking about it. I told myself that I'd let it go a long time ago, but every once in a while, those questions would pop into my head, reopening a door that I thought I'd closed a long time ago.

Before sitting down for dinner, I excused myself to use the bathroom so I could change out of my bathing suit and get cleaned up. As I made my way back, I overheard my name coming from the kitchen where Dex and his parents were talking, and paused briefly in the hallway to listen.

"Are you sure that you and Olivia are just friends?" Mr. Porter asked Dex. "Because from where I'm standing, it sure seems like there's more to it than that."

I heard Dex let out a deep breath. "We're close, that's all. I like being around her."

"She certainly seems lovely," Mrs. Porter chimed in. "You've never brought a girl around here before, so she must be awfully special. I can't help but notice how happy you are around her."

Her words sent butterflies into my stomach, and I couldn't stop the smile that formed on my lips. Dex mumbled something back too quietly for me to hear. I didn't feel right about eavesdropping on their private conversation any longer. I backtracked to the bathroom and walked into the kitchen with heavy footsteps so they would know I was coming.

My parents already loved Olivia. They hung onto her every word and kept casting approving glances in my direction and openly beaming when they caught me staring at her for longer than a few seconds. I couldn't help it. She was beautiful and funny, and sometimes I got caught up watching her. The way her blue eyes lit up when she laughed, the dimples that appeared on her cheeks if she smiled big enough, or how she bit down on her full bottom lip when she was nervous... it was hard *not* to look at her.

"Is your family around here?" my mom asked.

Olivia hesitated briefly, looking uncomfortable for the first time all night, before shaking her head. "I don't have any family. My dad left when I was three so my mom raised me, but she passed away in a car accident when I was eighteen. Her parents died when she was young and she was an only child, so now it's just me."

My mom gasped softly, guilt washing over her features as she placed a hand over Olivia's on the table. "My goodness, I'm sorry, honey. I didn't know."

"It's all right," Olivia smiled reassuringly. "It's been a long time now. I've gotten used to being on my own."

Her words were rehearsed and impassive, like she'd recited them a million times before, but I knew that there was pain on the other side of the walls she had built up around her. Hearing about all she'd been through—all on her own—my heart felt like it was being crushed inside my chest. I had the sudden urge to wrap my arms around her and never let her go, just so she would know that she wasn't alone. Instead, I settled my hand on her knee and gave it a comforting squeeze, needing her to know that I was there for her.

The conversation shifted to easier topics, and Amy arrived to join us after returning from her trip. While everyone chatted happily, I was stuck in my own head, unable to shake Olivia's words from earlier. I couldn't comprehend how she'd turned out to be as amazing, fun and cheerful as she was after the life she had. She'd been through so much... lost so much... and was still so strong. So much stronger than me. Yet another reason why I didn't deserve her.

"I should probably get Sadie home," Amy announced with a laugh as Sadie began to fall asleep at the table. "Do you want a ride home, Liv?"

"I can give you a ride home," I said a little too eagerly. "I mean... if you want to stay a little longer, you know, so you don't miss out on dessert." Man, I reeked of desperation. Even though we'd spent the last two days together, I really wanted to get a few minutes alone with her tonight. I ignored Amy's puzzled expression and tried to act nonchalant while I waited for Olivia's answer.

"Well, I can't say no to dessert," Olivia said, a smile playing at her lips.

"Okay, we'll probably see you tomorrow then," Amy replied, hugging both my parents and gently collecting Sadie from her chair without waking her. As she was leaving, she smirked at me and whispered in my ear, "I sure hope Mom actually has something for dessert."

Fortunately, my mom came through with a homemade apple pie, preventing me from looking like an even bigger jackass than I'd already managed. When we finally left for the night, the short drive to Olivia's house was quiet as I sorted out what I wanted to say.

I parked in her driveway, and before she had a chance to open the door to leave, I reached over and tucked her hand in mine, catching her off-guard.

"I'm sorry for everything you've had to go through, Liv."

"Thank you," she smiled weakly. "Sorry for springing it on you like that... I don't usually tell people. I don't want them to feel bad for me because of it. Not when there are so many people out there who have it way worse than I do, you know?"

Her compassion blew me away. I absentmindedly ran my thumb softly over hers in the hand I still held, drawing tiny circles on her delicate fingers.

"Maybe," I said, "but it couldn't have been easy for you. I can't begin to imagine what my life would be like if I didn't have my parents or my annoying twin sister around." My eyes shifted to her small hand enclosed in mine as I struggled with what to say. I cleared my throat, "Being in Iraq... so far away from home and everything familiar to me... there were times when the loneliness was suffocating. But I always knew that I had a home and a family to come back to. I'm not sure I would have made it through if I didn't."

The words poured out of my mouth before I realized what I was saying. I'd never spoken to her about my time in Iraq or the Marines. I didn't talk about it with anyone. Until now. Maybe it was because she'd shared a piece of her past with me that I'd felt the need to reciprocate, or maybe I simply needed her to know how much I admired her.

She looked down and took a deep breath, as if bracing herself for what she was about to say. "I've gotten used to being alone. Or, I thought I had anyway. The first couple months after my mom died were... really hard. Then I met Steven, my ex, and I let myself become dependent on him to make me feel whole. He became a fill-in for the family I didn't have. It made me ignore all the signs that he was wrong for me. I was so scared to be alone again that I let him turn me into someone that I wasn't." Her eyes shifted back up to mine and held them. "I thought I would be lonelier than ever starting over in a new place and being on my own, but for the first time everything feels... right."

"Well, I for one am really glad that you ended up here."

"Me, too."

It had been weeks since my last fight. If I didn't get one lined up soon, I was going to end up picking one with the next jackass who had the nerve to look at me funny. I'd been on edge ever since my parents handed me that letter, which now sat in my living room as a constant reminder of my failure. I was too much of a pussy to even open it and get what I deserved.

I was hanging out at Amy's with Nate and Olivia when I finally got a text that there was a fight for me that night. It was happening in an old commercial building about an hour away, so I would need to leave soon in order to make it there on time.

"You feel like going to a fight with me tonight?" I asked Nate. He usually came along, because even though I was an idiot most of the time, I knew it was better to have someone with me in case something actually happened and I got hurt.

"I can't. I uh…" He glanced over at Amy. "I have to work."

"What is this fight you're talking about?" Olivia asked.

It was a bad idea, but I couldn't help myself.

"Why don't you come with me and find out?"

chapter ten

Olivia

I had no idea what I was getting myself into.

After almost an hour of driving, Dex and I ended up in a deserted area surrounded by dark warehouses that appeared to be abandoned. A huge man stood at the entrance to the building, eyeing Dex questioningly as we approached.

"It's okay," Dex said to him. "She's with me."

He nodded, stepping aside and allowing us to enter. We were met with a huge crowd of people, and I felt completely out of place.

I'd agreed to this because I was worried about Dex and didn't want him to come alone, but I was also intrigued and wanted to see for myself what this whole thing was about. I'd been expecting some casual backyard fight between a few guys for fun, but this was... intense. It was organized, and I could tell that the people here took it very seriously. I couldn't believe something like this actually existed outside the movies.

Underneath a spotlight from the ceiling, there was a circle drawn on the floor that everyone gathered around. The air was stale and reeked of sweat, and I kept my head low, staying close to Dex as he pulled me through the intimidating crowd and escorted me to a raised platform that overlooked the big circle where the fight would take place. He boosted me on top of it and ordered me to stay put. Considering where I was and what was going on around me, I probably should have been terrified, but I couldn't help but feel safe when Dex was around. Even in a place like this. I knew that he would never put me in danger.

"You'll be safe up there, Liv. Whatever happens, do NOT move from that spot until I come back for you when the fight is over, okay?"

I nodded nervously, relieved to be out of the crazy crowd. Another guy who looked to be around Dex's age jumped up on the platform next to me.

"Keep an eye on her, Reece," Dex told him, his eyes threatening. "Keep her safe, and I'll make sure to put on a good show for you. If anything happens to her, my next fight will be with you."

"You got it, Porter." Reece offered Dex a quick handshake before gesturing toward the big circle. "You're on in five. You better get out there."

Dex peeled his shirt off and tossed it up to me, leaving him in only his old jeans and work boots. "Enjoy the show," he winked.

I was suddenly frightened as I watched him walk over to the circle and take his place inside it. The guy who stood across from him was huge—as tall as Dex, but easily about fifty pounds heavier—and the look on his face was chilling. He wasn't as toned or fit as Dex was, and I hoped that would work in Dex's favor.

The bell finally rang, echoing in the empty building and indicating the start of the fight. My eyes were glued to the ring, my stomach twisting with nervous energy. For a couple of seconds, they both circled the ring, studying each other and waiting to see who would make the first move. Dex's opponent moved first, swinging a fist into his side and making him stumble back a step. I expected Dex to retaliate, but he didn't. Three hard punches later, all landing on Dex, and he still hadn't done anything other than watch the other guy hit him.

For the next several minutes, Dex continued to get pummeled. I wasn't sure how much longer I could take it. His nose and lip were bleeding, and each time the other guy's fist connected with Dex's body, I cringed, growing more and more concerned about whether or not he would make it out of here in one piece.

Just when I thought the fight was over and Dex was beat, I saw something in his eyes shift, turning dark and dangerous. He straightened up, and all of a sudden, he sprang into action, his powerful body uncoiling with deadly force and lethal precision as he attacked his opponent.

The crowd went wild. The sound of their cheers filled every corner of the huge building. All I could focus on was Dex. He was covered in sweat, his muscles stretching and tensing as he unleashed himself against the other guy, never wavering or slowing down. He was powerful and intense, unlike anything I'd ever seen before.

I wasn't someone who condoned violence of any kind. I didn't watch wrestling, I wasn't into action movies, and I didn't think exchanging punches ever actually solved anything.

Yet, I couldn't help the excitement I felt when I watched Dex. It must have been some kind of automatic female reaction to seeing powerful, bare muscles covered in sweat, because I didn't have any other explanation for it. I'd had no idea what Dex was capable of. I couldn't decide if it was scary or sexy, but it was definitely turning me on.

Stupid hormones.

Dex won the fight easily, laying his opponent out completely within a few short minutes. After his victory was announced, he immediately came back over to me, cocky grin in place despite all the damage to his gorgeous face. Seeing it up close, I realized just how bad it was, and I hoped that we would stop on the way home to have a doctor take care of him. But knowing Dex, it didn't seem likely.

Dex collected his winnings from Reece. My jaw dropped when I saw the huge stack of cash he received. It had to amount to thousands of dollars, but they acted like it was an everyday thing. Did he make that much for every fight?

As I expected, Dex refused to see a doctor on the way home, instead opting to let me drive while he drank whiskey from a bottle he pulled out of the glove compartment. By the time we got to his house, nearly half the bottle was gone, and I hopped out of the truck to help him inside.

"Don't worry about me, Liv. I've had way worse than this," he mumbled. "Take my truck so you can get home, and I'll come by and get it in the morning."

"Can I at least help you take care of these?" I ran my finger over the tender areas of his face, making him wince. "You don't want them to scar…"

"Are you worried about my sexy face getting messed up?" he teased, but let me follow him inside.

I'd never been to Dex's house before. It was nothing like the bachelor pad I'd been expecting. It was simple and inviting, and right on the beach, close enough to hear the surf. I caught a glimpse of the view through the glass doors in the living room, and it was incredible.

Amy had explained to me that she and Dex had both inherited property from their grandparents. Amy chose to live in the house that she shared with me, and Dex lived in the beach house. It definitely seemed to me that Dex had gotten the better end of the deal.

I followed him into the bathroom, where he pulled out a first aid kid from underneath the sink. He sat patiently while I gently tended to him, never once taking his eyes off mine.

"Sorry, this is going to sting a little bit," I warned, dabbing his cuts with an alcohol swab as carefully as possible.

"I can take it," he said softly, unfazed by it.

"Why did you let him go after you like that?" I asked curiously as I applied ointment. "You're obviously a much better fighter than he is, so why take that beating when you didn't have to?"

"That kind of pain is nothing. I'm numb to it." There was sorrow in his eyes, but he covered it with a grin. "Besides, it makes for a better show if I let him think he has a chance. People don't want to watch a one-sided fight, and no one would ever want to go against me if I beat them easy every time."

"So, you're saying you always win?"

"Always," he smirked.

The sound of screaming woke me up. Through the haze of sleep, I looked around and realized I was still in Dex's living room. It had been really late by the time I got ready to leave, and I'd sat down on the couch for just a second. I must have fallen asleep.

I stood up on unsteady feet and began walking toward the front door to leave when I heard more screaming coming from Dex's bedroom. Rushing over, I pushed the door open and found Dex thrashing around on the mattress, his strangled cries filling the room. He was talking in his sleep, but his words were jumbled. All I could make out was *"Teddy, Teddy!"* He sounded absolutely terrified, and it broke my heart to see him in so much pain.

Moving to sit on the edge of his bed, I hesitantly reached out and grabbed his hand, whispering words that I hoped would soothe him. "Shh… it's okay, Dex. I'm here now. You're going to be okay…"

His body stilled, his cries beginning to ease. I lowered myself down next to him and started rubbing his back in a comforting rhythm, the same way that my mom used to calm me down during a nightmare. Sighing deeply, he pulled me in close and laid his head on my chest, his warm breath caressing my skin.

For a long time, I watched him, stroking his cheek gently until his breaths evened out and he fell back into a calm sleep. I wondered what was haunting his dreams and filling him with so much fear. He didn't talk much about his time overseas, but I knew a lot of people came back with PTSD. I hated the idea of Dex suffering that way. I held him protectively and continued to soothe him until I too drifted off to sleep.

The second blast is bigger, louder and closer. Too close. The sound is deafening as it throws me against the Humvee and pins me to the side while the waves of the explosion unfurl around me. I fall to the ground, disoriented. The only thing I can hear is the sharp ringing in my ear while the scene around me plays out like a silent film of terror.

I'm stuck in a daze for a moment, and then my body kicks into high gear. Maybe it's adrenaline or maybe it's just combat training, but it's something that happens in the most horrible situations. All I know is that my men are out there, and I need to get them to safety.

"The fucking sweep set off the secondary!" I shout, but I can barely hear my own voice over the ringing in my head.

I move toward the site of the explosion and see one of my men crawling through the black cloud of dust and smoke. It's Chase. His legs are mangled and his ashen face is twisted in pain. "One WIA, one WIA!" I yell into the radio as I drop to the ground beside him.

There's so much blood that I don't know where to begin. I rip a section of cloth from his uniform and tie it tightly at the base of his thigh, doing my best to stop the bleeding, but I need to get him to safety. I grab him below the shoulders and pull him back to the convoy.

"Tourniquet, we need a tourniquet!" I yell to the medic as he takes over. Chase is gesturing frantically to me, but I can't hear what he's saying. Finally I make out one word, "Teddy."

Jumping to my feet, I run back through the smoke and search the area for any sign of him. "Teddy! Where are you, Teddy?" I scream out at the top of my lungs. I can make out faint sounds now and through the chaos, I finally hear him.

"Dex!"

I try to move toward the sound of his voice, but I can only hear from one ear and the other one is useless. I can't pinpoint where it's coming from. Every time I think I'm getting close, I lose the sound completely.

"Hang in there, buddy, I'm coming!" I say, but I'm becoming more and more anxious as more time passes. Finally, I make out a shape a hundred yards away and run toward it. It's Teddy, but he's not moving.

I collapse next to him, grabbing his hand. "Teddy, look at me. Come on, man."

My eyes survey his injuries, my heart dropping when I see a large piece of shrapnel in his abdomen. It's bleeding too much, but I can't pull it out or he'll die in seconds.

His eyes flutter open and he looks up at me, full of fear.

"I need a medic! Get a fucking medic over here!" I scream desperately, tightening my hold on his hand and leaning toward him. "Hang in there, Teddy, you're gonna be fine. Just hang in there."

His grip on my hand is so weak, and his body is beginning to tremble as it goes into shock. I almost don't see it when he shakes his head slightly.

"Don't give me that bullshit, Teddy. Stay with me, okay? I need you, buddy, stay with me."

My words are left unanswered when his body stills, his hand going limp in mine, as the life drains from his eyes.

Out of the darkness I hear a voice that doesn't belong here.

"Shh… it's okay, Dex. I'm here now. You're going to be okay…"

I rolled over and opened my eyes to the blinding light of the sun through the window in my bedroom.

What the fuck?

I've never slept long enough for the sun to come through my window. My nightmares usually wake me up well before dawn, and I know I had one last night because I remember every vivid detail, so why didn't I wake up?

I sift through my memories from the night before and vaguely remember feeling a warm hand in mine. A voice… Olivia's voice… had pulled me back. But was it real, or was it just part of the dream?

I didn't want it to be real. I didn't want Olivia to ever see me like that, but when I saw the cool glass of water and bottle of pain reliever on my bed stand, I knew she had been here. She had tenderly held me and comforted me while I went back to sleep, chasing my demons and protecting me from myself.

She was gone now though, not that I could blame her. She was probably scared out of her damn mind.

"FUCK!" I screamed, knocking the water glass into the wall and shattering it. Olivia had witnessed the one thing in my life that I didn't want anyone to see.

Normally my nightmares tapered off after a big fight, especially if I drowned myself in whiskey afterwards, but lately, nothing had been able to stop them. I didn't know if it was because of the letter from Teddy's parents or because of the date on the calendar, but they had been getting worse with each passing day.

I didn't need to glance at the calendar to know what day it was. This day had been looming for months, and for the first time ever, it brought me pain.

July 11th.

Teddy's birthday.

I couldn't forget it if I tried. This would be the first time in more than twenty years that I didn't spend my best friend's birthday with him.

Now it was just another painful memory.

I threw on my sweats and sneakers and went for a run on the beach. I pushed my body to the limit, desperate for the adrenaline, not stopping until I could hardly breathe and my heart was pounding in my chest.

I reached into the back of my bookshelf, pulling out the picture frame that was hidden from view. It was a photo of Teddy and me on our last day of basic training, all decked out in our dress greens but still goofing around with huge smiles on our faces. We were so eager to get out there and fight for our country. There was no fear on the faces of the people in that photograph—a sure sign that we were brand new. We didn't have the hardened look of men who knew what they were walking into. We were two young Marines, eager to make our mark and be a part of something bigger, completely unaware of the kind of things we were about to face. We had no idea what war really meant. We should have been afraid.

If we had known… would we have done anything differently? If someone had told the people in that photograph about all the things they would be up giving up, would they have chosen a different path?

Deep down, I knew that, despite everything, we wouldn't have. Just like I knew that if it weren't for my busted eardrum, I would probably still be out there. It was who we were. Or at least, it used to be.

The person standing next to Teddy in that picture was fearless. He was brave, confident and determined. I was merely a fragment of that person now. I was weak and cowardly. If Teddy could see me now, he would be ashamed of what I'd become.

I grabbed a bottle of Jack and two shot glasses from the cabinet before heading out to my truck. It was time to go somewhere that, up until now, I'd been too scared to go to.

It was still and quiet. Rows of stark gray headstones protruded from the green grass, serving as a reminder of our immortality and the harsh reality of life. It was a surprisingly peaceful place, considering that it was where hundreds of loved ones were laid to rest.

The last time I'd been out here was for the funeral. Normally, I avoided the pain that it brought, preferring to keep myself numb, but for today I would let it have me. My best friend deserved to be mourned, and I deserved the pain.

I kneeled down in front of the headstone that read:

THEODORE C. ELLIS
US MARINE CORPS
Beloved son, brother and friend

A fresh bouquet of flowers had been placed in front of it, and I knew that I wasn't the only one thinking of him today. I pulled the shot glasses from my pocket, placing one of them on top of the headstone and filling it to the brim before pouring my own.

"Happy birthday, buddy…" I spoke to his grave, as though he could somehow hear me through it when I knew he never would. "We've never once spent a birthday apart, and I'm not about to break tradition. If you were still here, we'd probably be out fishing… or, more likely, drinking a lot of beer and pretending to fish. No matter what stupid shit we were doing, we always made it fun. Even during boot camp, which was supposed to be the most miserable time of our lives, you managed to put a smile on my face every single day."

Hanging my head, unable to face even his headstone, I choked out my next words. "I'm so sorry, Ted. I'm so fucking sorry. I hope that, wherever you are, you know that I would give anything to trade places with you. I wish it had been me instead."

I tipped back the shot, downing it easily before I turned and walked away.

chapter eleven

Olivia

Aside from the brief "I'm sorry" text that I received that morning, I hadn't heard anything from Dex since the night after the fight. We usually chatted back and forth all day, even when we were working, and I was worried about him. I got the feeling that whatever he was dealing with wasn't something that he had shared with anyone. He was so closed off, and it pained me to think that he was suffering alone.

I spent most of the dinner shift at the Seaside checking my phone incessantly, waiting for a response from him. It had been hours since I texted him to ask how he was doing, and if I didn't hear from him soon, I was going to stop by his house when I was done for the night.

After checking my messages for the one-thousandth time that night, I looked up to see Dex stumbling into the restaurant and taking a seat at the bar. There was a purple bruise on his jaw where he'd received a harsh blow during the fight the night before, but that wasn't the most shocking thing about his appearance.

I'd never seen Dex look anything less than gorgeous, but tonight he appeared… disheveled. His eyes were empty and unfeeling, and his usual confident smile had been replaced with a dark scowl. He hadn't registered me when he came in, and he didn't seem to notice or acknowledge anyone else around him either. There was no sign of his normally charming, funny self. Instead he quietly drank by himself in his own little world. He seemed… lost.

"Hey, Dex," I said, finally approaching him when I had a break in between tables. "Glad you're here. I was about ready to send out the search party."

"Well, no need. As you can see, I'm safe and sound…" His slurred words were dripping with sarcasm, and he barely even glimpsed at me when he spoke.

"Okay then…" I was at a loss for words. It was clear that he didn't want to talk to me, or anyone for that matter, so I figured I would give him some space while I finished my shift. "I have to close out these tables, and then I'll come back and sit with you."

He nodded tersely. I realized that was the only response I was going to get from him and reluctantly went back to work.

Once my section had finally cleared out for the night, I got started on cleaning up the wait station. One of our regulars approached me. Tony was a heavy drinker and a flirt, but he was mostly harmless.

"What's up, beautiful?" Tony said, aligning himself next to me at the counter.

"Not much Tony, working." I shifted my body away from his and busied myself with refilling the ketchup containers. "Can I get you something?"

He leaned in close enough that I could smell the booze on his breath and grinned. "You could get me your phone number."

"Nice try," I laughed humorlessly. "But I'm afraid that's not on the menu."

"Aw, come on..." He stepped closer and began running his finger lazily along the bare skin of my forearm.

"Tony, no..." I warned, lightly pushing his chest to halt him. Apparently, he'd had a few too many drinks for my usual method of laughing it off to be effective, so I would have to step it up a notch.

"She said no, so take your filthy fucking paws off her." Dex appeared behind me, glaring at Tony with a murderous look in his eyes.

"Hey, man, we're trying to have a conversation here," Tony argued, gripping my arm possessively.

He finally let go of me when Dex abruptly ripped him away and threw him against the wall, clutching fistfuls of his shirt as he stared down at him. "If you don't get the fuck out of here, I'm going to rip your goddamn arms off and shove them up your ass," he growled through clenched teeth.

"Dex, stop it!" I shouted anxiously, worried that he was going to seriously hurt him. I'd never seen Dex so angry. "What the hell is your problem?"

Dex turned to me and, registering my fear, released his hold on a very frightened Tony, letting him drop to the floor next to me.

"Whatever," Dex spat out dismissively. He spun around and left the restaurant, letting the door slam behind him.

I stood there frozen in place as I watched him exit, completely stunned by what happened. It was no secret that Dex had a temper, but what I'd just witnessed was something entirely different. He could always rein himself in, but this time his anger had total control.

"Hey, Mel, do you mind if I take off?" I needed to find Dex, whether he wanted to talk to me or not. Whatever he was going through, I couldn't let him do it alone.

"Sure, no problem," she said. "We're done here anyway."

"Thanks, I'll see you tomorrow!" I said, grabbing my purse from behind the bar and racing toward the exit.

I headed to the beach first. It was dark, but the moon lit up the sky, reflecting off the ocean's surface and casting enough light for me to see. I found Dex sitting in the sand, staring blankly toward the water.

"Mind if I sit?"

He nodded but didn't look up as I took a seat next to him, careful to leave some space between us so I wouldn't scare him off. For a few minutes we just sat there. The sounds of the gentle surf crashing onto the beach filled the silence between us.

"You know that you can talk to me, right?" I finally said.

"There's nothing to talk about."

"You probably don't think that I'll understand what you're going through, and maybe I won't... but I can still listen and be there for you, if you'll let me."

"You won't be there for me if I tell you," he muttered.

"Try me."

Dex took a deep breath, dragging his hands over his face. "Today is my buddy's birthday, or... it would be, anyway. For the first time ever, he's not here with me."

He hesitated, and I placed a comforting hand on his arm, silently encouraging him to keep going. I could see his internal struggle, and I knew how hard this was for him.

"Teddy and I were best friends since we were kids," he said. "We grew up together, joined the Marines together and went to Iraq together. It was what we'd always wanted to do. We were part of a special operations unit doing deep reconnaissance in unfriendly territory, and one night, all hell broke loose. We dealt with chaos every day over there, but this was different… it was one thing after another, and nothing seemed to go right for us.

"That night, our convoy was traveling along a deserted road when one of our trucks ran over an IED, detonating it on the spot. We all managed to get through it with only minor injuries, but while we were sweeping the area for additional devices, one of them went off. This time the explosion was right on top of us. I was on the outer edge of the impact zone so I didn't get it as bad, but it still tossed me around and scrambled my brain pretty good. My ears were ringing so fucking loud. I couldn't hear anything, but I knew I needed to find my guys and get them to safety."

Dex turned to me then, his eyes meeting mine for the first time since I sat down. "In war, especially in units like mine, we see this shit every damn day," he said softly. "Horror… cruelty… mayhem… it's normal for us. It's what we're trained for. There's no room for shock and emotion in war. It's our job to focus on getting through it and getting our men to safety.

"I made my way through the smoke, searching for my guys. The first two that I found had shrapnel injuries, they were bad but not life threatening. But the closer I got to where the bomb went off, the worse it got. I found my buddy Chase next, his legs blown to shit. As I carried him to the medic, he kept trying to tell me something but I could only hear out of one ear. When I realized he was saying 'Teddy', I forget every safety measure I was supposed to follow and ran straight into the blast zone. Teddy wasn't supposed to be out there, and all I could think about was getting to him."

He hung his head in his hands and his body trembled. "I couldn't fucking find him," he choked out. "He was calling for me, and I was running around in circles, wasting precious time because my own worthless body was failing me and my piece of shit ears weren't working right. When I finally found him and saw him lying there... his bloody, ruined body destroyed by shrapnel... it was too late. He knew it, too. I could tell. There's this 'look' that Marines talk about. It's a look that you see in the face of a dying man that conveys everything that needs to be said without a single word. That one look says that they're scared, it asks you to take care of their family, it tells you they love you and it begs you to never forget them. It's the worst fucking look you could ever see and that's what I saw in Teddy's eyes. I sat there helplessly and watched the life drain from him, all the while knowing that it was my fault. I should have gotten to him sooner. If the roles were reversed, Teddy would have been out searching for me as soon as that bomb went off. Injured or not, he wouldn't have let anything get in the way of finding me. I failed him."

Dex turned to me with tears running down his face, and only then did I realize that I was crying, too. Without saying a word, I wrapped my arms around him and held him until his body stopped shaking. My heart ached for him, for everything he'd been though, but I didn't say that I was sorry or tell him that it wasn't his fault, because I knew that wasn't what he wanted to hear. Right then, he needed someone to listen and be there for him, so that was what I was going to do.

I'm not sure how long we stayed like that, but I would have stayed there all night if that was what he needed. We eventually got up, and I reached for his hand, threading his fingers through mine as we walked off the beach.

I didn't want to leave Dex alone. Since he was still fairly drunk, I walked him home and helped him climb into bed. I lay next to him, neither one of us speaking a word, until I thought he had finally gone to sleep. As I shifted to climb off the bed, I felt a hand on my waist.

"Stay with me?" Dex asked, his eyes pleading with me. "Everything's better when you're around, Liv. You push the darkness away."

I nodded, pulling the covers down and climbing in next to him. Dex automatically pulled me close and wrapped his arms around me. The lines were starting to blur, but I didn't care. I snuggled in next to him and let him hold me, wanting to do anything I could to take his pain away.

We were still curled around each other when we woke up the next morning. I was relieved that Dex hadn't had any nightmares. He swept his fingers along my arm, a simple motion that warmed me all over to the point that I felt like I was going to combust.

"I'm sorry," he said quietly. "I don't usually let people see me like that, but it was a rough day."

I shifted my head from where it rested on his chest, meeting his eyes. "You don't have to apologize to me, Dex. Ever. You can always be real with me and talk to me about anything. No judgments."

"What I told you last night... I've never told anyone that before. Not even my family."

I nodded in understanding. "For a long time after my mom died, I never spoke to anyone about it. It was too painful. When I finally did, though, I felt like a weight had been lifted. I know it's not the same thing, but I do understand how hard it is to lose someone that you love. It's still hard for me to talk about my mom, and it still hurts, but it's easier when you have someone to share the burden with. So, for whatever it's worth... I'm glad you told me."

"Me, too," he said, tightening his arm around me. "Thank you… for being there for me."

"Always," I smiled, curling into him further.

Over the next few days, I was determined to put all that shit behind me. I felt better after talking to Olivia, even though it meant completely breaking down and unloading in front of her. I kept expecting her to look at me with sadness and pity, but she never did. When I looked at her, all I saw was understanding. She didn't push me or try to reassure me with empty condolences. She just listened.

I could feel something shifting inside me; in the way that I looked at her and the way I felt when she was around. I'd always been attracted to Olivia, but now it was something more. I could feel myself falling, and I didn't know how to stop or how much longer I could remain just friends and hide what I was feeling.

After our long, emotional night, Olivia and I had decided that we needed to take our minds off the misery and have a little fun. We made a plan to get our friends together and head into Charleston for a night out. Nate and Amy both came, as well as Olivia's friend Nora, her fiancé Jake, and their friends Susie and Ethan. Despite having just met Olivia's friends, they seemed like a cool group, and we all got along really well. By the time we were halfway through dinner—and a few drinks in—we were all laughing like we'd known each other for years.

I wasn't in the mood to lose control, so I stayed away from hard liquor and stuck to drinking beer for the night. By the time we got to the club, everyone else had a good buzz going, and even I felt pretty good. That was in mostly because of Olivia. She was being more affectionate toward me than usual—sitting close to me at the table, whispering in my ear, resting her hand on my thigh. I didn't know if it was because her feelings for me were also changing, or merely because she was drinking. Regardless of the reason, I couldn't help but sneak in the extra touches and flirtation… since she was actually flirting back for a change.

It was Friday night, so the club was packed by the time we got there. The girls immediately went out on the dance floor, dancing together in their own little circle and giggling with each other like teenagers. I loved seeing Olivia let loose. She looked so happy and carefree. With those bright blue eyes and dazzling smile, I couldn't take my eyes off her.

"How long have you and Olivia been together?" Jake asked me.

"We're not. I mean, not like that. We're just… friends."

"Well, you could have fooled me. Maybe you won't be 'just friends' for much longer," he said, tipping back the rest of his beer. "Now, if you'll excuse me… I gotta go join my girl on the dance floor."

Jake made his way through the crowd, coming up behind Nora and wrapping his arms around her waist. Her eyes lit up when she saw him, and he nuzzled his head into her neck, whispering something in her ear that made her smile even wider. They seemed so… happy. I wondered if I would ever have something like that—have someone to look at me like I was the greatest part of her day.

Ethan and Nate eventually joined them, and I was relieved that Nate had taken pity on Amy and was dancing with her. Only Olivia was left, and I could see a few guys nearby watching her like vultures, waiting to make their move.

Hell no.

I gulped down my beer and pushed off the bar, weaving through the crowd to get to Olivia. I came up behind her and gently placed my hands on her hips, careful to leave some space between us. I held her loosely at first but when she leaned into me, my grip tightened, and I pulled her close, enjoying her sweet, sexy smell.

She placed her delicate hands over mine, and I drew her in further, completely enveloped by her. The way she was moving her sexy little body against me had my dick stirring to life within seconds, but I couldn't help it. She felt so fucking good. With each swing of her hips and shake of her ass I was growing harder, and I knew she could feel me pressing into her. I expected her to move away in disgust, but instead my obvious arousal seemed to encourage her, making her dance more seductively and push her body even more firmly against mine.

I groaned into her ear, causing her to shiver slightly, and I felt like I might explode. She wanted me to want her. I could tell she was turned on by it, so I decided to let go and enjoy it. When I spun her around to face me, she didn't hesitate to drape her arms around my neck. Dropping my hands to the curve of her ass, I dragged her against me, pressing myself into her and letting her feel exactly how badly I wanted her. She let out a sexy moan, running her hands up my abs and over my chest, and I wasn't sure how much more I could handle. Everything about her drove me wild... Her smell, the way she touched me, her sexy giggle, the bead of sweat running down her neck that I wanted to lick from her skin... if there was even the slightest chance that she wanted me the way I wanted her, I knew I had to take it.

All of a sudden, she looked up at me, murmuring something about needing to get some fresh air before pulling away from me and turning to the exit. I thought she might be running away from me, but then she tossed a flirtatious smile over her shoulder, locking eyes with me as she walked away.

Was that an invitation?

Before bolting through the door after her, I paused. Now was the time to decide if I wanted to go for it, risking our friendship in the process. I'd never wanted anyone the way that I wanted her, but I didn't want to lose her as a friend. Despite my feelings for her, I wasn't sure I was ready to do the "boyfriend" thing. Could I really handle being there for her that the way she needed? The way she deserved? What if I failed her like I'd failed everyone else?

chapter twelve

Olivia

What the hell was I doing?

I knew it was a horrible idea to flash Dex that stupid "come hither" look, but let's face it... the alcohol was making me bold, and I wanted him. For once, I wasn't thinking about tomorrow, or the day after that, or the week after that. All I cared about was right now. Being pressed so close to him and feeling his thick arousal against me as he blatantly let me know how much he wanted me... It had put me in such a haze that I couldn't think clearly. All I could think about was the burn in my stomach that craved more.

Just when I thought Dex was going to leave me hanging, I felt him come up behind me and wrap his arms around me.

"You're driving me fucking crazy tonight, Liv... You know that?" He pressed his lips to my neck, and I couldn't contain the moan that escaped my throat. "You like that?"

All I could manage was a nod as he continued to move his mouth over me, licking and sucking my heated skin. His grip around me tightened as I melted into his body, overwhelmed with sensation and barely able to stand.

"I can't keep myself from touching you. You're so fucking perfect. You're gonna have to tell me when you want me to stop."

"Don't stop. Please," I begged. My body was screaming for his touch, and my brain was no longer in charge of the words pouring out of my mouth.

"Where do you want me to touch you?" His hands roamed down my ribs, grazing the sides of my breasts before settling on my hips. "Here?" He kissed a trail down my neck and over my shoulder, and I was desperate to feel his hands on me.

When his palm traveled back up my stomach and came close to my breast, I arched into his touch until his hand settled over it, his thumb teasing my hardened nipple through the fabric. I pressed my backside against his hardness and he growled, moving his other hand down to the top of my thigh and under the hem of my short dress, only inches away from where I needed him to be.

"How about here?" he whispered, tracing his fingers along the edge of my panties. "Do you need some attention here?"

"Yes," I nodded breathlessly.

His fingers finally met their mark, rubbing me through the thin silk of my panties. I moaned loudly, reaching one arm over my head to clasp him around the neck as I tilted my head back and pressed my lips against his throat.

"Fuck, Liv… You're so fucking wet." He reached underneath my panties, moving his clever fingers over my hot flesh. "I need to take you home so I can give this perfect pussy the attention that it needs." He dragged his hand up my side and cupped my breast with the other hand. "And I'm gonna kiss these amazing tits and suck on your nipple until you come."

By now my body was practically throbbing with the need for release. I wasn't sure I could wait until we got to his house, even though it was only a fifteen-minute drive. I rubbed my bottom against his hard length, but the feel of his arousal only turned me on even more.

Dex removed his hands from me, but before I could protest the loss, he turned me around to face him, crushing his mouth to mine. His tongue slipped through my parted lips and twined frantically with mine as he cupped my ass and lifted me up. My arms and legs automatically wrapped around him as he carried me over to his truck, never once separating his mouth from mine. He pushed my back against the side of the truck, his erection pressing perfectly against my center. Desperate for release, I gripped my legs tighter around him and rocked myself along his hard, perfect length, crying out loudly when he hit the right spot.

"We need to get out of here now," he groaned. "Or else I'm going to have to make you come right here, and I'd hate for someone to hear your sexy screams when I do." Throwing the door open, he put me in the passenger seat. "Wait here, baby. I'm going to go inside and tell them we're leaving. Don't move."

After grabbing Olivia's purse and hastily saying goodbye to everyone, I rushed back to my truck as fast as I possibly could—with a hard on—and peeled out of the parking lot. I was a little worried that in the few minutes I was inside Olivia might have changed her mind about what we were about to do, but she scooted across the seat and aligned herself right next to me. She started kissing my neck and reached into my lap, rubbing me through my jeans and nearly causing me to run off the road.

"God, you're killing me," I groaned, stomping the gas pedal down even further.

"You're so big... and hard," she giggled, looking up at me deviously as she continued to stroke my now rock-hard length.

"Well, my cock fucking loves you." I pressed my hand over hers in my lap, dragging it over every swollen inch and letting her feel what she did to me.

She leaned up, nibbling on my earlobe as she whispered in it. "Good, because I am *horny*," she giggled again.

Hearing those words tumble from her mouth made me want to pull over and bury myself inside her right there. Apparently she was drunker than I thought. If I were a better person I would probably put a stop to it, but I was way too far-gone for that. I needed her. Badly.

When we finally got to my house, I jumped out of the truck and practically carried her inside to my bedroom. My mouth found hers again, savoring the feel of her soft, perfect lips and the way her tongue tangled with mine. I was addicted to this mouth and couldn't wait to find out if the rest of her tasted just as sweet.

Olivia's hands found the hem of my shirt, pulling it over my head, and I wasted no time peeling that sexy little black dress off her body. Stepping back, I took a second to enjoy what was in front of me.

"You're so fucking beautiful, Olivia." She wore black, lacy panties and a matching bra that propped up those perfect tits that I was dying to put my mouth on. I had the sudden urge to pinch myself and make sure that this was real and not just the greatest dream I'd ever had.

I strode toward her, tangling my hand in her hair as I pulled her

mouth to mine and placed a gentle kiss on her full lips. She ran her hands down my chest and over my stomach, landing on the waistband of my jeans as she popped open the button and lowered the zipper. I kicked them off and backed her onto the bed, sinking her to the mattress and kneeling over her.

As I began kissing a trail down her chest, Olivia reached behind her and unclasped her bra, tossing it to the side and revealing the most flawless breasts I'd ever laid eyes on. I stared at them hungrily for a moment before covering them with my mouth and hand, kneading them and sucking her nipple into my mouth.

"Oh God…" she moaned, reaching into my boxers and wrapping her hand around my cock.

"Shit…" I hissed as her fist began stroking me up and down. "If you keep that up, I'm going to explode right now, baby."

"You feel so good, Dex. I want to feel you." She removed her hand and pulled me down on top of her. I settled between her thighs, and she wrapped her long legs around me so that my erection was right up against her pussy, pressing through the thin layers of clothing that separated us.

I rocked against her, agonizingly slowly, wanting her to feel every inch of me. "How's that feel, baby? Can you feel how much I want you?" She moaned, clasping her legs around me and clawing at my back as she tried to pull me impossibly closer.

"I want you inside me," she pleaded.

God, how long had I been dreaming of hearing those words fall from her lips? I'd never wanted anything more, and yet for some reason, it didn't seem right. At least, not now. She was drunk, and even though she said she wanted it now, I didn't want alcohol to factor into the decision. I wanted her to want me the same way I wanted her—no question, no hesitation, no doubt.

"Liv, I've never wanted anyone as much as I want you, and even though I would like nothing more than to bury myself inside you right now, I can't. Not now… not when you're drunk and there's a chance you might regret it later."

"Come on, Dex, since when has that ever stopped you?"

"Since it's you." I brushed the hair away from her face, dropping kisses along her neck and tilting my mouth to her ear. "You're different, Liv. When I finally do sink inside your willing body, I want you to feel everything. I want you to be completely aware of every touch… respond to every movement… remember every single second… and I want you to want it."

"I do want it," she whined. "I need you…"

"You have me, don't worry. I'm going to take good care of you, sweet Liv."

My lips traveled over her soft skin, kissing a path between her breasts and over her stomach as I slid down her body. I grabbed her panties and slipped them off slowly, tossing them to the side as I kneeled in front of her.

I ran my hands up her legs, parting them gently as I spread her in front of me. I kept my eyes locked on hers as I caressed the smooth skin of her inner thighs before finally dropping my mouth to her wet pussy. I teased her with my tongue, enjoying her taste as I pressed my lips against her and licked her sensitive flesh.

"Ah, yes…" she cried out, clutching the sheets in her hands and arching her body off the mattress.

Her response to me and the sexy sounds she made turned me on even more, and I nearly blew my load right then. When her loud moans turned into shameless begging, I finally went for it, licking and sucking until her body stilled and she cried out her release.

I hadn't finished devouring her yet. It wasn't until after her second orgasm, when Olivia was sated and tired, that I finally stopped. I refused to let her return the favor, covering her with the blankets and pressing a kiss to her forehead. Tonight was all about her and making her feel good. Despite my painful erection, that's how I wanted it. Instead, I opted for a shower, pumping my fist over my cock as I replayed the night in my head—the way she felt, the way she tasted, and the sounds she made—and came almost instantly.

Olivia was asleep when I returned to bed. I didn't want to wake her, so I crawled in beside her and pulled her close, amazed at how perfect it felt.

chapter thirteen

Olivia

I gathered up the clothes that had been strewn around Dex's bedroom and quickly threw them on. As nice as it had felt to wake up with Dex, when I thought back on the night before and reality set in, I automatically began to panic. I was humiliated about the way I'd thrown myself at him and needed to get out of there before he woke up.

With one last glance at Dex, his naked body tangled in the sheets and his handsome face so peaceful in sleep, I quietly snuck out of the bedroom. I crept around the living room, searching for my purse, and crashed into something, causing a loud noise to echo through the room.

"Shit!" I half-whispered, trying to get out the door as fast as possible.

"Liv?" Dex's voice called out from the bedroom, and I heard the springs of his mattress as he got up. "You okay, baby?"

I froze, briefly considering running out of the apartment at top speed so I wouldn't have to face him.

He appeared at the door wearing only his boxers and my idiotic heart immediately started racing at the sight of him.

"Where are you going?" His voice was heavy with sleep. "Come back to bed."

"I—I have to get to work," I stammered, gesturing toward the door.

"It's only six… Come back to bed and we can start the day off right." He grinned seductively and moved toward me. "Then we can grab some breakfast or something."

"I really need to get going," I muttered, backing toward the door. "Sorry about last night, I guess I was pretty drunk. How about we skip the awkwardness and pretend it never happened?"

"You want to pretend it never happened?" His expression was confused, and hurt.

"Yeah, it was a stupid mistake. No need to make a big deal of it." I tried to play it off but my words were forced, and I couldn't look him in the eye. "Besides, I thought random hookups were your specialty? Don't tell me you're getting sentimental on me?" I laughed awkwardly, ignoring the huge lump in the pit of my stomach.

Dex's face turned hard, his entire demeanor changing from hurt to angry. "If that's all it was, then fine."

"Friends?"

"Right. Friends," he hissed, turning and walking back to the bedroom, slamming the door behind him.

My stomach remained in knots during my shift at the aquarium and I felt... unsettled. Every time I remembered the pain I saw on Dex's face, I wanted to throw up.

I thought he'd be relieved with my decision to pretend it never happened. I'd let him off the hook. Dex was only interested in having a good time. If I let myself believe it could be more, he would only end up destroying me. Sure, he had seemed into it at the time, but he had also been drunk, and I'd been blatantly throwing myself at him. If I was going to salvage our friendship, I needed to play it off like it was no big deal... just sex. If I acted like a typical girl and got all attached and all "so what does this mean?", then it would only chase him away. He would end up being yet another person that I lost.

I couldn't handle losing Dex. I cared for him too much. I wanted him in my life. The feelings that were clouding my judgment were simply a result of the incredibly satisfying night we had, and I couldn't let that get in the way. Dex must have felt that on some level too, because—let's not forget—he turned me down! Dex, who had sex with any woman with a pulse, turned me down when I told him I wanted him inside me. The reminder made my cheeks redden with embarrassment. Forgetting the whole night was definitely the right decision.

So then why did Dex seem upset? He acted like he was genuinely hurt when I told him it was a mistake, but it wasn't as though he tried to correct me.

"You have me, don't worry... I'm going to take good care of you, sweet Liv."

His words from last night echoed in my head, making me question everything. Was it possible that Dex had real feelings for me? What would that even mean?

I couldn't get into a new relationship. I needed to gain my independence. Not to mention that I still practically had a tan line from my engagement ring! I had *just* gotten out of a long-term relationship with a man that I'd planned to marry. I couldn't consider starting another one so soon. What kind of person would that make me? It's not like I had feelings left for Steven—the guy was a cheating pig—but I wasn't someone who jumped from one relationship to the next.

One thing I did know was that I wasn't ready to put myself out there and risk getting hurt, and as amazing as Dex was, he had "heartbreak" written all over him. I couldn't handle that kind of pain. He had an endless supply of willing woman everywhere he went. How—and why—would he ever settle for just one? Dex didn't do relationships, and I didn't do random hookups. It was that simple.

"You have me."

I shook his words from my head. They only confused me more. It didn't help that the entire night kept replaying in my mind, over and over again. The words he'd whispered and the way he'd touched me... it got me so worked up that I had to step into the bathroom and splash cold water on my face to calm myself down. Somehow, I'd managed to have the best sex of my entire life without even *having* sex.

I wasn't sure if I would ever be able to look at him without thinking about last night and wanting him that way again. Part of me would always be wishing that we could be more. I knew I couldn't handle losing Dex's friendship, but could I handle *not* being with him?

My mind was running in circles. These were the times that I wished that my mother were still alive. She had always known the right thing to say to help me through my internal struggles. I missed having her to talk to. I missed having someone who would be there for me, and love me, no matter what. Through all my mistakes, and doubts, and fears. Through everything. There were times when I felt that I didn't have anyone, and I hated feeling so alone.

All the more reason to keep my friendships intact, I thought with a sigh, firming my resolve.

I'd crossed a line with Dex that I never intended to cross, and I needed to find a way back. I only hoped that our friendship wasn't beyond repair.

I stared at the crumbling plaster around the fist-size hole I'd punched in the wall after Olivia left. It was fitting, considering I felt like my entire life was crumbling around the edges, leaving a gaping hole that I couldn't seem to fill.

It had been a while since I took my anger out with this kind of destruction, but then again, I'd never experienced rejection like this before. It was an entirely new feeling for me, this combination of anger, hurt and confusion. I didn't know how to deal with it.

I threw on my gym shorts and sneakers, and went out to the beach for a run. Dealing with my emotions the only way that I knew how. Six miles later, my anger had taken a backseat but I was still as confused as ever.

I thought that Olivia and I were finally on the right track, finally where we were supposed to be. But now we were even farther away than before. If anything, it was like we'd gone backwards. One step forward and two steps back. It was a discouraging pattern that I didn't know how to break.

Since running and destroying things didn't seem to help, I decided that I needed a distraction. There was nothing like working on a car engine to occupy the mind, so I went into work early, beating everyone there, even Nate.

I was elbow-deep in the engine of old Dodge Charger when Nate came into the garage, whistling cheerfully and holding a cup of coffee.

"Getting an early start?" he asked.

"Couldn't sleep."

"Considering the way you and Olivia were dancing last night and then ran off on us, I'm not surprised you didn't sleep! Did you two finally hook up?"

I didn't bother lying about it, and he took my silence as confirmation.

"No shit, really?" he said, surprised. "It's about time. Good for you, bro."

I rolled out from under the car and sat up, grabbing a rag to wipe my hands off. "Don't get too excited. It was a mistake, according to Olivia. She wants to pretend it never happened."

"What about you? Did you think it was a mistake?"

"I didn't before, but now I don't know what the fuck to think," I shrugged. "I thought she was on the same page as me. Clearly, I was wrong."

"She's probably confused about the whole thing. I mean, she just got out of a relationship and totally uprooted her life. Maybe she's scared to make another big change. It's obvious that she has feelings for you though—anyone with eyes could see that. It's a matter of getting her to admit it... which won't be easy because she's determined to be on her own."

I considered what he was saying, and, surprisingly, he actually made a lot of sense. "When did you get so damn smart?"

"Some of that may have come from Amy," he grinned. "We've spent some time discussing your situation."

"Figures," I chuckled. My sister was notorious for sticking her nose where it didn't belong. She did have pretty good advice, though. I'd give her that.

"So the real question is how you feel about *her*… are you ready to give up all the casual sex and random woman, and be there for Olivia the way she would need you to be? Cause, if you can't do that, then the rest of this shit doesn't matter."

I hadn't thought about any other women in a long time, but that wasn't the part that I was worried about. The problem was whether or not I could get past my own problems and be the kind of man she needed.

"Olivia's different from anyone I've ever met. She makes me want to be different… better," I answered truthfully. "No one compares to her. I know that she deserves better than me, but the idea of her being with anyone else rips me apart. I would do anything for her."

"Well… there ya go. I guess you are ready."

"How do I get her to admit that she has feelings for me?"

"Give it time. She'll come around."

Sitting around and waiting was not my style. I was a man of action, making things happen. I'd been waiting my whole life for someone like Olivia. I couldn't just sit around and do nothing while she slipped through my fingers.

"What if you're wrong and she doesn't have feelings for me?" I asked.

"That's a risk you're going to have to take. Is it worth the risk?"

Without a doubt.

chapter fourteen

Olivia

It was busy at the bar that night. I went straight from waitressing the dinner shift to bartending for the remainder of the night. It was crowded for a weekday, but apparently that was the norm now that we had entered the hectic summer months. Despite my exhaustion, I was glad to be occupied. It was a welcome distraction from the thoughts that had been eating away at me all day.

I hadn't heard anything from Dex since I left that morning, which wasn't surprising considering how we'd left things. Still, I found myself missing the random, goofy messages he usually sent me. No matter how bad my day was, I could always count on him to put a smile on my face.

As my mind drifted back to more sexy images from last night, I looked up to see Dex walk into the bar, looking like my every fantasy come to life. I could feel the heat rising to my cheeks, as if my naughty thoughts were written all over my face.

He greeted a few people before nonchalantly strolling over to the bar, wearing a big smile and appearing as though he didn't have a care in the world.

"Hey, Liv. What's up?" he said, plopping down on a stool in front of me.

"I'm good... um, how are you?" I stammered, totally thrown off by how casual he was acting.

"Can't complain."

We talked briefly, completely avoiding the elephant in the room and the fact that his head had been between my legs less than twenty-four hours ago. I was desperately trying to appear as normal as possible despite the butterflies in my stomach and the tension that was radiating throughout my body. Everything about it felt off. Our conversation was forced, and Dex was far more standoffish than usual. There were no flirtatious comments, coy smiles, or excuses to touch me... and I missed it. I didn't like it this way. Maybe what had happened between us was too significant to pretend that it hadn't happened. Maybe we needed to talk about it if we were ever going to get past it.

Before I had a chance to say something to Dex, I got called over by a group on the other side of the bar. After making what seemed like a dozen drinks, I returned to find a busty brunette perched on the stool beside him. The dress she was wearing left little to the imagination, and she was leaning as close to him as possible, arching her chest out and practically shoving her boobs in his face.

I glared at her while I walked over to where they were sitting, annoyed that I couldn't step away for five minutes without the slut parade swooping in for him. I mistakenly assumed that Dex would send her packing when I came back, because that's what he normally did. I hated the fact that it hurt me so badly when he didn't.

"Brandy, this is Olivia," he introduced me. "She's a good *friend* of mine... right, Liv?"

He looked at me purposefully as he emphasized the word "friend," as if daring me to correct him.

"Yup, that's right," I snapped, wondering what kind of game he was playing. I didn't know if he was trying to prove a point or if he had just regressed back to his asshole self. The insecure part of me wondered if all I'd ever been to him was some kind of challenge.

Brandy and I continued to exchange bitchy looks until she finally excused herself to go use the restroom. Dex continued to sit there, cool as a cucumber, pretending as though nothing out of the ordinary was happening. Which only irritated me more.

"Back to trolling for bar trash, I see."

"That's what single guys do," he said with a pleased smile. "Would you prefer if I didn't?"

I could see the challenge in his eyes. He *wanted* me to admit to being jealous... to having feelings for him. But why? What the hell was he trying to prove? Whatever sick game he was playing, I wasn't going to let him win. No way would I give him the satisfaction of admitting to anything when he was being such a total jerk about it.

"By all means, troll away," I smiled back stubbornly. He wanted to play childish games? Fine. I could play, too.

We glared at each other across the bar, both of us refusing to give in. When Brandy came back, Dex stood up and grabbed her hand. "Come on baby, let's dance."

As he pulled her to the dance floor, she tossed me a huge, delighted grin over her shoulder that made me want to hurl. It wasn't long before they were grinding and gyrating against each other, her back pressed against his chest in the same way mine had been last night when it was the two of us dancing together. When the slut bent over, putting her hands on her knees and grinding her ass into Dex's crotch, my stomach twisted into knots. I felt like I was going to be sick. I kept trying to remind myself that he was only aiming to get a rise out of me, and I shouldn't let it bother me, but it did.

With each song, their disgusting performance on the dance floor got worse, until they were basically just dry humping each other in a crowd of people. Their sweaty bodies were fused so tightly together that it was difficult to tell where one whore ended and the other began. I tried not to look at them, but it was a train wreck happening right in front of me that I couldn't help but watch.

When they finally decided to come up for air, Dex sauntered over to me while Brandy stopped to talk to her friend.

"Hey, Liv, could you be a doll and get me a water?"

"I think what you really need is a shower," I hissed. "You're covered in skank sweat."

"Aren't you awfully snappy tonight," he grinned, resting his elbows on the bar. "I wonder why that is…"

"No, I'm just repulsed. Could you give me a heads up before you go out there for round two so I can go to the back and gouge my eyes out? Thanks."

"You jealous, Liv? Cause you know I'm all yours if you want me. Just say the word, and she's gone." Leaning over the bar, he reached out and brushed his fingers along my cheek.

I recoiled from his touch, furious. "How could you think that I'd want you? You make me sick. Go back to your stupid slut and leave me the hell alone."

His smile fell, pain sweeping across his face. But I didn't feel bad this time. Did he really think that *this* was the way to win me over? That he could act like an asshole and I would swoon at his feet?

Dex was never going to change. This is who he was. I was

delusional to think that any kind of relationship with him was anywhere in the realm of possibilities.

Without a word, he spun around and marched over to Brandy. Pulling her body against him, he dropped his mouth to hers and began kissing her intensely.

I felt like I'd been punched in the gut. Tears pricked at my eyes, and I wasn't sure if I was going to cry or throw up. I rushed outside through the back door before the first sob broke free.

This was a new kind of pain for me. I'd never felt this before, not even when I walked in on my fiancé screwing another woman… and we'd been together for four years! Dex and I were barely together for one night, so why did this hurt so much more?

This was different, though. It hurt more because Dex knew me— really *knew* me. I'd cracked my walls and given him glimpses of who I was, and that terrified me. It was one thing to be rejected by someone who barely knew the real me, but to be hurt by someone that I trusted enough to expose myself to… that was something else entirely.

I stood outside in the fresh air, taking deep breaths and trying to regain my composure. Every time I thought about his arms wrapped around her and his lips on hers—the same arms that had been wrapped around me, the same lips that had been on mine—fresh tears flowed down my cheeks.

I'd been hesitant with Dex because he knew me too well, and somehow he managed to crush me anyway. That was what happened when I let people in. That's how it always was. My dad, Steven and now Dex. All they ever did was hurt me and leave me.

Out of the corner of my eye, I saw Olivia freeze. Her face paled and her eyes filled with pain before she turned and ran out the back.

My heart dropped.

Immediately I knew that I'd gone too far and really fucked things up. I hadn't even meant to do it, but when I heard her say all that shit about not wanting me and how much I disgusted her, I was so pissed off and so fucking hurt that I just lost it. I hadn't been thinking. All I'd wanted to do in that moment was hurt her the way she hurt me.

But the look on her face… shit. It broke my fucking heart to see that. The pain in her eyes, the anger, the sadness… I never meant to do that. It gutted me. That look hurt more than getting ripped apart by shrapnel.

I tore my mouth from the whore I was kissing and pulled away.

"Where you going, baby?"

"Get the fuck off me, I have to go." I pushed her into the arms of a random guy nearby. "Here you go. I bet he'll fuck you."

Ignoring her shocked expression, I stormed out of the bar. I wanted to find Olivia, but I knew I was the last person she would want to see. I didn't want to make it worse than it already was, so I began walking to nowhere in particular, trying to clear my head.

All I could see was the look on Olivia's face.

I sat on the hood of Olivia's car, waiting for her to come out at the end of her shift. I don't know long I was out there—a couple hours maybe—but I refused to go home without talking to her first. Everything had spiraled out of control, and I was powerless to stop it. I felt weak. In the Marines, we were trained to alter our circumstances and regain control when a situation got out of hand. When you lost the upper hand in war, you became vulnerable and exposed. I felt that way now, only this was a different kind of war. One that I was unfamiliar with. There were no definitive boundaries or a chain of command to follow. I'd worked long and hard to become a successful Marine, but I was inexperienced when it came to life outside of combat. My training couldn't help me with this.

Olivia finally came outside, her eyes narrowing angrily when she glanced up and saw me there.

"I'm so sorry, Liv."

"What the hell are you doing out here?" she said, stopping several feet away from me. "You sure made quick work of that girl in there. Did you decide to do her out here in the parking lot instead of taking her all the way back to your place?" Her hands rested on her hips defensively, and she wore an angry scowl, but there was vulnerability in her eyes that couldn't be hidden by her tough exterior. I hated that I was the one who put it there.

"I promise you, I didn't sleep with her. I left without her."

She scoffed, "Well, that's a first."

"Can we please talk?" I said, stepping toward her slowly.

"There's nothing to talk about, Dex. You were out there dry humping and making out with some random slut right in from of me,

140

less than twenty-four hours after we... whatever, it doesn't matter." She tried to move past me to her car, but I blocked her path.

"I know that I fucked up. I know that. But I was only doing it to make you jealous. I was upset about what you said, and I was stupid. I wanted to hear that you have feelings for me and that it wasn't a mistake. I wanted to be more than that."

She was quiet for a moment, staring at the ground between us. I thought I had finally gotten through to her. When her eyes met mine, though, they were firm.

"Even if I had feelings for you then, I sure as hell don't anymore. Nothing will ever happen between us because guys like you never change." She stepped forward into the space between us until she was only inches away from me. "Now, if you care about me at all, then you'll leave me alone and get out of my way so I can go home and pretend that the last two days never happened."

Defeated, I stepped aside and let her climb into her car. I watched helplessly as she drove off, never slowing down or glancing back.

chapter fifteen

Olivia

I stayed as busy as possible over the next week, picking up extra shifts at the restaurant and spending a lot of my free time at the aquarium. I had little time to myself, which was exactly how I wanted it. When I wasn't working, I thought too much about all the things I had sworn to put behind me.

I'd barely seen Amy, except in passing, because I was rarely home. She'd called me a few times and I felt bad for ignoring her, but she was Dex's sister after all. I wasn't sure what, if anything, she knew about what happened between Dex and me. If he'd filled her in, then she would most certainly try to talk to me about it, and that was the last thing I wanted to do. I didn't want to think about it, and I most definitely didn't want to talk about it.

So I did the mature thing and avoided her instead.

Dex had done as I'd asked and was leaving me alone. He hadn't been to the restaurant while I was working and I hadn't seen him visiting Amy's house, either. He'd managed to drop out of my life entirely. It was exactly what I wanted… so I didn't know why it bothered me so much. It wasn't as though I expected him to chase after me—Dex didn't chase after women—and clearly I was no exception.

I woke up to pounding on my front door, and groggily looked at my phone to check the time. It was after eleven in the morning, but since it was my day off and I had nothing better to do, I'd decided to let myself sleep in.

The knocking continued, and I dragged myself out of bed to get the door. I opened it to find Amy and Sadie standing there in their beach gear.

"Oh, gosh, I'm so sorry to wake you," Amy said, noting my disheveled appearance. "I haven't seen you all week, and when I saw your car sitting in the driveway, I didn't want to miss my chance."

I was a terrible friend. "No worries, I was getting up anyway," I lied. "I'm sorry I haven't been over to see you guys. I've been working like crazy this week."

"I figured it was something like that," she said. "We were just getting ready to go to the beach. Do you want to come?"

I thought about saying no, but the idea of sitting at home alone on this beautiful day was way too depressing, even for me. "Sounds great. I'll get changed and meet you out front."

We went to our usual spot on Folly Beach, which wasn't easy considering how crowded it had become now that summer was in full swing. Just as we were getting settled in, Sadie started jumping up and down, waving her arms excitedly.

"Dee! Over here!"

My heart jumped into my throat when I looked up and saw Dex and Nate walking over to us. I noticed Dex hesitate for a second when his eyes linked with mine, clearly surprised to see me there, and my pulse began to race.

I glanced over at Amy. "I didn't know that they were coming…"

"I told them to meet us here. I hope that's okay." She turned to me with a questioning look. "Is there something going on with you and Dex?"

Apparently he hadn't filled her in on what happened. The last thing I wanted to do was draw attention to the situation and make things uncomfortable, so I did my best to brush it off. "No, of course it's fine. I just, uh, thought that he'd be working today, that's all."

"Not today, finally. He's been totally MIA all week doing who knows what. I had to resort to putting Sadie on the phone this morning to beg him to come meet us. I knew he couldn't say no to her," she said with a laugh.

As the day went on, I avoided looking at Dex, who had been quiet ever since he arrived. Instead, I buried my nose in my book, pretending to be completely absorbed in what I was reading. It worked for a while, until Nate and Amy took Sadie to go swimming, and Dex came over to me.

"I'm sorry, I didn't know that you were going to be here. I swear," he said sincerely. "I can make up an excuse to leave if you want me to."

I started to feel guilty. He was avoiding his family because of me—because I'd instructed him to stay away from me. And yet, I didn't want him to leave. Being near him turned me into a jumbled mess of emotions, and I was losing track of how I was supposed to feel. I was furious with him, but I adored him at the same time. I wanted nothing to do with him, but my traitorous body craved him, responding to every lingering glance and aching for his touch. Everything about him pulled me in.

Something was off about him, though. The easygoing smile was missing from his face, and there was no trace of his usual goofy humor. He looked as tired as I felt, and I could see the dark circles under his eyes. I worried that his nightmares were keeping him awake at night. It pained me to recall him thrashing and screaming in his sleep, terrified by the images in his head. Then I reminded myself that I wasn't supposed to care.

"No, it's fine… stay," I told him, sorting through my conflicting emotions. "There's no reason we can't hang around each other. I mean, we're all friends here, right?"

He smiled sadly. "Right."

During the weeks that followed my horrendous fuck-up, the only time I saw Olivia was when Nate and Amy were around. She hardly spoke to me or even looked at me. I wanted so badly to talk to her and try to explain everything, but I was afraid to piss her off more. She was barely tolerant of spending time with me in a group setting, and if I tried to push, she might stop seeing me altogether. And when it came down to it, being around her in a limited capacity was better than not seeing her at all.

I missed everything about Olivia. Her friendship, the cute little smiles she saved for me, her laugh, the way her eyes found me in a crowd or across the room and looked at me like I was actually something special. Every once in a while, I thought I caught her looking at me that same way, but she would glance away so quickly that I couldn't be sure if it was really happening or if I were simply imagining things. Either way, I longed for those moments because it was all I had left. At this point, I would settle for any little piece of Olivia that I could get. I let myself imagine that she felt something for me because it was the only way I could get through the day.

My nightmares were coming more frequently, waking me up nearly every night and leaving me tense and anxious throughout the day. I tried to take the edge off by running, spending more time at the gym and fighting whenever I could, but nothing seemed to help. I refused to resort to my previous method of using random woman to numb the pain, because I knew it would only drag me deeper into the depths of my misery. I only wanted Olivia. After being with her for that brief moment in time, anything else felt wrong.

When Nate and Amy invited me to grab lunch with them at the Seaside, I readily agreed since I knew that Olivia was working. Being near her put me at ease in a way that nothing else could. It didn't matter if she ignored me; her presence alone brought a fleeting sense of relief to my pathetic existence.

"Hey! What brings you here?" Olivia greeted us as she led us to an empty table in her section. She seemed surprisingly happy to see us—even me—and I wondered if perhaps we were turning a corner. If maybe there was a chance for us to get closer to where we were before I took it upon myself to destroy everything.

Amy answered, "You've been working so much lately that we decided to come to you."

We sat down at the table, and Olivia brought over the menus. She handed one to me and for a split-second her finger brushed against mine, sending a volt of electricity shooting through me. Her smile faltered, and I knew she felt it, too, but for once she didn't jerk away from me. Her cheeks flushed a faint shade of pink before she resumed taking our orders, and I reveled in the idea that I still had some kind of effect on her. I missed making her blush.

The restaurant was fairly quiet, so Olivia made frequent stops at our table to visit with us. It didn't last long though. Two guys came in and sat down in her section, forcing her to get back to work. They were dressed in khakis and polo shirts, looking like they'd been out golfing or something, and were probably about thirty or so. They had light hair and were clean shaven, and definitely seemed soft: the type of spoiled rich guys whose idea of living dangerously was taking a risk in the stock market or having an extra light beer at their Sunday tee-time. Bunch of fucking pussies.

I watched as one of them trailed his eyes trailed over Olivia appreciatively. My fists immediately clenched at my sides as my protective nature kicked in. Nate shot me a look across the table, warning me to calm down. I took a deep breath and relaxed my hands, without taking my eyes off her.

Richie Rich immediately began flirting with Olivia, sending clever smiles her way and flashing his pearly whites in her face. I wanted to knock those damn teeth right out of his fucking mouth.

As though he could read my mind, Nate leaned over to me and whispered, "Dude, calm down. Liv gets hit on in here all the time, but it's not like she ever goes for it."

This was different, though. I knew it. These weren't skeezy drunks or stupid frat guys, and Olivia wasn't doing her usual "polite but not interested" routine. Instead she was hanging around their table to chat, laughing with them and falling for their stupid rich-boy charm. At one point, she placed a hand on Richie Rich's shoulder, and I couldn't take it anymore. All I wanted to do was go over there and stake my claim—tell him that she was *mine*. Tell *her* that she was mine.

But she wasn't mine.

She wasn't mine, and it was my own fault that I lost her. But I couldn't just sit around while this asshole swooped in and stole her away from me. I knew his type. They appeared all suave and polite on the outside, but inside, they were no better than me. In fact, they were worse than me because they hid it underneath polo shirts and fancy hair-cuts. At least I was honest about it. These guys charmed women left and right, pretending to be gentlemen until they got what they wanted. They were self-entitled, and the only thing they cared about was their bank accounts and having some pretty young thing on their arm who they could control. Olivia was better than this guy, and I wanted her to know it.

Instead, I fought every instinct I had and stood up from the table, throwing down some bills and mumbling a quick goodbye to Nate and Amy as I walked out.

chapter sixteen

Olivia

I wasn't entirely sure what I was doing anymore. Normally, I didn't give men the time of day when they flirted with me, but for some reason, I'd gone along with it today. Not only did I flirt back, but I'd agreed to go on a date with the guy.

Brian was good-looking and seemed nice enough, but deep down, I knew it had less to do with him and more to do with the fact that Dex had been watching from ten feet away. I hated playing games, but an overwhelming part of me had wanted to make Dex jealous and give him a taste of how he'd made me feel. But when I saw Dex slink out of the restaurant, my stomach immediately twisted in response.

Was I being a total hypocrite? Perhaps our emotions led us to do stupid things where our hearts were concerned, and maybe I'd been too hard on Dex for what his made him do.

I wouldn't let myself go down that road. It was time for me to move on. From Dex, from Steven... it was time to start fresh. I couldn't mope around forever, and it was just one date. I hadn't agreed to marry the guy. And who knew? Maybe Brian would end up being the perfect guy for me if I gave him a chance.

Despite the pep talk, when Sunday evening rolled around, and it was time to get ready for my date, I was beginning to seriously question my decision. First dates were supposed to be all about excitement and anticipation and nervously trying on six different outfits before finding the one that would leave him speechless. I wasn't feeling any of those things.

I pulled a cute dress out of my closet, eyeing it briefly before hanging it back up and grabbing a pair of jeans. No sense in pretending this was something it wasn't.

I knew better than to let some stranger know where I lived, so I was meeting Brian at the restaurant instead of having him pick me up. Since I put little effort into getting ready, I had some time to kill before it was time to meet him.

I began looking through the first batch of photographs that I'd gotten back from being developed. They were all the ones that I'd taken when I first arrived. The photos from the pier on the morning when I first met Dex, various places around Charleston, and all the pictures that I'd taken when I was with Amy, Sadie, Dex and Nate. I flipped through the photos from our first trip to the beach, snapshots of Dex and Sadie building sandcastles together, laughing and smiling. There was no darkness in these images of Dex. I missed his easy smile and carefree laugh. I missed seeing him happy.

As I continued to thumb through the photos, I found ones that I hadn't taken, and I vaguely remembered Dex playing around with my camera one day on the beach.

They were all of me.

Snapshots of me and Sadie playing in the ocean, and of me and Amy laughing together while we exchanged stories. There were some of me when I hadn't thought anyone was paying attention—gazing out over the water, sitting in the sand, and close-up shots of my smile… They were meaningful and beautiful.

There was adoration and significance in those photos, and I was taken aback to think that Dex was the one behind the camera. People always said that a photo tells more about the photographer than the subject. If that was true, then what did these photos mean?

All of a sudden, the idea of going on this date seemed wrong. I wasn't sure I could go through with it. I picked up my phone to call Brian and let him know, but when I saw the time, I realized he was probably on his way there already and it would be rude to cancel now.

I sighed, glancing down at the photos one more time before heading out. Amy and Sadie were in the driveway when I stepped outside.

"Hey Liv," Amy greeted me happily. "We were just on our way to Sunday dinner at my parents' house. Do you want to come? They're dying to see you!"

My heart dropped. "I can't… I have a, um, date."

"With who?" she asked. "That guy from the restaurant?"

I nodded and an obvious flash of disappointment crossed her face.

"Okay, well have fun, and be safe," she said. "Maybe next week."

I smiled sadly. "Yeah, maybe next week."

Dex

We were halfway through dinner when my parents asked where Olivia was and why she hadn't come with us this week. She had become a frequent guest at our weekly dinners over the past couple of months, and they'd come to expect her there. It was no surprise that they adored her. It was impossible not to.

Amy didn't answer their question right away, glancing around the table and chewing her food slowly. Finally, she swallowed, her eyes shifting to mine. "Olivia had a date tonight."

"Liv's on a date?" My stomach lurched, coiling painfully as her words sank in. "With who?"

My voice came out sharper than I intended, and Amy eyed me hesitantly without answering.

"Don't even tell me she's out with that jackass from the other day…"

She sighed regretfully. "Sorry, Dex."

"FUCK!" I pounded my fist on the table so hard that the plates shook as I stood up, knocking my chair over in my haste to get away.

I stormed through the woods behind my parent's house until I found myself at the swimming hole. Everything was spinning out of control, and I needed to slow it down and clear my head. I wasn't angry anymore, I was… crushed. It was worse than anger, because yelling or hitting something couldn't make me feel better. I wasn't sure that anything would. I finally found someone who meant more to me than anything else, someone who understood me and really saw me… and I'd lost her.

When the stakes were high, I failed.

I sat at the edge of the water, studying the way the stars reflected off the dark surface and created a mirror image of the sky above. For some reason, I often found myself by the water when I needed to escape. There was something about it that calmed me down and made me feel… safe. Probably because it was one thing that would never bring back memories of my time in Iraq. Everything in Iraq was hot, sandy desert, and the only water I came into contact with was from a bottle as it crossed my lips. Now, no matter how fucked up things got in my head, I could go near the water and be reminded that I was home.

The leaves rustled behind me, and I didn't need to turn around to see who it was. My sister could always find me. It was some kind of "twin intuition" or something.

"Want to finally tell me what's going on between you and Olivia?" she said, sitting down next to me. "And don't you dare say 'nothing' because I've seen how tense it's been with you two lately."

I explained everything, from the night we hooked up, to the morning after when she acted like it was a mistake, and of course my stupid plan to make her jealous and how she'd told me that she wanted nothing to do with me.

"I really fucked up," I told her.

"No shit, you fucked up!" she scolded, staring at me in bewilderment. "What kind of an idiotic plan was that? It wouldn't work on anyone, but especially not Olivia."

"I know, I was upset and I…" Her words caught up with me, and I paused. "What do you mean *especially not Olivia*?"

"Because of how things ended with her fiancé."

I shot her a puzzled look and waited for her to explain what the hell she was talking about.

"I figured that Olivia told you," she muttered guiltily. "They broke up because she walked in on the bastard screwing someone else in their apartment."

I groaned, feeling even worse than before. "Why didn't she tell me?"

"She's probably embarrassed about it. There's nothing worse than feeling like you're not good enough or you're lacking something."

"That's bullshit. Olivia is perfect... her fiancé is a fucking jackass." He was lucky to be all the way in New York, because I was tempted to find him and show him what happens to guys who hurt amazing, beautiful girls like Olivia. Then I remembered that I was one of them, and I hated myself even more.

"I know that, but it's hard to see it when you're the one who got cheated on," Amy explained.

"How can I fix this?" I asked desperately. "Please tell me I can fix it."

"Have you tried talking to her? Groveling at her feet for a second chance?"

I shook my head. "She told me to leave her alone. I didn't want to make it any worse."

"Wow, you really don't know anything about women, do you, bro?" she said, shaking her head. "Of course she told you to leave her alone. She was angry and hurt. That doesn't mean you give up. You have to fight for her and show her that you're serious. Are you serious?"

"I'm dead serious when it comes to Liv," I told her. "I may have zero experience with this shit, but I would do anything for her."

"Then you need to quit playing games and be honest about how you feel. You got so angry because she wouldn't admit her feelings, and yet… have you ever once told her how *you* feel?"

Apparently I was the jackass.

Amy sighed. "So far, all you've done is show her that you're incapable of an actual relationship, and are no better than her dumbass ex. You need to prove to her that you can be different. Can you handle that?" She eyed me curiously, "Are you sure it's what you really want? Because there's no going back after that."

"Liv is what I want," I said firmly, without hesitation. "I don't want to go back. She's all I want."

"Do you love her?"

I sucked in a breath, letting the question hang in the air between us. I hadn't put a label on what I was feeling. If I hadn't admitted it to myself yet, there was no way I could say it out loud to my sister.

She smiled, giving me an encouraging pat on the back. "Well, then, go get her, you idiot… and don't fuck it up this time!"

chapter seventeen

Olivia

Brian took me to a cute little restaurant downtown that wasn't overly fancy. I was relieved that there didn't seem to be any added pressure to try and turn the date into something it wasn't. We talked easily, chatting about mindless topics such as our favorite areas in the city and what we enjoyed doing for fun. Typical first date conversation and straightforward, robotic answers. He told me a little bit about his job, which had something to do with finance or banking, and my eyes began to glaze over. I realized early on in the date that I felt the same way with him that I had often felt with Steven—bored and distant. There was no spark, no excitement... nothing drawing me in. Spending time with Brian wasn't moving on, it was moving backward; reverting to the same life I had before coming to Charleston.

Needless to say, I was glad when the date was over. Not because I had a bad time—he was nice, smart, and charming—but my heart just hadn't been in it. When we finished dinner and he suggested going out for a drink, I told him that I had an early morning and needed to call it a night. He hadn't pushed it. I was sure he could tell that I wasn't into it, and when I apologized for wasting his time, he handled it like a total gentleman, thanking me for being honest and wishing me luck.

There had been a time when he would have been exactly what I was looking for—safe, easy, and predictable. It was the same reason I'd ended up with Steven: because I'd been searching for the stability that I never had growing up.

Dex had given me a taste of what it felt like on the other side—passionate, spontaneous, and unpredictable, but with the comfort of a best friend who made me feel protected. Now that I'd felt that, I didn't want to settle for easy anymore. I wanted someone who set me on fire with a single look, someone who thrilled me and made me feel safe and vulnerable at the same time. I wanted something real.

I pulled into my driveway and was climbing out of the car when I noticed Dex hidden in the shadows on my doorstep, slumped over and distraught. He lifted his head when I approached, and my heart automatically started beating faster as excitement vibrated through me.

Slowly I began walking over, my pulse racing. My emotions were all over the place. I didn't know what to say or how to act. I couldn't remember if I were mad at him or happy to see him... If I hated him or wanted to be with him.

He stood up nervously when I got closer. "I only need a minute, Liv. I know you don't want to see me or talk to me. I know you probably hate me, but please let me get this out and then I promise to leave you alone and never bother you again."

With a nod, I leaned against the porch rail, unsteady on my feet as I waited anxiously for him to say what he had come here to say.

"I'm so fucking bad at this," he started, "But it's only because

I've never felt like this before. For anyone… ever. You're all that I think about, Liv. You're my first thought when I wake up and the last thing on my mind when I go to sleep. Your smile… the sound of your laugh, the way your eyes light up when you're happy, the way your lips taste, the way you feel pressed up against me… God, Olivia… I want you so bad. You're all I want."

My breath hitched in my throat, and I couldn't respond. I tightened my grip on the railing, afraid that if I let go I might fall.

He took a step toward me. "Since I came back from Iraq, I've been a shell of the person I used to be. I'm so afraid of what people will see if they get to know me that I keep them out so they never have the chance. Then I met you. Without even realizing it, you crashed through my walls and brought light back into my life… you brought *me* back. War may have broken me in a lot of ways, but you're putting me back together, piece by piece, day after day. I'm far from being whole, and I know I have a long way to go, but every time I'm with you, I find a little piece of what I lost." With cautious steps, he moved to stand right in front of me. "You pulled me from the darkness, Liv, and I'll be grateful to you for the rest of my life."

My eyes welled with tears, and it wasn't long before one escaped, sliding down my cheek and falling to my shirt. It broke my heart to know how much pain he held inside and the burden he carried with him every day. He saw himself as broken, but I knew without a doubt that he was the strongest, bravest person I'd ever known.

Dex reached up and cupped my cheek with gentle hands, brushing my tears away with his thumb. "I know that I've totally fucked this whole thing up and that you deserve so much better than me, but you're it for me. It will only ever be you. I promise, if you give me a chance, I'll never hurt you again. Seeing you in pain is worse than any nightmare I've ever had, and I swear, I'll be better. I would do anything for you, Liv. You're everything to me, and I fucking love you—"

I crashed my mouth against his, closing the space between us and throwing myself into his arms. His words resonated inside my chest, shattering whatever defenses I had left and opening my heart to him. I was done being scared and running away from what I wanted. Seeing him with someone else, real or not, had torn me apart. There was a chance I would end up brokenhearted, but it was a risk I was willing to take.

Dex was like gravity. Right from the beginning, he had pulled me in, drawing me to him in a way that no one ever had. I was tired of fighting the pull and tired of fighting my heart. I felt more connected to Dex than I'd ever felt to anyone, tethered to him by some invisible force that was stronger and more powerful than both of us.

He didn't hesitate to pull me close as his lips began moving frantically with mine. I draped my arms around his neck and stood on my tiptoes, aligning my body with his so I could feel the wild beating of his heart against my chest, pounding in a rhythm that echoed my own. His hand tangled in my hair as he explored my mouth and clutched my body to his, pressing me against the railing. He slipped his hands underneath my bottom and lifted me up, wrapping my legs securely around his waist. As soon as his hardness made contact with my aching center, I moaned into his mouth and rocked my hips against him, desperate for more.

"Fuckkk," he groaned, pulling me tighter against him. "I can't wait to bury myself inside you."

He carried me inside, kissing me lovingly all the way to my bedroom before laying me down on the mattress. With his eyes fastened on mine, he stood up and pulled his shirt off, tossing it to the side before climbing over me. Dropping his mouth to my stomach, he began peeling my blouse off while his lips blazed a trail up my torso and between my breasts, not stopping until he reached my mouth and brought my shirt over my head.

He gazed down at me, his tender eyes burning into mine as he ran a finger down my cheek. "I'm yours, Liv. Tell me that you're mine."

My voice caught in my throat. I nodded, placing my palm over his heart. "I'm yours."

His lips moved slowly over my skin, worshipping every inch of my body and driving me wild. He pulled off my jeans, his eyes leisurely raking over me before he lowered himself on top of me.

"I can't get enough. I want to taste every inch of you," he murmured, removing my bra and staring hungrily at my naked breasts. He kneaded them gently and ran his thumb over my nipple, watching it harden beneath his touch. I felt like my body was going to ignite at any moment, and when he dropped his lips to my breast and pulled my nipple into his mouth, I had no control over the cries that poured out of my throat.

Sliding a hand into my panties, he began teasing my wet, sensitive flesh with his fingers while simultaneously sucking my breast. I reached down and began fumbling with his jeans, writhing desperately underneath him as desire coursed through my body.

"I want you now," I whined, pressing my lips to his neck. "I've been waiting so long. I can't wait any longer."

"Don't worry, baby. I got you." He withdrew his hand from between my legs and stood up, dropping his jeans and boxers as he grabbed a condom from his wallet.

My eyes ran over his perfect form, taking in every muscle and ridge before landing on his thick, hard length. I watched him slide the condom over himself, marveling at the fact that he would soon be inside me, and my body tingled in anticipation. I'd never wanted anyone more than I wanted him.

I bit my lip, absorbing his hungry stare as he stalked forward and kneeled on the mattress. Hooking his thumbs into my panties, he slid them off and settled between my legs, positioning himself at my entrance. Placing a gentle kiss on my lips, he slowly pushed inside, inch by precious inch, until he filled me.

"Christ, you feel so fucking amazing," he groaned, stilling once he was deep inside. "You're so tight and perfect. I just need to feel you for a minute."

My body stretched pleasantly to accommodate him. I felt so amazingly and completely full in a way that I never had, but I was anxious for more. I ran my hands down his back and grasped his toned backside, pulling him into me as I lifted my hips, encouraging him to move. "I need you, Dex."

He finally began to shift, drawing himself out and plunging back in, deeper than before. His pace was slow and deliberate, allowing me to feel everything more intensely. Each movement was amplified, and I was all sensation, my entire body a live wire frantically waiting for a spark to combust. I wrapped my legs around his waist, and he immediately began increasing the speed of his thrusts, moving faster, harder and deeper. I clawed at his back, moaning loudly as the quiver in my belly began to intensify and my muscles tightened around him, begging for more.

"Oh God, yes," I wailed. "Right there, don't stop…"

He pulled my nipple into his mouth, sucking and biting it gently while he continued driving into me until I exploded around him, screaming out his name as I flew over the edge. He absorbed my cries with his mouth, drawing out the waves of pleasure as his movement accelerated.

Grabbing his neck, I brought my lips to his ear and whispered, "You feel so fucking good inside me."

With one last powerful thrust he stilled, loudly groaning out my name as he shuddered and found his release. He collapsed on top of me and my arms automatically went around him, holding him close to me. After a few labored breaths, he gazed down at me and placed a soft, sweet kiss on my lips.

"I missed you so damn much," he breathed.

My heart swelled in my chest. I reached up, brushing my hand along the rough stubble of his cheek. "I missed you, too."

I woke with Olivia in my arms, her head resting on my chest and her warm body pressed against mine. Her sweet smell invaded my senses and clouded my mind with images from the night before. I pulled her closer, needing to make sure she was really there and I wasn't dreaming. She nuzzled against my chest but stayed asleep, and I didn't dare wake her after the long night we'd had.

We'd been denying ourselves for so long that the first time had done little to curb our appetite for one another. The simplest touch ignited our hunger, and within minutes, we had wrapped ourselves up in one another again, lost in our frantic need and desperate for more. We had taken our time learning each other's bodies, exploring every inch of one another. I'd discovered that I could make her toes curl by kissing her neck, and she found that nibbling on my earlobe drove me wild.

I could have kept going all night, and it still wouldn't have been enough.

Olivia shifted, watching me with lidded eyes as she ran her hand up my stomach and settled it on my chest.

"Good morning," she smiled, her voice heavy with sleep.

"I love waking up next to you. I can't tell you how long I've been waiting for this."

"Me, too," she said. "I'm sorry for pushing you away. I was stubborn and scared. Scared of getting hurt or left behind... but mostly, I was scared of my feelings for you. Waking up with you that morning, I felt so happy and peaceful, and whenever I feel that way, something always seems to come along and rip it away from me. I didn't want to lose you, Dex. You're so important to me."

"I'm not going anywhere," I told her, running my hand over her silky smooth skin. "You have nothing to apologize for. I'm the one who fucked up, not you. I'm just glad you're here now. Part of me was worried that last night was the best dream I've ever had, and I was going to wake up alone."

She laughed gently and trailed her hand down my stomach, tracing my abs with her fingertips. Her hand disappeared below the sheet and I sucked in a sharp breath when she wrapped her hand around my already rock hard cock.

"If you were dreaming... would I do this?" she said playfully, stroking up and down my length.

"Ahhh... yes," I groaned. "Yes, this is exactly what you'd be doing if I was dreaming..."

Keeping her eyes locked on me, she shifted on top of me and slid her body down mine. "What about... this?" Her warm mouth covered my dick and her tongue brushed over the swollen tip.

"Oh shit…" My body tensed, struggling to hold back as she wrapped her lips around me, licking and sucking and driving me crazy. "Damn, baby, that's so fucking good. Just like that," I cried out, slipping my hands into her hair. My eyes kept trying to roll into the back of my head, but I held them on her. Normally I closed them, only caring about how it felt, but this was different because it was Olivia. I watched her suck me and, holy shit… it was erotic as hell. She took me deep until I touched the back of her throat and when her hand joined in to stroke the base of my cock, my control snapped. "Fuck yeah baby, suck it… just like that, don't stop. You're fucking amazing, Liv, feels so damn good… I'm gonna come, baby…"

She didn't pull back, and I came hard, groaning loudly as I poured into her mouth. My whole body shuddered, and she didn't stop until she pumped every last drop from me. Licking her full lips, she gazed up at me deviously. "How'd that compare to your dreams?"

"Damn… that was beyond my wildest dreams. You're incredible, you know that?" I flipped her on her back and hovered over her. "I was planning on spending the morning inside of you, but now…" Reaching my hand down, I found her pussy soaking wet. She moaned, pushing her hips against my hand. I crept down her body until my head was between her legs and looked up at her eagerly.

"… I think I'll have you for breakfast instead."

We finally got out of bed a while later. I resisted the urge to follow Olivia into the shower, deciding to make breakfast for her instead. When she emerged—looking unbelievably sexy with damp hair and wearing my tee shirt—I handed her a cup of coffee and led her to the table where I had two omelets waiting for us.

"Wow," she said between bites. "Where did you learn to cook like this?"

"Teddy," I answered. "Throughout high school and boot camp, he was always the guy who took care of everyone. We'd wake up hung-over after partying too hard the night before and Teddy would have these huge breakfasts laid out for us. He drank just as much as the rest of us, but somehow he always woke up cheerful and ready to go. It used to drive our friends crazy, especially when they were fighting wicked hangovers, but it's the way he always was." Pain twitched in my chest at the memory. "He had such a great attitude about life… like he was just grateful to be here. Total glass half-full type, you know? He took everything in stride. No matter what happened, he was always positive, loving life. It was impossible not to be happy around him. He had this infectious personality that pulled people in. I always wished I could be more like him."

"Sounds like a really great guy," Olivia said, placing her hand over mine.

"He was."

I never discussed Teddy, with anyone, ever. It was too painful for me to talk about him, and yet, here I was chatting to Olivia about him without even thinking. She made it easy to open up and share those parts of myself that I kept hidden from everyone else. I was completely hypnotized by her. She knew what it was like to lose someone who she loved, and she understood a lot of what I was going through.

Olivia didn't ask any more questions or press for details, and she didn't tell me how sorry she was. I loved that about her. It was as though she could sense how much it hurt for me to talk about him, so she changed the subject to make it easier for me.

There was still a part of me that worried what she might do if I opened myself up to her completely. There was so much bad shit inside me. I couldn't help but fear what would happen if she saw the darkest parts.

Olivia had to leave for work shortly after we finished eating, so I walked her out to her car before we went our separate ways. She was working for the next three nights, and I wouldn't be able to spend much time with her. At this point though, I was glad to have any time with her at all.

We stood at her car, looking at each other awkwardly for a moment, neither one of us knowing what to say. After spending the last twelve hours in our own perfect little bubble, it was time to get back to the real world.

"So, what now?" Olivia laughed. "I guess I'll, um… see you later?"

I put my hands on her hips and pulled her toward me. "Now, you give me a kiss… a good one… and call me when you're done working. No matter how late it is."

She smiled. "That can be arranged." Standing on her tiptoes, she wrapped her arms around my neck, softly brushing her lips against mine. I swiped at her bottom lip with my tongue, and with a faint moan, she parted her lips. Because I couldn't help myself, I took full advantage and deepened the kiss until my mind was hazy and we were both breathing heavily. Then, after placing one last soft kiss on her lips, I reluctantly let her go and turned away.

chapter eighteen

Olivia

Despite the fact that I was stuck working the next few nights, Dex and I managed to find time to see each other. We would go out to lunch in between my shifts at the aquarium and the restaurant, or he would come in when I was working to have dinner or grab a beer. Not to mention that he sent me sweet—and sometimes dirty—text messages throughout the day, and every night when I got off work, we would talk on the phone. He hated the fact that I got home so late after my shifts at the restaurant, and I knew he wouldn't sleep until he could confirm that I'd gotten home safe.

For someone who didn't do relationships, Dex sure was good at it. When I teased him about it, he would say that it was easy with me because he wanted to do all this stuff anyway, so he didn't even have to try.

Pretty damn sweet, right? Yeah, I was in trouble.

Aside from a few lingering kisses here and there, we hadn't done anything physical since our first night together. I was aching to be with him again. Never once had it been this way with Steven, or anyone else for that matter. Every little touch from Dex left me heated and eager for more. I lay in bed with images of him drifting through my head and no way to cure the ache.

In other words, I was horny as hell.

Fortunately, I only had one more night shift at the restaurant, and then I would have a couple days off. Dex would be taking me on our first official date, and I was practically counting the minutes.

I met Nora in Charleston to go shopping for something to wear, since my clothing selection was limited, and I wanted to wear something nice that Dex hadn't seen before. I didn't have a lot of money to spend, but Nora suggested a boutique thrift store downtown with a selection of high-end clothing, most of which had been dropped off by wealthy women after being worn once or twice.

After browsing through multiple racks, I found a coral dress that caught my eye. It had a low neckline and was fitted through the bodice with a slight flair at the waist. It was the perfect combination of pretty and sexy, and it fit like it was made for me.

"That's the one. it's absolutely perfect!" Nora said when I stepped out of the dressing room.

"I don't think I have any shoes to wear with it…" I mentally went through the three or four pairs of shoes I had in my closet and came up empty.

She smiled. "No, but I do. Pay for that dress and then let's go raid my closet."

We hurried over to the house that she and Jake were staying in, and she immediately brought me inside and led me to her closet. It reminded me of college when she would dress me for big dates, job interviews, or anything that required me to look somewhat decent. She'd always been so generous.

"How's the wedding planning?" I asked while watching her dig through her closet.

"Good! I mean, we haven't given it a ton of thought, but it's not as though we're in a rush. Right now, we're getting used to our new life and enjoying being together." Nora got a dreamy look in her eye whenever she spoke about Jake and for the first time I understood it. "We're probably going to do something small, keep it simple, you know?"

"Simple is nice," I agreed. "No sense in putting more pressure on yourselves. It should be the happiest day of your life, not something to stress over."

"Exactly! We thought about doing a beach wedding, but then Jake had the idea to do it at his grandfather's old fishing cabin where we had our first date. He recently fixed it all up, and it's beautiful. It's right on the water with a dock that we could turn into a makeshift aisle, and there's a field nearby where we could set up a tent for the reception... it would be really special. And you should have seen how excited Jake was with the idea; it was adorable!"

I laughed. "He's a sweetheart, that one. I can see why you held out for him all those years."

"Totally worth it," she smiled. From the corner of her closet she pulled out a pair of tan strappy heels. "Aha! Found them!"

After finding me the perfect shoes and a chunky, teal necklace to go with the dress, Nora and I spent the rest of the afternoon getting our nails done at a salon down the street. I was happier and more relaxed than I'd been in a long time, and I couldn't wait for my date tomorrow.

I said goodbye to Nora and got in the car. As I was driving away, she called out to me, "Have fun tomorrow. I'll be expecting details!"

A few minutes into my shift at the Seaside, Melanie approached me with a weird look on her face.

"Do you know that guy over there?" she asked, pointing to the man she had seated in my section. "He requested you, which seemed a little strange, so I wanted to give you a heads' up."

He was an older man, probably in his fifties, with gray hair and a rough look about him. I didn't recognize him, but I must have known him from somewhere if he asked for me specifically.

I shrugged. "I don't think so, but I've seen so many people in here that it's hard to keep track. I probably waited on him at some point and made a good impression."

Grabbing a menu, I walked over to his table with a friendly smile. "Good evening, sir… how are you doing tonight?"

He barely smiled in return, and he didn't look at me with any familiarity. Instead he seemed to examine me; his hard, steel gray eyes probing me as if searching for something. When his lips turned up in a half smile, it seemed forced, like he was hiding behind it.

"I'm good," he answered. "How're you doin', Olivia?"

Obviously, he knew me somehow, unless Melanie had given him my name, which was unlikely.

"Great, thank you," I replied. "Can I start you off with something to drink?"

"Scotch, neat."

By the time I returned with his drink, his intense demeanor seemed to have toned down a bit. Shortly after that, when I brought his food over to him, he was actually somewhat friendly.

"Have you lived here long?" he asked casually, grabbing a handful of fries from his plate.

"A few months or so," I answered vaguely, wanting to avoid personal conversation. "It's a great place though."

"Yeah, it seems like it. It's my first time here. I'm passing through on my way back to New York. I wish I could stay longer."

I was momentarily distracted when I saw Dex and Sadie walk into the restaurant, and I couldn't help but smile. My customer noticed when I stopped paying attention and followed my gaze across the room to where Dex and Sadie were waving at me.

"That your boyfriend?"

My focus snapped back to him, and I blushed furiously, searching for a way to steer the subject toward something else. "You, uh, said you're from New York?" I muttered, hiding my flushed cheeks. "I used to live up there."

"Is that so?" His lips curled in amusement. "What brought you here?"

"Just a change of scene, I suppose." The topic of conversation made me uneasy, and I really wanted to get out of there. "Can I get you anything else?"

His eyes flickered to where Dex was sitting before he answered, "Just the check, please."

I did my best to shake the awkward feeling before heading over to Dex and Sadie's table. It was adorable to see them sitting together, and my mood immediately brightened. Fortunately, it was still early for dinner, and they were my only other table so I could spend a little bit of time with them.

"Well, it must be my lucky day," I said, walking over to them. My heart jumped in my chest at the way Dex's eyes greedily took me in, making it difficult to keep my composure. "What brings you two here tonight?"

"Well, I wanted to get pizza," Sadie told me excitedly. "But then Uncle Dee said that if we came here, he would take me out for ice cream after!"

"Oh, yeah?" I turned to Dex, who was grinning.

"What can I say? The service here is excellent... I can't get enough of it," he said cheekily.

I dropped the mystery man's check off while he was outside talking on the phone so I wouldn't have to endure any more uncomfortable interaction with him. I noticed him watching me while I was talking to Dex and Sadie, and it gave me an eerie feeling.

"Who is that guy?" Dex asked, noticing my discomfort.

I knew how protective he was, and I didn't want to make a big deal out of what I was feeling when it was probably nothing. "Nobody. Some customer from a while back that I can't seem to remember. He was a little nosy, that's all," I reassured him.

They left when they were finished with dinner so that Dex could take Sadie to get her ice cream, as promised. He gave me a quick kiss goodbye and leaned in close.

"Can't wait to see you tomorrow," he whispered. His warm breath caressed my neck and a shiver ran down my spine as I watched him walk away.

When I next looked up, the creepy, mystery man was already gone. It wasn't until later that night when I finally picked up on something he said. *"This is my first time here,"* he'd told me. So, if he had never been in here before, then why did he request me? And how did he know my name?

Since Olivia and I had already slept together—which I was *not* complaining about, by the way—it felt like we'd skipped ahead and missed a few steps. I'd never even taken her out on a proper first date, and I wanted to make up for it. I was determined to do everything right with Olivia. If that meant taking a step back from the physical stuff and keeping my dick in my pants, then I would do it. I didn't want to do anything to mess this up, and I definitely didn't want her to think I was only interested in sex. I mean, yeah, I couldn't stop thinking about it because it was hands-down the best sex I'd ever had and I was dying to do it again, but it was only a part of it. I loved everything about her, and I wanted her to know it.

After three agonizingly long days, she finally had the night off from work. I was taking her out for a nice dinner in Charleston. I'd even dressed up for the occasion, something I almost never did. I felt awkward and uncomfortable wearing a navy blue dress shirt and gray slacks with a matching tie that I'd let Amy pick out for me. I was starting to regret my decision to do a fancy dinner, until Olivia opened her door and literally took my breath away.

She was in a gorgeous dress with her hair falling loose over her shoulders and sexy heels that made her legs look like they were ten miles long. Every inch of her was fucking flawless. I stood there with my heart in my throat as my eyes wandered over her, speechless, frozen in place and suddenly nervous.

When I didn't say anything, she eyed me with concern. "Dex? Are you all right?"

"You're beautiful."

"Thank you." She smiled shyly. "You're looking pretty darn good yourself, Mr. Porter. Where are you taking me?"

"You'll have to wait and see, Ms. Mason." I led her to my truck and helped her climb inside. Her sweet, tantalizing smell filled the cab, and I wasn't sure I could make it all the way to the restaurant without pulling over to get a taste of her.

As we walked down the cobblestone street to the restaurant, I reached for her hand and wove her fingers with mine, unable to go any longer without touching her. She looked at me with her gorgeous smile, and my chest tightened. I couldn't believe that she was here with me… that I was lucky enough to be with her.

The restaurant I took her to was on the rooftop of a hotel overlooking downtown Charleston and the harbor. The setting sky glowed with the city lights—specks of blazing fire dancing across the twilight. Olivia's eyes brightened when she took in the view, with a look of pure enchantment that thawed my heart and made everything worthwhile.

It was a warm summer night, but with the breeze from the rooftop, the temperature was perfect. There were only a few other tables besides ours, so our meal was quiet and peaceful with the twinkling lights and the city below serving as an ideal backdrop. The conversation came naturally between us, as it normally did, and we stuck around for drinks once we finished dinner. The longer we sat there, the more difficult it became not to touch her. We kept inching closer to each other, unable to fight the pull between us, until we were nearly touching. She leaned back, crossing her legs and causing her dress to ride up even further, exposing the soft skin of her thigh that I was aching to run my hand over. The way she licked her lips when she looked at me, like she wanted a taste, drove me crazy and made me want to devour her mouth and suck on those perfect lips. I could hardly stand it.

"You're making it really hard to keep my hands to myself," I told her softly, sloping my body toward hers.

Resting her hand on my thigh, she smiled. "What makes you think you have to keep your hands to yourself?"

Her touch fired electricity through my veins, and I sighed. "Because, this is technically our first date, and I promised myself I would do it right, which means taking it slow."

"What if I don't want to take it slow?" she said, a pout forming on her lips. "What if I want you?"

Christ, she was going to make this difficult. "I want to give you everything that you deserve," I told her. "And you deserve charm and magic... and perfection. I want you to know how much you mean to me." I brushed her hair to the side and gently touched my lips to the spot below her ear. "Even if it means resisting the urge to rip your panties off and sink inside you right here." She sucked in a breath, and I loved how much I affected her. When I pulled back, she had a determined smile on her face.

"We'll see," she said cunningly. "Now if you'll excuse me, I have to use the ladies room."

I used her time away to try and get myself under control. The fact that she wanted me as badly as I wanted her was such a fucking turn-on, I could hardly stand it. When she came back to the table, there was a mischievous look in her eye that made me wonder what she was up to. As she sat down, I noticed that there was something hidden in her closed fist.

"Would you mind holding onto these for me?" She held her hand out and pressed something into my palm. "They were getting awfully damp, so I decided to take them off."

I looked down, groaning loudly when I saw what she handed me. Her panties. She took off her fucking panties and handed them to me. Tiny, sexy, black lace panties that most certainly didn't cover much before, but now covered nothing. My cock was instantly hard and straining against the front of my slacks.

"You play dirty, Ms. Mason..." I said through gritted teeth. All I could think about was her bare, wet pussy underneath that dress, and it was driving me crazy. She smiled playfully, like she knew exactly what she was doing to me, and began seductively tracing her lips with her finger.

Damn, she was frisky. It was sexy as hell, and if she wanted to play... we would play.

I deliberately let my napkin slide off the table to the floor. Leaning down to pick it up, I placed my palm on her ankle and slowly ran my hand all the way up her leg, settling it on her thigh beneath her dress, obscured by the tablecloth. Her breath began coming in faster and her legs parted slightly. With my eyes locked on hers, I pushed my hand between her legs, running my finger over her wet heat before slipping it inside her, causing a breathless moan to escape her lips.

Drawing my hand back, I sucked my finger into my mouth while she watched with rapt attention. "Delicious..."

Her cheeks flushed pink, and she sat there wordlessly for a moment, making me think our little game was over. Then, she scooted closer to me and shoved her hand beneath the tablecloth, landing on my lap and positioning it over my massive erection. She began stoking me through my pants, and I gripped the edge of the table until my knuckles were white.

"You're killin' me, Liv..." I closed my eyes and let my head fall back, pleasure flooding through me. She began rubbing me harder and when my eyes snapped open there was desire written all over her face.

Touching me was turning her on, and the fact that she needed me so badly was the last straw.

"Fuck it, let's go." I threw more than enough cash down to cover our meal as well as a generous tip, grabbed Olivia's hand and hauled her out of the restaurant.

We couldn't get back to my house fast enough. As soon as we made it through the front door, I had her up against the wall, locking her hands above her head and pressing my body against hers.

I'd never experienced this kind of need before. Obviously, I loved sex, but this kind of visceral, desperate, uncontrollable need was something I only felt with Olivia. I wanted to possess her—mind, body and soul—and I wanted her to possess me the same way. I craved her with an intensity that went beyond anything else and made me feel out of control.

"Feel that, baby?" I pushed my hips into her so she could feel just how badly I wanted her. "You make me so hard... I'm so fucking hard for you."

She moaned, and I ran one of my hands down her body, pulling her tightly against me. "I was kidding myself thinking I could control myself tonight," I murmured. "It'd be one thing if I hadn't been with you yet and I didn't know what I was missing. But now that I know what you taste like..." I brought my lips to her neck, sweeping my tongue across her skin, "... what you feel like..." I dropped my hand between her legs, dragging it over her slick pussy, "... what you sound like..." I sank two fingers inside her, causing her to moan loudly. "There's no way I can resist plunging myself deep inside you tonight."

She rocked her hips into my fingers, breathing heavily.

"Do you want this as much as I do?" I asked, looking down at her.

She pulled her bottom lip between her teeth and nodded.

"I want to hear you say it." I unbuttoned my pants and pulled the zipper down as I thrust my fingers inside her.

"I want it, Dex," she replied with breathless anticipation. "I want you."

My lips crashed against hers. She grabbed my tie, pulling me closer and kissing me with the same urgency I felt. I reached for a condom from my wallet and rolled it on while she devoured my neck, making it difficult to concentrate.

As soon as I was covered, I hiked up her dress and grabbed her thighs, driving into her hard and fast against the wall. She cried out, wrapping one leg around my waist and gripping my shoulders forcefully, letting her head fall back against the wall. I was so far beyond taking my time, I couldn't have slowed down even if I wanted to. Fortunately, Olivia seemed to want it that way.

"Oh God... Harder... please, Dex... Harder."

I shifted my hips, pulling almost all the way out and then thrusting back in, over and over again until she tightened around me and screamed my name. I followed her immediately, growling my release as I exploded inside her.

Our chests heaved together as we caught our breath. I rested my forehead on hers and loosened my grip, continuing to hold her.

"Holy shit," she breathed.

"Yeah... but I'm not nearly done with you yet, baby."

chapter nineteen

Olivia

Dex carried me into his bedroom and laid me on the bed before standing up to throw away the condom and grab another one. I watched him get undressed, enjoying the sight of him slowly and shamelessly getting naked in front of me. There was no way I would ever tire of seeing his powerful body and defined muscles, marked with the prominent black ink of his tattoos. Now that I knew what he could do with that body, how much pleasure he brought me, it only made him sexier.

He crawled over to me, and I sat up on my knees, letting him pull my dress over my head and remove my bra. Immediately, he took my breast in his mouth, and I grabbed his neck, holding him against me as he sucked my nipple, sending currents of pleasure shooting through my body. He made me come less than five minutes ago, and yet somehow, I already wanted more.

Dex lay down on his back and looked up at me expectantly. "I had you the way I wanted you, now it's your turn." His eyes twinkled,

"How do you want me, Liv?"

My eyes traveled up and down his body, unable to decide where to start. He was already hard again, his arousal standing proudly, and I was tempted to run my tongue over it and taste his silky smooth skin. Instead, I climbed over him, letting my breasts graze his chest as I kissed all the way down his neck to his stomach, running my tongue over the ridges of his abs in the way I'd been wanting to ever since I saw him that day on the beach.

"Olivia." His voice was rough and unsteady. "I know I told you to take control, but if I don't get inside you soon I might lose it."

I smiled against his skin and sat up, reaching for the condom behind me. "Patience, Mr. Porter…" With eager fingers, I slid it over his hot, thick length and positioned him at my entrance. I braced my hands on his chest as I sank down on him, moaning noisily as he filled me.

I rocked my hips against him, slowly at first, enjoying the way he felt so deep inside me. As I began moving faster, I grabbed his hand and placed it over my breast, desperate for more contact.

"I want your hands on me. I love the way you touch me," I said.

He kneaded me with his large palm, teasing and caressing my sensitive nipple as I arched into his touch and let my head fall back.

"God, you're so sexy," he said gruffly. "I love watching you come apart. I'll never get enough, Liv. Never. I fucking love being inside you."

His words spurred me on, and I moved faster as he gripped my hips, driving himself deeper. It felt so unbelievably good and I let myself go, grinding my hips against his and riding him hard until I sent us both spiraling over the edge.

"Okay, I need a break," I panted, trying to catch my breath.

Dex and I were going for a run together, and even though I exercised regularly on my own, I wasn't in nearly as good of shape as he was.

He slowed to a walk beside me. "I'm impressed, Liv. Not many people could keep up with me as long as you did."

I laughed. "Well, I would have stopped a long time ago if I wasn't trying to impress you!"

He threw his arm around my shoulder and pressed his lips against my sweaty temple. "Don't be silly, babe. You don't have to do anything to impress me because you've already amazed me in every way."

Whenever he said sweet things like that, which he did often, my heart melted a little bit more. I couldn't understand how one person could be so sweet and so incredibly sexy at the same time.

"How deep are we in the middle of nowhere?" I scanned the area around us, looking for anything familiar. We were in a rural part of town, along a quiet dirt road with historic looking country homes. I'd told Dex I wanted to see more of the area, since I hadn't really been anywhere other than the beach and the city, so he took me out to do some exploring.

"Not far," he said. "This road loops back to where we started."

We approached a driveway with a wooden mailbox in the shape of a house, and for some reason, it stuck out to me. It was one of those unique handcrafted ones, designed to look like the house it stood in front of. It had miniature wooden shingles covering the roof and an intricate little front porch with dark green shutters. I could have sworn I'd seen it before. Obviously, that didn't make any sense, but when we got closer I noticed that "EVANS" was painted on the side, and I stopped.

"Dex..." I gestured to the mailbox with a bewildered expression on my face. "That's my name."

"What are you talking about?" He looked at the mailbox and then back at me, confused. "Your last name is Mason."

"Mason was my mother's last name," I explained. "I changed it when I turned eighteen because I wanted nothing to do with my dad... his last name is Evans."

"It's a pretty common last name. I'm sure it's just a coincidence."

I shook my head. "I've seen that mailbox before and the house... I recognize it. On the other side, is there a tire swing hanging from a big oak tree?"

I knew this place, but I didn't know why. It was like I'd seen it in a dream, and all I could remember were bits and pieces and a few foggy images that were floating around in my head. I didn't know what was real and what wasn't. For some reason, I recalled swinging on a tire swing, laughing with someone whose face I couldn't see.

Dex jogged ahead to check the other side of the house, and his puzzled expression confirmed it. "How'd you know that swing would be there?"

"I can remember swinging on that swing, Dex. Why do I know this place?" It was a big white house with a two-story front porch, and there was a huge yard with big oak tree in the front, draped with Spanish moss. It was nothing like any of the places I'd ever lived, and yet it was familiar to me. The more I looked around, the more foggy memories began to surface. "It doesn't make any sense."

An older woman walked out the front door, heading in our direction. Her gray hair was cut above her shoulders and her jeans had mud on the knees, like she'd been working outside in the garden.

"Why don't we talk to her and find out?" Dex motioned in the old woman's direction. "Maybe you visited this place when you were a kid or something."

"Can I help you folks?" she called out from her front steps.

I grabbed Dex's arm and tried to pull him away. "No, let's just go. I'm sure it's nothing."

The woman moved closer, and when her eyes landed on me she froze, shocked.

"Olive? Is that you?"

The nickname tugged at a memory, and I studied her face, trying to put the pieces of the puzzle together. "How do you know me?" I asked her.

She seemed shaken, staring at me for a long moment before replying. "I'm Rose. I'm… I'm your grandmother."

My stomach did a somersault, and I took a step away from her. "No, that can't be. I don't know you," I sputtered, unable to wrap my head around what she was trying to say. "This is too much, it doesn't make any sense. I—I need to go."

There was disappointment on her face, but she nodded. "I'm sorry for springing it on you like that. I don't quite know what to say. I'm having a hard time believing that you're really standing here in front of me. I know this is strange… but if you want to talk, if you want me to explain… you just come by anytime, okay?"

Dex

"Are you okay?" I asked Olivia as we walked home.

She was quiet, and I was worried about her. I couldn't imagine what must have been going through her head. Coming across your long-lost grandmother during your afternoon run? It was a hell of a lot to process.

"I'm okay," she said. "Just confused, I guess. It doesn't seem possible... and yet, I remember being there."

"What made you think that you didn't have any family left?"

"That's what my mom told me. She always said that it was just the two of us, but it didn't matter because all we needed was each other. Why would she lie to me?"

I wondered the same thing. It seemed cruel to keep a child from her family. If Olivia had known she had someone out there, then she wouldn't have been on her own for so many years. I couldn't say that to her, though, so I just shrugged. "Maybe Rose can fill you in. Do you think you're going to go back and talk to her?"

"No... I don't know," she sighed, her hands twisting anxiously at her sides. "My mom must have had a reason for keeping her from me, so maybe it's best if I stay away. My whole life it was my mom and me, she was my best friend. I never had any reason not to trust her before, and now that she's gone, it doesn't seem fair to question her motives, you know?"

I didn't say anything because I knew she was trying to convince herself more than me. Her eyes were full of questions that she was scared to answer because she didn't want anything to tarnish her memory of her mother. I only hoped that she wouldn't let her love for her mother stand in the way of finding out the truth about her past and where she came from.

"I hate that I can't ask her," she said softly, eyes welling with tears. "She hated my dad for leaving us, and I could see how much it upset her when I talked about him, so I avoided it. I thought that if I waited to ask about him until she was happy with someone else, then it would be easier for her. I never wanted her to think that I didn't appreciate her, or that asking about him meant that I loved her any less. Now she's gone, and it's too late. I just... I really wish she was still here."

"I know, baby." I wrapped my arms around her and pulled her close. "I know."

It was then that I realized I wasn't the only one with ghosts. We were both anchored to the past, haunted by our own regrets and unable to move forward or let go. In a lot of ways, Olivia was still a three-year old little girl, scared and confused about why her dad was no longer there. I was stuck in a desert halfway across the world, watching my best friend die in front of me and wishing more than anything that I could stop it or take his place.

What kind of a future could we ever have together if we were both constantly looking back?

After Olivia went to work that night, I went home and stared at the envelope that Teddy's parents sent me. It had been sitting on my coffee table for months, taunting me with its presence and daring me to open it. The only way I would ever have a future with Olivia was if I confronted my demons and accepted the consequences, and reading this letter was the first step.

How do you make yourself read a letter that will verify all the worst thoughts that you already have about yourself? Hearing it from people who I loved would make it all the more real, and I wasn't sure I would ever be able to recover from that. My fingers hovered over the envelope, ready to tear it open and face the truth, but I couldn't do it. Fear shot through me and I chickened out, as usual.

Instead, I hid in my bedroom, where the letter wouldn't mock me, and waited for Olivia to finish her shift. Sometimes she would come here afterwards and I hoped that tonight would be one of those nights. When she was with me, I didn't have to think about the past or worry about the future – all I cared about was the present.

This is it. After months and months of endless training, tactical preparation and pushing our bodies to the limit, we are finally shipping out to begin our first tour overseas. All our blood, sweat and tears have led to this moment, but in a way, it's only the beginning.

Teddy and I wait to get on the flight that will take us to Iraq, surrounded by our parents who insisted on seeing us off. It's more for them than it is for us. We chose this, but I know that our parents haven't quite come to terms with it yet. I can see the fear in their eyes, and I know that my mom is barely holding it together. She's gripping my dad's hand so tight that it's turning white. I'm glad that Amy didn't come. She's nearly nine months pregnant and about to pop, and I don't want to upset her any more than she already is. Teddy's little sister didn't come either; she's too young to deal with this. It's hard enough with our parents here. They have to watch us walk away and wonder whether or not we're going to come back on our own or in a wooden box draped with the flag of the country we're fighting for.

We already had the hard conversation – you know, the one where you sit down and talk about how you want to handle stuff if you don't make it back. My mom had to leave the room during that one, but my dad sat there graciously while I explained what I want in the case of death or serious injury. It's a real shitty fucking conversation to have, but the Corps drilled it into our brains how important it is to have it.

I can see the other men from our unit starting to make their way to the boarding area and I know it's time for us to go. I look over at Teddy and he nods.

"We better get going or else we'll miss out on the in-flight cocktails," Teddy jokes, trying to lighten the mood. He glances sideways at me. "I hope they have those little umbrellas in them, I love those."

"Don't be ridiculous, Ted." I scoff, rolling my eyes at him dramatically. "Of course, they have those little umbrellas!"

We laugh, but as usual our parents are less than amused by our antics. My dad steps forward first and pulls me into a hug.

"I love you, son. We're so proud of you," he says, clutching the back of my neck and squeezing me tight. "Be safe out there, you got it?"

I nod. "I will, Dad. I love you, too."

My mom looks like she's going to burst into tears at any moment, and my dad has to guide her over to me.

"Get over here, Mama Bear," I smile. "I need a good hug for the road." I lean down and wrap my arms around her, lifting her a few inches off the ground. "I love you. Take good care of that little niece of mine and send me pictures when she gets here, okay?"

She nods tearfully against my chest. "I love you, honey. Promise me you'll be careful."

"I promise."

I hug Teddy's parents, too. They've been like a second family to me all my life, and it's almost as hard to say goodbye to them as it is to my own mom and dad.

"You two need to take care of each other," his mom says to me. "You make each other stronger, you always have, and as long as you're looking out for one another, I can sleep better at night. You boys keep each other safe, okay?"

"You know we will," I tell her. "We're a team. We're in this together. Always."

I felt warm arms come around me, pulling me out of my bad dream. Olivia's comforting smell and gentle touch carried me out of the shadows and brought me back to reality.

As much as I wanted to be the one protecting her and keeping her safe, the truth was that she was the one saving me. She cast light into my life, but unfortunately the darkness was always close behind, knocking on the door with a harsh reminder of my past.

I couldn't rely on her presence to keep my demons at bay. My only chance at a decent future was to push them away for good, but I just didn't know how. My nightmares felt like a punishment for my past, and I was afraid that they wouldn't go away unless I found a way to come to terms with everything I'd done... but that was something I might never be able to do.

chapter twenty

Olivia

I was alone in bed when I woke up the next morning, and I could hear the sound of the shower in the bathroom. Dex always let me sleep in after working late, but he usually came back into bed with me. I decided that since I was already up, I might as well surprise him.

He was having a nightmare when I came by his house after work the night before, and while it wasn't as traumatic as the last time I'd seen it, I recognized the torment he was going through. I knew how much they affected him and I wanted to cheer him up and take his mind off it.

Undressing quickly, I snuck into the bathroom as quietly as possible. I could make out his naked form through the textured glass of the shower, standing motionless under the stream of hot water.

"Good morning..." I sang out, sliding the door open and stepping inside.

"Mmmm... morning, baby." He caught my hips and pulled me underneath the water with him. "When did you get up?"

"Just now. I was lonely in there without you…" Brushing my lips against his, I immediately felt his arousal against my belly. I trailed my hand down his chest and stomach before taking him in my hand and stroking his length.

He groaned, tightening his hands on my hips. "I can't have my girl feeling lonely… let's see if we can fix that."

Grabbing a condom from the vanity, he covered himself in record time, and whirled me around to face the wall. He grazed his lips over my neck and slowly entered me from behind, filling me perfectly and completely. And just like that, all our worries were momentarily forgotten.

It was quiet at the aquarium during my shift that day, which meant there was no one to distract me from all the thoughts that had been colliding in my head since I met Rose. I couldn't stop thinking about what she said and whether or not I should go talk to her. As much as I wanted to find out the truth, I was scared of what it might mean.

I didn't want to believe that my mom would hide family from me, especially when we had no one else. I loved my mom more than anything. She was the one who stood by me and was there for me all my life, and I didn't want to hear something that might tarnish that.

At the same time, there was a whole piece of my life that I was missing. There was so much about my past that I didn't know and didn't understand, and I wanted answers. I'd been feeling that void for as long as I could remember, but would getting the answers make it better or worse?

I rested my elbows on the edge of Myrtle's tank and watched the turtle drifting lazily around in the water by herself. "How 'bout you

Miss Myrtle… do you have a little turtle family of your own waiting for you?" I sighed, "I probably shouldn't complain since you turtles have it way worse than me. Your mom laid her eggs in the sand and then left you all alone to hatch and find your way into the ocean. You poor little turtle babies have to learn to survive all on your own… that's pretty brutal. I guess life is cruel that way. It can be a lonely world out there. I suppose that if I have a chance to find my family, I should take it, huh?"

I was talking to a turtle. Myrtle was a cool chick and all, but I was probably starting to lose it.

When Frank appeared beside me, my cheeks heated in embarrassment. I hadn't even heard him come in and there I was, talking to an animal like a crazy person.

"Myrtle here is a pretty decent conversationalist, isn't she?" he chuckled, resting his arms next to mine on the tank.

"Busted," I grinned. "They left me to my own devices down here and look what happened."

"Hey, I'm not judging. Sometimes the best ones to talk to are the ones that don't talk back and let us work stuff out on our own instead." His eyes shifted from me to Myrtle. "You know, turtles are solitary creatures by nature, but that doesn't mean they're always alone. A lot of them migrate to the same places, along the same routes and sometimes they even travel in groups. They might not have family, but I like to think that they find some friends along the way."

I had a feeling we weren't talking about turtles anymore.

"Do you think that's enough?" I said softly.

"I guess it depends," he shrugged. "Family is important, there's no doubt about that. But not all family is related by blood. Sometimes, the strongest bonds we have are the ones we form along the way. That being said, it's important to know where we come from. Often times, we have to look back before we can really move forward."

"You're a wise man, Frankie." I turned to him with a questioning look. "Are you sure you weren't a therapist before this?"

He laughed. "Nah, just stumbled across a lot of life lessons in my time, so I like to pretend I know a thing or two. It's come in handy around here – you're not the first person to talk to the animals, and you won't be the last!" He gave my shoulder a reassuring squeeze. "We're all just navigating our way through life, Livie girl. Some paths are trickier than others. There's no harm in making a few wrong turns along the way."

With that, he turned to go back upstairs, leaving Myrtle and me to try and absorb everything he said and make sense of it. Before I had a chance to sort through my thoughts, I felt my phone vibrate in my pocket. Normally, I ignored it while I was working, but since no one else was around, I pulled it out and glanced at the screen. The call was from a blocked number so I didn't answer, assuming that whoever it was would leave a message. They didn't though, and kept calling.

After the third call, I finally gave in and picked it up. "Hello?"

No answer.

"Hello, can I help you?" I repeated, getting frustrated. I thought I heard noises on the other end, but there was still no answer, so I hung up.

I was a little creeped out about who it could be. When I left New York, I got a new, unlisted number, and only a handful of people had it. None of them had a blocked number, and if it was a wrong number, then they would have realized it after hearing my voicemail message and wouldn't have called back.

For a split second, I wondered if it might be Rose, but then I laughed at the idea. The nice old woman who claimed to be my grandmother didn't look like someone who even owned a cell phone, so unless she was secretly some kind of tech-savvy computer whiz, there was no way she found my number.

Deciding that it must have been a persistent telemarketer, I brushed it off and got back to work. Phone calls were the least of my problems.

"Hey man, it's Porter… Dex Porter. I know this is out of the blue, but I was hoping I could come by today."

The voice I heard on the other end of the phone was a familiar one; one that I heard every night when I fell asleep. Hearing that voice shook me and made me want to turn around, but I pressed on.

A three-hour drive into Wilmington, North Carolina wasn't exactly what I'd planned on doing today, but after having another nightmare last night, I knew I had to do something. Olivia had very successfully distracted me in the shower, but I knew I couldn't keep burying my problems. As soon as she left for work, I'd hopped in my truck and started driving.

My directions led me to a quiet street lined with houses on each side. It was a nice neighborhood, full of family homes with white picket fences and children playing in the yard. I thought I might have gotten the street wrong until I pulled up to the house and saw a truck in the driveway with a "USMC" bumper sticker. I took a deep breath and climbed out, stuffing my hands in my pockets as I walked to the front door.

Before I could knock, the door swung open.

"Holy shit, Porter... it's good to see you," Chase said, pulling me in for a hug. "After more than a dozen unanswered phone calls, I'd given up on hearing from you, until you called me this morning."

I rubbed the back of my neck awkwardly. "I know, I'm sorry. I just..."

"It's okay," he stopped me. "I know how it is. I'm glad you're here now. Come on in."

After grabbing two beers and cracking them open, he led me into the living room. He walked with a slight limp, but I doubted if it was noticeable to anyone else. When we sat down, I took a long pull from the beer he handed me. It was still early afternoon, but this kind of situation required one.

"How's the leg?" I asked.

"Pretty damn good, actually." He pulled up his pant leg to reveal the prosthetic leg he had underneath. "It's incredible what they've done with these things. It hardly bothers me at all anymore. Obviously it took some getting used to at first, but it's a small price to pay. I'll take losing a leg any day if it means getting away with my life."

I wondered what was wrong with me. My friend lost half his leg and still found a way to move on with his life and be positive about it. Me? Aside from a slight loss of hearing, I'd escaped in one piece, and yet I couldn't seem to move past it.

"It's because of you that I got out of there at all," Chase said. "If you hadn't dragged me out, I wouldn't be here right now. I wouldn't have had a second chance." A huge smile formed on his mouth. "I wouldn't be a daddy."

My head snapped up. "You have a kid? Are you fucking with me?"

"Not quite yet, but in another couple weeks, yeah."

"Wow, congratulations. That's… incredible," I smiled, shaking my head. "Didn't waste any time, did you?"

"Hell no!" he laughed. "As soon as I got out of the hospital, I asked Lila to marry me, and we went down to city hall. We decided we didn't want to wait to start a family, and now… here we are."

"Here you are," I echoed. "I'm so happy for you. You deserve it."

"You wanna know what we decided to name him?"

"It's a boy?"

"Yup," he replied with a nod. "Austin Porter Scott."

"What?" My throat tightened, and I looked at him, "Why?"

"You saved my life, Porter. You saved all our asses out there. More than once. I can only hope my son turns out half as brave as you."

"I'm not brave," I mumbled, focusing on a spot on the floor. "I'm a fucking mess, man. Sometimes I feel like a part of me is still over there. I wake up from a nightmare, and all I want to do is throw on my gear and go hurt someone. I'm constantly looking around for threats, like any minute an enemy combatant is gonna sneak up behind me and take me out. I can't get my shit together and my head… God, my head is so fucked up. I don't think I'm ever gonna get past it."

"Yes, you will," he told me. "I've been where you are, and it sucks. The nightmares, the guilt, the paranoia… it's enough to fuck anyone's head up. You can't live through what we lived through, see what we saw, and expect anything to be normal after. That shit wasn't normal, and we're all probably going to carry it with us for the rest of our lives. We all left a part of us over there."

"Not me, I didn't just leave a part of myself… I left my best fucking friend over there to die. I failed and I don't deserve to move on."

"How did you fail?" he questioned me. "By running out into the smoke even though you couldn't hear shit, and your brain had just gotten rattled to shit inside your skull? By dragging half our goddamn unit to safety so we could return to our families? That doesn't sound like failure to me, Dex."

"I failed Teddy!" I screamed, no longer able to keep it inside. "He was dying, he called out for me, and I couldn't fucking find him! I couldn't save him!"

"No one could've saved him!" Chase yelled, standing from his seat and staring me down. "He never called your name, Dex. I know you thought you heard him, but you didn't. His injuries were too extreme, and there's nothing that you or anyone else could have done to save him. You've got to understand that."

I dragged my hands over my face in frustration. "I understand what you're trying to say, I do. My logic tells me one thing, but I just... can't feel that way."

"It's all part of the PTSD. It's like all your wires get crossed, and even though you want to feel one way, you just can't. It gets better, though."

"How?" I asked. "How do I get better?"

"You talk about it. Talk, talk, and talk until the mess in your head starts to unravel. We internalize all this shit, and it eats us alive. They have counseling and therapy and all that shit to help us sort it out and give us the tools we need to move on."

"It doesn't feel fair, somehow. Why should I get to live a happy, normal life when Teddy can't?"

"You really think Teddy wants you to punish yourself for the rest of your life? Just because his life had to end doesn't mean yours does, too. He wouldn't want that for you." A small smile formed on his lips. "That kid would have your ass if he knew you weren't out there living life to the fullest."

He was right about that. "Are you happy?"

"Fuck yeah, I'm happy. I'm not sure I'll ever truly get past it, and I'll probably struggle with it for the rest of my life, but I've learned to deal with it and move forward. I keep up with the therapy, I've got a good woman who's always there for me, and every day is a little bit easier than the last." He looked at me with a sideways glance, "You got a good girl, Porter?"

I was quiet for a moment before a smile tilted my lips and I nodded. "Yeah, I do."

"You'll work it out, I know you will. If anyone can get through this, it's you."

I spent the rest of the day there and got to meet his very-pregnant wife, Lila, who invited me to stay for dinner. We kept the conversation light, catching up and exchanging embarrassing stories about each other while Lila laughed so hard I thought the baby was going to pop out right there in the dining room.

Before I left, Chase handed me a card for the veteran support program that had referred him to his therapist, who specialized in Post-Traumatic Stress Disorder, and told me that they could refer me to someone as well.

"Thank you… for everything," I said as I took the card.

"No thanks necessary. Don't be a stranger, okay?"

"I won't," I said. "I want to meet that little boy of yours when he gets here."

"You better. Stay safe, brother. Semper fi."

"Semper fi."

chapter twenty-one

Olivia

"Have you decided what you're going to do about Rose?" Dex asked.

It had been a little over a week since the "grandmother" incident, and I'd been avoiding the topic. I knew that Dex thought I should go see her, but aside from a few hints here and there, he had left it alone. Until now.

"Not yet." I really hoped that he would drop it, but the look on his face said otherwise.

"I know it's a lot to think about, Liv… but aren't you curious? She might be able to answer some of the questions you have and fill in the gaps from your childhood."

"Of course, I'm curious," I snapped. My tone came out harsher than I intended but I couldn't help it. "But it's not like she's filling me in on last week's episode of Grey's Anatomy… we're talking about my *life* here! It's a big deal."

"I know it is," he acknowledged. "I'm not trying to push you, I just… I'm worried that you'll regret it if you don't. She's not going to be around forever and I don't want you to spend the rest of your life wondering."

Since when did everyone else think they knew what was best for me?

"This coming from a guy who has an unopened letter from his best friend's parents that's been sitting on his coffee table for months now. Why don't you take your own advice, Dex?" I blurted it out without thinking and immediately regretted it when I saw the pain flash across his face. He was trying to help me and I was getting defensive. I was frustrated and confused, and I was taking it out on him.

Dex quietly walked out of the room, and I felt like the worst person on the planet. I was about to jump up and go after him when he came back in.

"I'm sorry, Dex. I'm being such a bitch. I didn't mean that, I know it's not the same thing. I'm confused, and I'm taking it out on you when you're only trying to help. I'm so, so sorry."

"No, you're right." He sat down on the couch next to me, gripping the letter in his hand. "I've been avoiding this letter because I'm afraid of what's inside, but it's time to face it. Good or bad, we can't hide from the past forever. It has a way of catching up with us whether we like it or not."

He was far more understanding than I deserved.

"So I was thinking," he continued. "What if we did it together? You can sit with me while I open this letter, and then we'll go over to your grandmother's house. Let's just rip off the band-aids and get it over with."

"You would really do that for me?" I asked.

"I would do anything for you."

Looking into his eyes, I was totally overcome by the amazing, kind, wonderful man in front of me. The fact that, for me, he was willing to open himself up to the pain that would come with reading that letter… it blew me away. In that moment, I finally admitted something to myself that I'd probably known for quite a while but had been too scared to acknowledge. I was totally and completely in love with Dex.

Of course, it was one thing to admit it to myself and entirely another to actually say it out loud. Dex had said it once on the night he admitted his feelings for me, but he hadn't said it since then. I knew how he felt about me—he had proved that to me—but I couldn't risk putting it out there if we weren't ready.

Still, that realization made me realize something else – that I couldn't let him rush into opening that letter. He needed to do it on his own time, when he was ready. As sweet as it was that he was willing to do it for me, I loved him too much to let him.

"Actually, Dex… if it's okay with you, could we rip my band-aid off first?" I said. "I'm afraid I'll chicken out if I wait too long."

"Sure thing, babe. Whatever you want."

His relief was obvious, and I knew I made the right decision. I had no doubt that he would find the courage to do it soon, but I couldn't let him do it for me. He needed to do it for himself.

The old station wagon was sitting in the driveway when we pulled up to the house, so I knew Rose was home. It was hard to believe that I'd ever lived here as a kid. All the places that my mom and I lived were tiny, cramped apartments in busy neighborhoods, but this place was completely different. It had a huge yard to run around in, trees to climb, and there was only one other house close by. It sat on the edge of the river, and there was a small dock that led to a little raft. There were rocking chairs on the front porch and a carefully tended garden bursting with colorful flowers. It was the kind of place that every child dreams of growing up in. I only wished I could have remembered my time here.

"Do you want me to come in with you or stay out here?" Dex asked, helping me out of the truck.

I looked at him nervously. "Could you come in with me?"

"Of course I will." He took my hand and gave it a gentle squeeze. "We're in this together, remember?"

I nodded and took a deep breath. "Let's do this."

We climbed up the brick steps, and I hesitantly knocked on the big wooden door. When there was no answer, I knocked again, this time a little louder.

"I'm coming, I'm coming. Hold your horses!" called a voice from inside.

Rose opened the door, a smile appearing on her face when she saw me. "I was starting to wonder if you were ever going to come by and see me." After a few seconds of awkward silence, she took a step to the side, ushering us in the house. "Well, come on in, honey."

All of a sudden, I had no idea what to say or do. Thankfully, Dex held his hand out to her. "Hi, ma'am. I'm Olivia's boyfriend, Dex Porter."

"Rose Evans," she smiled, shaking his outstretched hand. "It's nice to meet you, Dex."

"Sorry, I'm a little nervous," I admitted shakily.

"That's perfectly all right. I'm a little nervous myself," said Rose. "I'm just glad you came. Why don't you have a seat in the living room, and I'll go fetch us some lemonade?"

She led is into a cozy room with a couch and two chairs situated in front of a stone fireplace. There were French doors that opened up to the porch, letting in a cool breeze from outside. As I looked around, I was flooded with hazy memories and glimpses into a childhood that I didn't recognize.

There was a cluster of framed photos displayed on a bookshelf, and when I stepped forward to take a closer look, my eyes fell on one in the center. In a round, antique silver frame was a picture of Rose and me. I was probably about three years old, so it must have been taken right around the time we left. We wore matching smiles and my little arms were wrapped tightly around her like I was holding on for dear life. It was easy to see how much those two people loved each other.

"You were a cute kid," Dex said.

"How do I not remember?"

Rose came up behind us, "It was a long time ago, Olive. You were so young when your mama left. Let's sit down so we can talk." She handed us our glasses of lemonade and sat down in one of the chairs.

"I don't even know where to begin…" I said, taking a seat next to Dex on the couch.

"How about we start at the beginning?" she suggested, taking a sip from her glass. "As you may already know, your parents—Laura and Tom—were high school sweethearts. Laura lost her mother when she was young and was being raised by her daddy, who didn't know a damn thing about raising a daughter on his own. When Laura found out she was pregnant shortly after graduating high school… boy, was he was furious. He had big plans for her to go off to college and make something of herself, and since being a mother didn't fit into that plan, he gave her an ultimatum – give up the baby or get out."

I inhaled a sharp breath. My mom had never told me any of this.

She didn't talk much about her parents, but she always made it sound like both her parents died at the same time. I was beginning to realize that I didn't know as much about my mom as I thought I did.

"But your mama... she was a tough cookie, that one," Rose continued. "Fierce as a lion, but with a heart of gold. She loved you from the moment she found out you were in her belly, and she fought for you. Packed her bags, held her head high, and never looked back. I took her in here in a heartbeat. I loved that girl so much, and she was already like a daughter to me.

"Tom knew he needed more than a high school diploma if he was going to provide for a family, so he went off to college in the fall. He was only a few hours away, so he came home for weekends here and there to see you and your mom, but for the most part, it was just the three of us. As time wore on, he started coming home less and less, telling us he had to study or was busy with this and that. I knew it bothered your mom, but she never spoke up. He was the one person she could never stand up to, because she loved him so much and was afraid of losing him. She would make excuses for him and say that it was okay that he spent all that time away because he was working hard at school to make a better life for them. She thought that once he was done with school, he would come back, and you would be a happy family.

"Then, one weekend after months of him not returning home, Laura went up there to confront him. What she found out was that, while she had been at home raising you all on her own, my scumbag son had been seeing someone else for over a year. Laura was devastated, and the worst part was that Tom didn't even seem remorseful. He said that they had been growing apart for years, and he wasn't ready to be a family. It was all total bull, of course, but that's just the way Tom was... selfish beyond belief, with no regard for the feelings of those around him. Don't know where he got it from, because his father—God rest his soul—was nothing like that. As awful as it sounds, I always knew that Laura was too good for him, but I guess I hoped that he would turn out to be something other than what he was and prove me wrong."

My mom's story was remarkably similar to my own, and yet so much worse because she had a child with the man who betrayed her. It broke my heart to think about how much pain he caused her. She carried that pain with her for the rest of her life, never truly moving on or letting go.

Rose took a deep breath before continuing. "Laura came back completely heartbroken and determined to get as far away from him as possible. I begged her to stay with me, telling her I would do whatever it took to keep her here – even if it meant cutting ties with my own son. I would have done it too, and perhaps that makes me an awful mother, but what Tom did was unforgivable and all I cared about was protecting you and your mom. You two were my family."

"It sounds like you really loved her," I said softly.

"Oh, honey, I did." She wiped a tear from her cheek. "I truly did."

"Then why didn't she stay with you?"

"She said that it wouldn't be fair to Tom or me if I chose her over him," Rose said tearfully. "Truthfully though, I think it was simply too hard for her to be here. Everything about this place, and me, made her think of Tom, and she no longer wanted anything to do with him or this life. So she took you, and she left." She pulled out a handkerchief to dab her eyes. "It broke my heart, but I knew how much she was hurting so I tried to understand. When weeks and then months went by and I didn't hear from her, I realized that I probably never would. She felt she needed to cut ties completely, and I'm guessing that's the reason she never told you about any of this. I still regret letting her walk away, and I want you to know that not a single day has gone by when I didn't think about you and your mom. I've missed you every day."

My eyes welled with tears, and Dex reached for my hand, giving it a reassuring squeeze. "How did you find out about my mom… about her accident?" I asked.

Rose stood up and walked over to the bookshelf, pulling something out from behind the frames and handing it to me. It was a photo taken of my mom and me at my high school graduation, only a few weeks before she died. It wasn't in a frame and it was worn, the edges ragged, like it had been handled often. I flipped it over and saw that there was a message written on the back in my mom's handwriting.

I miss you. I'm sorry.

"She mailed that to me before it happened. I couldn't believe my eyes when I opened it. After all those years, she was finally reaching out to me. There was nothing else inside, but there was a return address on the envelope, so I wrote her a letter begging her to contact me. When she didn't respond, I wrote another, and another, until one day they were all returned to me, unopened. I called the Postmaster in New York, and they were the ones who told me she passed. It destroyed me, and all I could think about was you, Olive. I didn't know if your mom had moved on and there was someone in your life to take care of you, or if you were out there all alone. I tried to find out, but no one could ever tell me anything."

"We moved around a lot," I explained, trying not to choke on my own words. "We were never in one place long enough to get to know anyone. My mom never moved on… there was never anyone else. It was… it was just us."

"Oh, Olive…" she cried, tears racing down her cheeks. "I'm so sorry that you had to go through that all on your own. I should have been there for you… I should have tried harder to find you. I just didn't know how."

"It's not your fault," I assured her. "When I first met you, I was angry that my mom kept you a secret from me, but I think she wanted to tell me… she just had to do it in her own time. Unfortunately, she never got the chance. I'm sure things probably would have been a lot different for me if she'd reached out to you sooner, or told me about you from the beginning, but I did all right on my own, and I'm stronger because of it."

"You're so much like her, you know that?" Rose smiled. "Laura had a way of putting everyone around her at ease. Simply being around her could brighten my day, and even as a little girl you were the same way."

"I'm starting to remember certain things," I said. "Nothing specific, mostly foggy images here and there of you and my mom, but nothing about my dad. He and I weren't close, were we?"

She shook her head, "No, not really. Like I said, he was hardly around, and frankly, he didn't know how to be a father at all, let alone a good one. Most of the time, he was watching from the sidelines, preoccupied with his own life. It got to the point where you stopped asking for him and didn't even really notice him when he was around."

"Did he ever try to find me? Or even talk about me?" The question fell from my lips before I had a chance to stop it. Deep down, I knew the answer but I couldn't help but ask it anyway.

Rose bowed her head sadly. "I can't be sure whether he did or not, but if you want the truth… I would be surprised if he did. He did love you, though, Olivia. I know it sounds strange, given the circumstances, but in his own twisted, selfish way, he loved you."

I nodded, ignoring the ball in the pit of my stomach, trying not to let it bother me. "Where is he now?"

"He's a few hours away in Columbia, but he does a lot of traveling for work, so he's rarely home."

"Does he have a family?"

She nodded slowly. "He married the woman he met in college, and they have a daughter. Now, don't start thinking that he turned into some great family man… because he didn't. He's still the same man that he was before, but this time, when he got the girl pregnant, her rich daddy threatened to kill him if he didn't marry her. He's absent from his daughter's life, and his wife is no better. They send her off to boarding schools and sleep-away camps, and up until this year, she spent every summer here with me. If you ask me, you were better off without him, Olive. I really mean that."

"I have a sister?" I'd never considered the possibility, and the idea made my head spin. I wasn't entirely sure how I felt about it. I would've thought that I might feel some kind of bitterness or jealousy toward her for getting the perfect family I never had, but from what Rose was saying, her life was far from perfect. I may have grown up without a dad, but at least I always had a mother who was there for me and loved me.

"Yup, you sure do," Rose answered. "Her name is Harper. She's nineteen, and she's an absolute sweetheart, probably because her parents never spent enough time with her to tarnish her. She's the only reason that Tom is a part of my life. I resented him for what he did to your mother, but when Harper was born, I knew that she needed to have someone in her life to love her and take care of her."

I already hated my father for what he had done to my mom and me, but now I hated him even more for what he was doing to this poor girl. I didn't even know Harper, and yet somehow I felt strangely protective. "Does she know about me?" I asked.

"Yes, she does. She doesn't know that you're here, but she's known for a long time that she had a half-sister out there somewhere. She always wanted a sibling growing up, and she never quite understood why she couldn't meet you." Rose looked over at me tentatively. "I'm sure that you're going to need some time to process all this, but when you're ready... if you're open to it... I know that she would love to meet you."

It was all so overwhelming and I hesitated for a moment, mulling it over in my head. "I would like that," I told her. "I'm not quite ready for it yet, and I might need some time to get used to the idea, but eventually... I would really like to get to know her."

"You take all the time you need, darlin'. She'll be there whenever you're ready."

After a while, Dex and I got up to leave. I promised Rose that I would come back again soon. She walked us to the door and pulled me in for a hug, holding me close for a long time.

"Olivia Rose Mason." I recited my full name out loud, finally understanding the meaning behind it. "I remember once asking my mom where my middle name came from and she told me that it was a family name. She said that it came from the most important person in her life, and someday she would tell me all about her. I'm so glad that I found you, Rose."

She smiled, her eyes pooling with tears. "Me too, Olive. More than you'll ever know."

I glanced over at Olivia after we pulled out of Rose's driveway. She seemed a little shell-shocked, but after everything that Rose just told her, how could she not be? There were times during that conversation that I had to ball my hands into fists just to contain my anger. Olivia's dad sounded like the most worthless piece of shit on the planet, and I hated him for not giving her the childhood she deserved.

"Are you okay?" I asked her. It was a stupid question because, of course, she wasn't, but I didn't know what else to say. I was afraid that if she had too much time to think about it, she would end up torturing herself.

"Yeah, I am," she said. "It was just strange to hear some of that stuff. There's so much that I didn't know about and it was… different than I expected. After hearing the whole story and realizing how difficult things were for my mom, I don't blame her keeping that stuff from me. I thought I'd be angry, but instead I feel strangely relieved. My mom is still the person I always thought she was. There's no way she could have predicted that she would die before having the chance to tell me about my past… sometimes these things just happen."

"You got here eventually, that's all that matters."

"It's crazy, isn't it?" she let out a laugh. "Of all the places that I could have ended up, I happened to end up here, where I started. When I first visited with Nora, I felt an immediate connection to this place. I knew part of it was because my mom was born here, but it went deeper than that. Now I know why. It's… home."

"So, about your dad…" I began, trying to pose the question in a way that wouldn't upset her. "Do you think you'll ever reach out to him?"

She turned to stare out her window without saying a word. I thought I may have crossed a line, but after a while, she finally answered. "No, I don't want anything to do with him. It's not that I hate him, or resent him… I just don't feel anything toward him. He wasn't a big part of my life even when he was around, and he never tried to find me or be a part of my life after that. He let me go and now I'm letting him go. I'm better off without him."

I couldn't blame her. I was relieved that she didn't have any plans to open herself up to someone who didn't deserve her and would probably hurt her. Some people were inherently bad and weren't capable of changing or worthy of a second chance.

One of my worst fears was that I was one of those people.

"You know what I do want?" Olivia took a deep breath and turned toward me. "I want to get my mind off all this serious crap. Even if it's just for a little while."

"Done," I grinned, knowing exactly what to do.

The narrow dirt road was so overgrown that I was afraid my truck might not make it to the end. There were huge potholes that made it nearly impossible to navigate unless you were in a lifted truck like mine. The area was remote, to say the least, and not many people knew of the spot I was taking her to. We used to light a huge bonfire and party out there when I was in high school, because it was so deep in the woods that no one would ever stumble upon us. I hadn't been there since before I went overseas for my last tour, but if it was anything like I remembered, then it was ideal for what I had in mind.

"Where are you taking me, exactly?" Olivia asked.

"You'll see," I evaded.

Finally the road opened up to a big clearing in the middle of the woods. It was perfect. Last night's rainstorm had left enormous puddles in the dirt and practically the entire area was all mud.

"I really hope this isn't your idea of romantic," she mused, eyeing me suspiciously as I rolled up all the windows.

My grin got wider. "Buckle up, baby."

She tossed me a confused look, and I hit the gas. The tires spun, fighting for traction as mud flew up and spattered the windows, painting the outside of the truck. Olivia screamed, bracing herself against the dashboard as we sped over a steep bump and splashed into the puddle at the bottom.

"Are you crazy?" she laughed, unable to contain the smile on her face.

"What, you've never been mudding before?" I glanced over at her. "If you're gonna be a southern girl, then it's something you gotta do!"

My entire truck was coated in brown mud, and we could barely see through the windows, but all that mattered to me was Olivia's carefree laughter echoing through the cab. If anything could make her forget about all that complicated shit, it was this. There was something liberating about whipping through the mud in a truck, flying into the air over a bump, and that lofty feeling you got in the pit of your stomach on the way down. It was exhilarating in the best way and made you let go of all the other bullshit. It brought me back to when I was a kid and the most fun happened when I was doing things that involved getting dirty. Adults are always going out of their way to avoid messes and stay clean, but sometimes you need it.

Being messy is a part of life. A fun part.

Every once in a while, when I hit a steep trench or sped up, Olivia would let out a little scream, but the huge smile hadn't left her face since we started. I loved that smile. I would do anything for that smile.

We kept going until the sun started to set and the sound of our growling stomachs alerted us to the fact that we hadn't eaten anything since breakfast. We stopped for dinner on the way home and when we passed the beach, Olivia told me to pull over.

"What is it?" I asked, concerned that she was going to be sick or that the day had finally gotten to her, and she was about to have some kind of emotional breakdown.

Her eyes twinkled mischievously. "There's another carefree, reckless thing that I want to do."

She hopped out of the truck, scampering over the sand and into the darkness. I jumped out to follow, scanning the beach futilely for any sign of her. It was pitch black and the only light came from the pale glow of the moon in the sky. My eyes began adjusting to the dark as I moved further down the beach and I nearly tripped over a pair of shoes in the sand. Olivia's shoes.

I picked them up and kept walking. When I came across the pale pink tee shirt that she'd been wearing, my face broke into a grin, and I started moving faster. I followed her trail of clothes, finding her denim shorts, bra, and finally her panties. I looked up, and when my eyes fell on her, wading into the water without a scrap of clothing on, I damn near swallowed my tongue.

Her soft skin was radiant in the moonlight, illuminating the sloping lines of her gentle curves against the dark ocean. Her blonde hair cascaded down her back, billowing in the soft breeze and caressing her slender shoulders.

I'd never seen anything more beautiful in my entire life.

She glanced over her shoulder, her eyes twinkling as they found mine. "Well, aren't you going to join me?"

I couldn't get undressed fast enough.

Throwing my clothes in the sand, I waded in behind her. The water felt amazing and refreshing, warmed by the hot summer sun during the day.

Coming up behind her, I aligned my body with hers and wrapped my arms around her waist, pulling her tightly against me. I dropped my lips to her ear and whispered, "You take my breath away, Liv."

She trembled slightly and curved her body into mine, pushing her round, perfect ass against my firm cock in the most tempting way. I moved my hand down her stomach, dipping it between her legs and running my fingers over her slick heat. She moaned, her head falling back against my shoulder as I took her breast in one hand and continued rubbing her pussy with the other.

I pulled her into the deeper water. The ocean was calm and relatively still, lapping against our shoulders as I turned her around to face me.

"Thank you for today," she said softly, wrapping her arms and legs around me. Her lips brushed softly against mine, but I needed more. I wove my hands in her hair, deepening the kiss and gently nipping her soft bottom lip. She parted her mouth and let me inside, winding her tongue with mine as sweet, sexy sounds escaped from her throat and vibrated in my mouth.

She was pressed perfectly against me, and it would have been easy to slide inside her, but this was too incredible to rush. I wanted to take my time and enjoy the way her wet, sexy body was slipping against mine. The way her nipples pebbled in the cool night air and grazed against my chest. The way the ocean water swirled between us, warming every inch of our already heated skin.

I began kissing my way down her neck, along her collarbone and over her cleavage. She bowed her back and I took her breast in my mouth, licking and sucking her nipple as she writhed her body into mine. Her skin was salty from the ocean and the taste on my lips was driving me wild. I hauled her against me, dragging her along the hard length of my cock until neither of us could take it anymore. Shifting my hips I sank inside her and a loud growl escaped my lips. Nothing felt better than this. She was tight and fucking perfect, our bodies fitting together like two pieces of the same puzzle.

Her hands clasped my shoulders as she rocked her hips into me. "Oh my God, Dex… you feel so good baby, just like that." Gripping her ass in my hands I began thrusting into her, no longer able to slow down or hold back.

"Shit, Liv, I don't have a fucking condom," I choked out, finally realizing that the reason she felt so incredible was because there was no barrier between us.

"Don't stop, please don't stop."

I knew she was close, and I was too far gone to stop now. Clenching my jaw, I began pounding into her, hard and fast until I felt her tighten around me. I pulled out just as my own release tore through me and reached between her legs, drawing out the rest of her orgasm with my fingers.

Once she caught her breath, she looked at me questioningly. "You didn't have to pull out," she said with a slight pout. "I'm on the pill, Dex. I thought you knew that."

"I didn't know if you were… cool with that… or whatever," I stammered.

She laughed. "You know that I trust you." Pressing her lips against my ear, she swiped her tongue along the spot that she knew drove me crazy. "Don't do it again… I want to feel you explode inside me when you call out my name."

My cock immediately got hard against her and she giggled softly while I groaned. "If I don't get you home now, I'm going to fuck you until our skin is pruned and wrinkled from being in the water too long."

"Mmmm," she murmured against my lips. "It might be worth it."

"You're trying to kill me, aren't you?" I drew her close, pressing my mouth to hers and slowly coaxing it open with my tongue. I was fully prepared to stay in the water for another round, no matter how wrinkly we got, when I felt her tense in my arms and pull away from me. "What's wrong?" I asked.

"I just saw something in the dunes over there... like a flash of light or something," she said worriedly. "Are you sure there's no one around?"

I turned toward the beach, looking for any sign of light or movement, but all I saw was darkness. "I doubt it, but I'll go check it out just in case."

She grabbed my arm to stop me. "No, let's just get out of here."

"Okay," I agreed. She seemed nervous, and I didn't want her to be. "I'm sure it was nothing, probably just a headlight or a weird reflection. It's way too dark for anyone to see anything anyway. Don't worry, babe."

chapter twenty-two

Olivia

We dressed quickly, and even though I didn't see anything else unusual as we made our way off the beach, I still couldn't shake the feeling that we were being watched. I could have sworn that what I'd seen earlier was a camera flash of some kind, but I hoped that I was wrong. I kept telling myself that my mind was playing tricks on me, or that Dex was right about it simply being a headlight from the other side of the dunes.

I wasn't normally so paranoid, but lately, I'd become increasingly wary. After all the weird phone calls and the strange visit from the mystery guy at work, I often found myself glancing over my shoulder and was constantly on the lookout. It was nothing more than a feeling—like the hairs on the back of my neck standing up—and so far I hadn't seen anything to justify it. I hadn't mentioned any of it to Dex because I knew how protective he was and I didn't want him to worry when it might be nothing. It was probably all the stress over my past that was causing me to act irrationally, and I was creating unnecessary drama in my head to distract myself from the real drama in my life. I needed to stop making something out of nothing.

Dex paused as he pulled into my driveway, his eyes fixed on something further down the road. "I think that's Nate's car," he said, parking the truck and climbing out. "What the hell is he doing here?"

I followed his gaze and sure enough, Nate's old Camero was parked on the side of the street, almost completely out of sight and concealed behind a cluster of bushes. It would have been impossible to see if not for the bright orange paint job, and I wondered why he didn't just park in the driveway.

"He must be looking for me," Dex said. "Shit, what if something happened to Amy or Sadie?"

He began tearing up the stairs to Amy's apartment, and I followed behind him. I had a sneaking suspicion that Nate had other reasons for being there, but before I could stop Dex, he was barging through the front door. He stopped suddenly when he got inside, causing me to nearly run right into him.

When I realized what had stopped him, I wasn't sure whether to scream, laugh, or slither away in humiliation.

We had walked in on a shirtless Nate, who was on top of an equally shirtless Amy, making out on the couch like two teenagers breaking curfew on a school night.

"What the fuck is going on here?" Dex yelled angrily.

Nate jumped off the couch faster than a bat out of hell, his eyes going wide as the color drained from his face. Dex's expression was furious, and I worried he was going to go after Nate the same way he went after his opponents in the ring.

"Dex! What the hell do you think you're doing?" Amy screamed, throwing her shirt on to cover herself up. "You can't just bust in here like that. Get out!"

"I saw Nate's car parked outside. I thought something was wrong!" Dex had the decency to look a little bit ashamed, but it disappeared when he turned to Nate. "And clearly I was right. What the *fuck* are you doing with my sister?"

"This is none of your business, Dex." Amy stood protectively in front of Nate, who was still frozen in place and too stunned to speak. "I'm a grown woman, not a teenager. You're not responsible for what I do."

"Where's Sadie?" Dex asked. "It's not very mature of you to do this while your daughter is in the next room."

Amy rolled her eyes. "She's at Mom and Dad's house, you idiot."

"Seriously, dude?" Dex looked at Nate, who had thankfully found his shirt and managed put it on. "Of all the girls for you to screw around with, you had to choose my sister?"

"I'm not screwing around with her," Nate replied, finally speaking up. He stepped up beside Amy and put his arm around her waist possessively. "I love her."

Clearly, Dex was not expecting that. "You better not be fucking around with me. The last asshole who told me that he loved her got her pregnant and then took off. How the hell do I know that you aren't going to do the same thing?"

"Oh, come on, don't compare me to that jackass," Nate said, taking a tentative step forward. "I'm your best friend, Dex. You fucking know me, and I'm telling you that this is for real. I've had feelings for Amy for a long time now, and I'm sick of pretending that I don't."

"And what about Sadie, are you really ready for all that?" Dex said, "Because in case you haven't noticed, they're kind of a package deal."

"Of course, I know that, and you know I love Sadie, too. I'll be in her life however Amy will let me, whether it's as a dad or just as a friend. I would never hurt either of them, you know that."

Dex stared at them both for a moment before finally fixating his eyes on his sister. "This is what you want?"

Amy nodded, gazing at Nate with a smile I'd never seen her wear before. "Yes, absolutely," she said. "I've wanted this for a really long time, and I'm sorry for keeping it from you… but he makes me happy. I haven't been this happy in a really long time." Her eyes narrowed, glaring at Dex. "You're my brother and I love you, but if you try to mess this up, I will hurt you. You don't scare me, Dex Porter!"

"Well, fuck," Dex said with a laugh, shaking his head. "I guess that's that then."

I grabbed his hand and started pulling him out of the room. "Let's leave these kids alone. I'm freezing my ass off over here. I say we hit the shower."

Amy eyed us curiously, finally noticing our wet hair and damp clothes. "Yeah, what the hell happened to you two, anyway?"

The idea that we had busted in on them making out on the couch, shortly after we had been out mudding and skinny-dipping, was too much. I started laughing hysterically. Here we were, a bunch of so-called adults, running around like teenagers.

I loved it.

There are certain kinds of fun that you never get too old for.

#

As disturbing as it was to walk in on Nate and my sister, it had been a wakeup call for me. Everyone around me was moving forward and I was stuck in place. I was tired of feeling trapped in my past, and I was finally ready to do something about it.

Early the next morning, I called Olivia and asked her if she would go somewhere with me. Her voice was heavy with sleep, and I could tell that I'd woken her up, but she agreed and I picked her up shortly afterward.

She smiled when she saw me, and I was amazed that she could look so beautiful only fifteen minutes after waking up. There wasn't a stitch of makeup on her face, and her hair was twisted into a messy bun on top of her head. She had the type of beauty that came naturally, and I loved seeing her that way.

"Where are we going?" she asked, settling into the seat next to me and fighting a yawn.

"Confronting some ghosts." She didn't ask me to elaborate, and I was grateful.

I parked outside the cemetery and walked around to the passenger side to open the door for her. She studied me carefully, as if wanting to make sure that I was okay before taking my hand and following me along the winding paths that led to Teddy's grave.

The shot glass was still sitting on top of the headstone from the last time I was there, and the flowers had dried up and shriveled in the hot sun.

"Is that from you?" She gestured to the shot glass, and I nodded.

"Do you come here often?"

"Only once since the funeral. On his birthday," I said. "Mostly I've avoided it, like I did everything else, but it seemed like the perfect place for me to finally face it all." Reaching into my back pocket, I pulled out the letter from Teddy's parents and handed it to her. "Would you read it to me? I don't think I'll be able to get through it on my own."

"Of course I will."

I sat down in the grass, leaning my back against the big oak tree that stood a few feet away from the stone. Olivia sat down next to me, carefully opening the envelope and I braced myself for what I was about to hear. I was terrified, but I owed it to them to read it. They had a right to tell me how they felt, to express their anger about the promises I'd failed to keep and to blame me for what happened. They had every right to hate me.

This letter had the power to break me, but I couldn't hide from it any longer. I'd been anchored to the past for too long, and the only way I would ever pull free was by breaking the chains.

As Olivia unfolded the sheets of paper, something slipped from the pages and fell into her lap. I recognized the clinking sound as she passed it to me, and I closed my hand around the rounded, aluminum I.D. tags that I knew were Teddy's. I let the long chain slither out of my palm and ran my finger over the imprinted letters of his name, delicately tracing the edges as though it were sacred, because to me, it was.

I held the dog tags in my fist and glanced toward Olivia, waiting for her to begin. With a deep breath, she finally began reading the letter.

Dear Dex,

We've been meaning to write you this letter for months, and I'm sorry it took us so long. We could never quite figure out the right words to say to you, because words are simply not enough to express to you just how grateful we are to you.

Not many people are lucky enough to experience the kind of friendship that you and Teddy had. You were only little kids when you met, but the bond you formed was something special. From then on, it was you and Teddy against the world.

The greatest kind of friends are the ones who bring out the best in one another, and that's what you and Teddy did every day. You made each other stronger, wiser and braver, and you learned from each other. Most importantly, you stood by each other, right until the very end.

We are eternally grateful to you for being there by his side in his final moments. For holding his hand and letting him know that he wasn't alone and that, even in death, someone he loved was there with him. We take comfort in knowing that he didn't leave this world alone.

There's no doubt in our minds that you did everything you could to try and save him, Dex. We know that there's nothing you could have done differently, and we can only hope that you know it too. Not everyone can be saved – sometimes God has a greater purpose for the ones we love, and we must fight through the pain and learn to accept that they are somewhere far better than here.

We know that you miss him, and we miss him too... every single day. But with each day that passes, it becomes a little bit easier. Some days are harder than others, but our frowns no longer outweigh our smiles. *We no longer cry when we see his pictures around the house, and memories of him no longer bring pain to our hearts, but instead put a smile on our faces as we remember who he was. We all must honor his memory by focusing on what we gained by having him in our lives, rather than on what we lost when he passed. It's what he would have wanted for all of us.*

Teddy loved life. He reveled in the simple things, and he saw a positive light in even the worst situations. He would never want his death to bring you sadness or to rob you of the joys of life. He would want you to remember the good times and focus on the memories of him that make you smile – because he is someone who could make anyone smile!

You have such a big heart, Dex, and because of that you've always felt things a little bit stronger and more deeply than everyone else. Don't let your grief weigh you down. Don't carry the burden of your loss with you forever. Our scars become a part of us, but you cannot let them define you. We will carry him with us in our hearts forever, and moving on does not mean that we're forgetting him or leaving him behind. It means choosing to live.

Thank you for being a part of our son's life. Of our lives. You brought so much joy and laughter to his time here on this earth, and we will forever cherish those moments. Take solace in your memories of him, do not let them bring you pain. Teddy loved you so much, and he always will. So will we.

Love,
April and Doug

My eyes were closed tight, but a few tears still managed to escape. I wiped them away, and when I finally looked over at Olivia, I saw that she was crying softly. Her tears fell more freely, and she reached over to grab my hand, holding it tightly in hers.

The whole time she was reading, I kept waiting for the blow of pain and disappointment to hit me at full force, but it never came. Instead, their words brought me relief, drifting through me and stirring me back to life. I could feel the weight fall from my shoulders when it hit me – they didn't blame me. Their lives weren't full of sorrow and heartbreak, and they had no feelings of anger or resentment, only words of hope and healing. If they could move on, then shouldn't I be able to?

I always thought that if I was no longer sad, then it meant I no longer missed him or had forgotten about him. There were times when I would find myself laughing or smiling about something and the guilt would hit me full force—*How can you be happy when you lost your best friend?*

His parents were right, though. Teddy would want us to focus on the positive and remember the good times, not dwell on the pain. That's the type of guy he was; always caring about others and going the extra length to make them smile.

"Are you all right?" Olivia asked. "I know that's a really stupid question..."

"No, it's not stupid," I broke in, running my thumb softly over her knuckles. "I think I am, actually. I've been carrying this guilt with me for so long that I started to lose perspective. I've been blaming myself all this time, for not being able to save him or protect him, because I desperately needed someone to blame, someone to direct my anger toward. I was so sure that his parents would blame me too. Maybe I needed to hear it from them in order to start believing it myself. That letter was a big wake up call for me. As crazy as it sounds, I kinda feel like they set me free."

"That doesn't sound crazy to me."

Toying with the dog tags in my hand, I felt closer to Teddy than I had in a long time and yet, the sadness was no longer crippling. "I didn't know how to move on without leaving him behind. I've been so caught up in the guilt and pain that I never let myself think about all the great times we had together and how much fun we had, and that isn't fair to him. Forgetting the good times we shared is worse than forgetting him. He deserves to be remembered and I'm sick of hiding from the past. I want to be able to laugh at the memories and tell stories about him with a smile on my face. I want to remember the way he lived, not the way he died."

And that's exactly what we did. As we sat under that tree next to Teddy's grave, I told Liv all about my best friend. I told her about all the stupid shit we did when we were teenagers, and all the crafty ways we managed to stay out of trouble. And for the first time since he died, I actually smiled when I thought about him.

Before we left, I held up Teddy's tags and looped the chain around my neck, tucking them under my shirt and letting them settle over my chest. The guilt was still there, as was the pain, but I didn't think those feelings would ever completely go away. I could only hope that, like Teddy's parents said, it would get easier over time. I still had a long way to go, but for the first time, I actually had hope.

chapter twenty-three

Olivia

In an attempt to try and make up for barging in on them a few nights before, Dex and I had agreed to watch Sadie so that Nate could take Amy out for dinner. It was sort of their first "official" date, and they were totally adorable. Amy spent over an hour getting ready, asking for my help to pick out what she was going to wear and how to do her hair. When Nate showed up, he was visibly nervous and had actually cleaned himself for the occasion. There were no oil stains on his hands or clothes, and he was wearing khakis and a dark sweater.

Dex and I watched them leave, feeling like proud parents who were sending their kids off to their first dance. It reminded me of my first date with Dex. Despite the fact that we'd been out together a million times before, that night was different because it marked the start of something bigger. It felt like so long ago, but it was really only a couple of months. It was odd to consider that we'd become so attached and so close to one another in such a short span of time.

What I'd had with Steven felt like a junior high romance compared to what I had with Dex, and as much trust as I had in him and in our relationship, there was still a part of me that was terrified. My feelings for him left my heart vulnerable to getting broken, and that fear was the one thing that kept me from opening myself up to him the rest of the way. I'd lost so many people already and losing Dex wasn't something I could survive.

"I like Nate," Sadie announced while munching on her slice of cheese pizza. "He always plays with me, and Mommy is way happier when he's around. Do you think he likes me, too?"

"Of course, he likes you, Sadie girl," Dex said, tugging playfully on her pigtail. "You're the most special little girl in the whole world."

I think my heart exploded. Dex was constantly reminding me of his sweet and sensitive side that existed beneath the tough exterior. His demeanor had changed a lot over the last couple of weeks, and I was so proud of him for everything that he was doing to overcome his past. He seemed a lot less angry and lot more playful, which was another side of him that I loved. Of course, he still had the same intensity in the bedroom and definitely wasn't shy about taking the lead between the sheets… which completely turned me on, by the way. Like the night before when he pressed me up against the…

My inappropriate sexual fantasy was interrupted when Sadie turned to me and asked, "Are you and Uncle Dee gonna get married?"

I choked on the water I was sipping, nearly spitting it across the table. I couldn't hide the shocked expression on my face and I felt like a deer in headlights. "Uh…" I turned to Dex for help, but he just grinned back at me in amusement, showing none of the discomfort that I was currently feeling about this topic.

"Who wants an ice cream pop for desert?" Dex called out, successfully distracting Sadie and saving me from having to respond.

Getting up from the table, he winked at me as he walked over to the freezer.

My phone rang while we were eating our popsicles, and I cringed when I glanced over and saw "PRIVATE" pop up on the screen. I hit the ignore button, not bothering to answer it since I knew that no one would be on the other end.

"Who was that?" Dex asked, noticing my reaction.

I forced a smile, not wanting him to worry. "Some heavy mouth breather who has the wrong number. I'm sure it's nothing."

"Are you sure?" He frowned, looking concerned. "If someone is bothering you, just tell me and I'll take care of it."

His offer was tempting, and I didn't doubt that he would take care of any problem I had, but I still wasn't sure if I actually had a problem or if I was just being paranoid. I didn't want to add more to his plate when he was already dealing with so much. "I'm sure. It's really no big deal," I answered as nonchalantly as possible.

I knew he wasn't convinced, but he let it go and we all went into the living room to watch a movie. Turning my phone off, I shoved it in my pocket so I wouldn't have to worry about any more calls.

After falling asleep on the couch during the movie, I woke up in my bed with a hazy memory of Dex carrying me from Amy's apartment when she returned home. I could hear the shower on in the bathroom, so I knew that he was still here. Stripping down to my underwear, I threw on one of Dex's tee shirts before climbing under the covers and drifting back to sleep.

My eyes fluttered open when I felt a warm body pressing against my back and Dex's strong arms wrapping around me. I automatically melted into him, snuggling into his touch with a contented sigh. He nestled his head in the curve of my neck, and I could feel his breath on my ear as he whispered, "I love you, Liv."

My whole body immediately became tense, and I started to panic. I knew that I loved him, and I desperately wanted to say it back, but all of a sudden, I wasn't ready. The words got stuck in my throat. I'd said those three words before, to Steven, but I'd never truly meant them. With Dex, it would mean everything. It would mean putting my heart in his hands and trusting him with it.

I attempted to steady my breathing, hoping that he would think I was still sleeping instead of realizing that I was a coward. After a few minutes, I heard his breaths even out, and I knew that he had fallen asleep. I opened my eyes, letting the tears that had welled up behind them slowly slide down my cheeks, and wondered what the hell was wrong with me.

This gorgeous, sweet, caring, beautiful man—who I loved—was lying next to me, telling me that he loved me, and I couldn't even muster up the courage to say it back. I wanted to say those words. I wanted to look into Dex's eyes, press my lips against his, and tell him that I loved him. But I couldn't. Nothing in my life had ever been permanent, and I hated the part of me that still believed that nothing ever would be.

"So, exactly how long have you had a thing for my sister?" I asked Nate over beers at the garage. I still wasn't particularly thrilled about the idea of him and Amy together, but I would probably feel that way no matter who it was—that's the way brothers are. I had come to my senses, though, and I realized that there was no one else I trusted more than Nate to treat her right and take care of her. He was my best friend, and he was a great guy. Even if it did creep me out a little bit.

"I don't know, man… a long time," Nate laughed. "I had a thing for her in high school, but she was your sister, so she was off limits."

"How the hell did I not know about this?"

"I didn't want to risk a beating from you, so I hid it well," he said. "Then you left for basic training so I didn't see her that much, and that scumbag Duncan swooped in, got her pregnant and fucking left her." He clenched his fists angrily at his sides, shaking his head. "God, I fucking hate that kid…"

"You and me both," I agreed. "At least he got a little bit of what was coming to him when he broke his arm and lost that football scholarship."

"You totally broke his arm, didn't you?" Nate said with a grin. "I fucking knew it was you!"

I held up my hands defensively. "I'm not admitting to anything…"

"Hey, I'm not judging," Nate said. "Do you remember his BMW that he loved so much?"

"Uh oh, what'd you do to it?"

"Rice in the radiator. Clogged the whole damn engine and destroyed it. I'd do it again in a second, too. After what he did to her, he got off easy."

Seeing how protective Nate was of Amy made me feel better about leaving her in his hands, but it didn't change the fact that I'd let her down in the first place. "I never should have let that pathetic asshole anywhere near her. I should have known he was no good."

"Oh come on… there's no way you could have known that

Duncan would turn out to be such a prick. He had everyone fooled with his bullshit 'golden boy' act."

"Yeah, but I'm her brother. It's my job to watch out for her."

"And you do. You always have," Nate said. "You carry around the weight of the world on your shoulders, and if you keep holding yourself responsible for the bad things that happen to the people around you… one of these days it's going to break you. Sometimes bad things happen. It's a part of life and it's not always anyone's fault. You can't change it, all you can do is move on."

I'd been hearing that a lot lately – from Chase, Teddy's parents, and now Nate. Fortunately, I was finally listening. "You know, that reminds me… I actually need to take a day off next week. There's some business I need to take care of down near the base in Parris Island."

"What kind of business do you have there?" he looked at me skeptically. "It's not a fight, is it? I thought you promised Olivia you were done with that shit."

I smiled, remembering how adorably nervous Olivia had been when she asked me if I was still going to fights. Knowing that she cared enough about me to worry made it an easy promise to make.

"No, not a fight," I said. "I actually, uh… I visited one of the guys from my unit last week, and he told me that the counseling stuff really helped him out. He put me in touch with his therapist, who recommended I attend this group therapy session for veterans with PTSD. I figured I might as well give it a shot," I shrugged, feeling a little embarrassed about the whole thing.

Nate looked a bit surprised but there was no judgment on his face. "Good for you, Dex. I think that's really great. I won't pretend to know anything about what you're going through, but it makes sense that talking to people who *do* understand… who have been through some of the same things you have... would help. I'm proud of you, man. Seriously. It takes a lot of balls to do what you're doing."

"It's something I probably should have done a long time ago," I admitted. "Better late than never though, right?"

"Absolutely." He shot me a coy grin. "This new attitude wouldn't happen to have anything to do with a certain beautiful blonde, now would it?"

"She deserves better than me, Nate. I can't help but feel that I'm selfish for being with her... that I'm only going to drag her down with me or fuck things up somehow."

"That girl is lucky to have you. You're a great guy, despite what you choose to think about yourself. Olivia sees what we all see in you, what you refuse to see—the good—broken parts and all. She'll be there for you while you work on putting the pieces back together, if you let her. You're always taking care of other people... let her take care of you, because you deserve to be happy. Does she make you happy?"

"Every single day."

"Then hold onto her," he said. "Fuck everything else. Let yourself be happy."

I wish it were that easy.

"You know..." Nate went on, "There's a great salvage yard out near Parris Island. If you want, maybe we could drive out there together. I'll rummage through some parts while you go to your session."

I doubted that there just happened to be a salvage yard in the same town where I was going for therapy, but I appreciated the fact that he wanted to be there for me. It was nice to know that I wouldn't have to do it alone.

"Yeah, that sounds great. Thanks, man."

chapter twenty-four

Olivia

I'd been feeling moody and on edge all day, and I couldn't seem to snap out of it. I didn't know if it was because of the creepy phone calls, or my relationship with Dex and my cowardly reaction to him telling me that he loved me, but something felt... off. Like any minute, the bottom was going to drop out and all the happiness I'd been feeling lately would be shattered into a million pieces.

I hadn't seem much of Dex over the last couple of days because of work, so he was having a drink at the bar and patiently waiting while I finished my shift. There was tension between us, but I didn't know if it was just me, or if he felt it too. He hadn't said anything about my response—or lack of response—the other night, so I didn't know *what* he was thinking, or if he had simply believed that I'd been asleep and hadn't heard him say that he loved me.

It was busy behind the bar. When I looked up from making a round of drinks, I saw that a woman had sidled up to Dex, taking the open stool next to him and had begun talking to him. Jealously and anger immediately sliced through me. Deep down I knew that I was being irrational because Dex wasn't doing anything wrong. I trusted him. He wasn't flirting with her or encouraging her in any way. He was barely even looking at her! Yet, the jealous part of me wondered why he couldn't just tell her to leave him alone and stop talking altogether.

My feelings for Dex combined with my fear of losing him were making me act crazy. I couldn't bear the thought of him being with anyone else, and it raised questions that I didn't want to have. What if he got bored with me? It wasn't so long ago that he had a different woman every night. Had he really changed *so* much in such a short amount of time, that he no longer had any interest in other women? That seemed unlikely, and the thought made me sick to my stomach.

He'd given me every reason to believe that he was in this—that he wanted me and *only* me. Hell, I was the one who was holding back. There was a part of me that still had an irrational fear of abandonment that haunted me with the notion that happiness was fleeting, and I couldn't shake it.

My shift was almost over, but I needed to get out of there. I told the other bartender that I wasn't feeling well and needed to head home a few minutes early. After grabbing my stuff from the back, I approached Dex on my way out.

"I hate to *interrupt*… but I'm heading out. Feel free to stay here if you want." Dex stared at me with a confused look on his face, but I ignored it, turning on my heel and walking out the door. I knew I was acting like a bitch and wasn't being fair, but all my rational thoughts were in the backseat and jealousy had taken the wheel.

I pulled up to my apartment a few minutes later, and it wasn't long before Dex's truck came screeching in behind me.

"What the hell was that about?" he asked angrily, stopping me from going inside. "You're just gonna storm off without any explanation?"

I crossed my arms stubbornly. "You seemed busy with your new *friend*... I didn't want to intrude."

"What, you're jealous?" He looked at me in disbelief, "Oh, come on, Liv... You were busy working and I was just being polite. It's not like I was interested in her... I barely said three words!"

"Well, she was certainly interested in you."

"So what if she was!" he shouted. "I can't control her. Don't you trust me by now?" There was hurt in his eyes when I didn't say anything. "That's it, isn't it? After everything, you still don't trust me."

I had no response because there was nothing I could say to try and explain what I was feeling. It didn't even make sense in my own head.

"This is bullshit, Olivia! I've been completely devoted to you since the moment we got together. I don't even look at other women anymore because you're the only one that I want. I've made my feelings perfectly clear from the beginning, but I have no idea where you stand because you never open up and tell me. You keep me at arm's length, and I feel like I could lose you at any moment... like you're going to run off scared and just disappear." He took a step toward me, his eyes bearing into mine. "You don't even mention the fact that I told you that loved you. I know you heard me say it. What I don't understand is why you pretended that you didn't."

I hung my head in shame, staring at the ground as my eyes welled up with tears. "I don't know why."

Dex let out a frustrated breath. "I'm not the one holding back here, Liv. Why don't you let me know when you figure out what it is that you want?"

He marched off, and I stood alone in the driveway, wanting to go after him but unsure what to say. He was right about everything, but I didn't know how to make it right.

I went inside, closing the front door behind me and plopping my keys down on the table. As I went to go turn on a light, I noticed a silhouette in the living room.

"Hello, Olivia."

"Steven?" I said, flicking on the light and taking a tentative step toward him. "What the hell are you doing here?"

"I'm here for you."

Fear twisted in my stomach. He'd never given me any reason to be afraid of him, but the slightly crazed look on his face was not one that I recognized. "How did you even find me?"

"I have my ways… it wasn't hard to track you down. Nowadays, anyone can be found if you have the right tools and the means to do it." He smiled menacingly and stood up, moving toward me. "You didn't think that I was just going to let you go, did you?"

"You sent someone to find me and follow me, didn't you?" It all made sense now. The creepy guy in the bar, the person taking pictures of Dex and me on the beach, the phone calls, and all the times I'd felt like someone was watching me… it hadn't all been in my head.

"I missed you so much. There's so much I've been wanting to say to you," he said. "I tried to say it over the phone, but every time I heard your voice, I lost my nerve. I knew I needed to see you face-to-face so we could work this out and go back to the way we were." His voice was pleading, but the look in his eyes was demanding.

"It doesn't matter what you have to say. It's over between us," I said firmly.

Steven stepped closer. "We were great together, Olivia. Think of the life we could have! I know I fucked up, but you can't throw away four years together because of one mistake. Please come home with me so we can fix this."

"It wasn't one mistake, Steven. We weren't right together. Deep down I always knew, but I was scared to be alone. I turned into someone else because I wanted to fit into your world, but it wasn't right."

His demeanor changed and anger flashed across his features. "Is this because of that jackass that you're with? You don't belong with him, Olivia. He has nothing to offer you."

"This has nothing to do with—"

He ignored me. "You think I'm just going to sit back and let another man have you? After everything I've done for you?" He stepped forward, not stopping until he was directly in front of me. "I'm not leaving here without you. One way or another, you will come back with me."

I backed away from him until I felt the wall against my back and there was nowhere else to go. Every instinct was telling me to run but I couldn't move. I wanted to believe that I wasn't in danger; that I'd spent four years with this man, and he wouldn't hurt me, but when I looked in his eyes, I saw someone else. This wasn't the man that I knew. That realization was terrifying because I had no idea what he was capable of. I kept hoping that Dex would walk through the door, but then I remembered that he was gone. I had stupidly pushed him away when all I wanted to do was pull him close. He wasn't coming back to rescue me. Amy's lights were off, meaning she wasn't home… there was no one to help me.

I was alone.

Dex

I stormed off in the direction of my truck and kept walking. I didn't know where the hell I was going, but I was too angry to get behind the wheel just yet. I needed to blow off some steam.

All this time, I'd thought that Olivia and I were on the same page about our relationship and how we felt about each other, but now I had no fucking idea what was going on with us. It wasn't about her not telling me that she loved me – I said it to her because it was how I felt and I wanted her to know, not because I needed to hear it from her. I could accept the fact that she wasn't ready to say it back yet, and it was okay because I already knew that she loved me. I knew it from the way she touched me, the way she looked at me, the way she kissed me... the words weren't important because she showed me how she felt every day.

The problem was trust. I couldn't get past the fact that she still didn't trust me. In all the time that we'd been together, I'd never given her any reason to doubt me. I'd opened myself up to her in a way that I never had with anyone else, and that meant something to me. She owned me—mind, body and soul—and if she didn't trust me now, I wasn't sure that she ever really would. If we didn't have trust, what *did* we have?

I had almost reached the end of the road when I stopped suddenly. I had a nagging feeling in the back of my head; a voice telling me that something was out of place, something didn't fit. Something wasn't right.

If there was one thing that Marine training taught me, it was to always trust my instincts and listen to my gut. It was the attention to detail and awareness of our surroundings that could often mean the difference between life and death, so I learned never to ignore it.

I began retracing my steps, focusing on everything around me and searching for anything I might have seen that would have set off the warning bells in my head. Most of the houses already had their lights shut off and the road was dark, with only a few street lamps lighting the way. About halfway back to Olivia's apartment, I noticed a black sedan parked off to the side of the road, and the bright orange New York license plate caught my eye. It struck me as odd to see that particular license plate here, especially considering that Olivia just-so-happened to be from New York. No way was that a coincidence. Something didn't add up.

Glancing through the car window, I saw a map spread out on the passenger seat and immediately got a horrible feeling that something was wrong. Breaking into a sprint, I ran back to her apartment, thinking back on all the weird phone calls and seemingly paranoid behavior that she would try and brush off, and wishing I'd paid more attention to it.

When I got closer, I heard a loud crash coming from inside, and I really started to panic. The prospect of something bad happening to her had me moving as fast as I possibly could, desperate to get to her. The thought of losing her was too much to bear and I would never forgive myself if something were to happen to her. I needed to protect her. I'd let so many people down in my life, but I couldn't let Olivia down.

I heard her muffled screams as I broke through the door to her apartment. There was a man inside, and he had her pushed up against the wall with his hands on her throat, roughly restraining her to try and keep her from screaming. Rage tore through me, pulsing through my veins and thumping inside my skull. I grabbed him by the back of his shirt and ripped him away from her, tossing him violently to the ground before checking on Olivia.

"Are you okay, baby?" I gently cupped her cheek, looking down into her beautiful eyes that were full of fear. "Did he hurt you?"

She shook her head, and while I was distracted, something hard hit me on the back of the head and knocked me to the floor. My head was spinning, but when I heard Olivia scream, I was on my feet in an instant. I pulled him away from her and stood between them, not letting him get anywhere near her.

"Liv, get out of here," I ordered, never taking my eyes off him. "Go somewhere safe and call for help. Now."

She hesitated but finally backed out of the living room. I was calmer now that I was facing him head on because I knew that, just like everyone else I'd faced in the ring, he didn't stand a chance against me. Unlike my other opponents, though, this guy had messed with my girl, and there was nothing that was going to stop me.

I watched him, waiting. But instead of making a move toward me, his lips turned up in a cunning smile as he pulled out a knife, pointing the sharp, shiny blade right at me.

"This isn't some fucking fist fight," he snarled. "Your underground fight club bullshit won't work here."

I cocked my head to the side. "Maybe not, but I'm warning you… if you take a shot at me, you damn well better make it count, because it's the only one you're gonna get."

I resisted the urge to attack first. This wasn't two guys exchanging blows in a makeshift ring anymore. I needed to be smart. I remained still, studying him and waiting for him to make the first move. As soon as he came at me, I was ready, bending away from the knife and striking him with a hard blow to the side. I heard the crack of his ribs, and he stumbled back, but I wasn't finished. I threw a powerful punch to his jaw, then another, and another.

He got a couple of hits in, but nothing could stop me. Adrenaline pumped through me as I landed one shot after another until he was no longer fighting back. I would have kept going, probably until he was dead, but a gentle hand on my arm stopped me.

"That's enough. Come here." Olivia's voice shook as she pulled me back.

Letting his body flop to the ground, I kneeled next to Olivia, frantically looking her over to make sure that she was okay.

"I'm sorry, Liv. I shouldn't have left you. I'm so sorry."

She shook her head, wrapping her arms around me. "No, I'm sorry. I can't believe you came back. I thought you were gone and I was so scared..."

Her whole body was shaking, and I kissed her forehead, holding her tight against me. "Shhh... it's okay. You're okay."

She pulled back suddenly, glancing down and noticing the tear in my shirt and the blood that covered it. Her face blanked and she looked back up at me. "Oh God, Dex..."

Carefully, she lifted my shirt and saw the long gash in my skin where his knife had made contact. The cut wasn't too deep, but it was bleeding a lot. Olivia began crying hysterically, frantically trying to stop the bleeding with a dishtowel from the counter.

"Baby, it's only a flesh wound," I assured her, stroking my hand along her damp cheek. "I'll be fine, I promise."

"I love you," she cried into my shoulder. "I love you so much, Dex. I don't know why it took me so long to tell you because I've loved you for so long. I was scared, and I was being an idiot... and of course, I trust you. I trust you with my life. I'm so sorry for acting the way I did, and oh God... I can't lose you, Dex..."

"You won't ever lose me, Liv. It's going to be okay." I ran my thumb over her trembling lips, tracing along the edges before softly brushing my mouth over hers.

"I love you more than anything," I whispered.

chapter twenty-five

Olivia

I hated hospitals. I'd learned the hard way that nothing good ever happened in a hospital, and being there made me nervous. It brought me right back to the day that my mother died, when I'd gotten the phone call telling me that she'd been in a car accident and I needed to get to the hospital right away. When I'd arrived there, no one would tell me anything. All I'd wanted to do was see my mom, but no one would let me, and I couldn't understand why. One of the nurses kept patting my arm and telling me that everything would be okay, and for a short time I actually started to believe her. Until a somber-looking doctor wearing blue scrubs walked up to me with a look on his face that told me everything I needed to know—that my mother was gone, and I was alone. I'd barely heard a word he said after that, but I continued to stand there, frozen in place, pretending to listen. When the truth hit my stomach, I ran out of there as fast as I could, emptying the contents of it behind a bush near the entrance. I didn't bother going back inside, because what was the point? My mom was gone, and there was nothing that anyone in there could do to change it.

Dex kept insisting that his injury was minor, but I didn't relax until I heard the doctor confirm that he was going to be fine. It hadn't been easy to get him into the examination room because he was more worried about me than himself, even though he was the one bleeding all over the place. Despite my concern, the doctor told us that the wound looked a lot worse than it actually was, and after a few stitches he would be able to leave.

I'd never been so relieved. The fear I felt when I saw Dex's shirt covered in blood was unlike anything I'd ever experienced before. It had completely consumed me… terrifying me and breaking my heart at the same time. In the moment when I thought I might lose him, everything that I'd been afraid of and all my reasons for holding back became irrelevant. The only thing that mattered was how much I loved him. I realized then, that the only thing worse than losing him, would be losing him without ever telling him how I felt.

Cringing, I watched as the doctor began stitching up the wound. Dex only smiled at me, completely unfazed by the pain as he held my hand in his, gently running his fingers over mine as if to remind us that we were both okay. He hadn't let go of my hand since we left the apartment. When the doctors tried to keep me from going into the exam room with him because I wasn't family, Dex had made it very clear that he wasn't leaving my side, even if it meant going home without any treatment. Fortunately, they had decided to make an exception for us, given the circumstances.

Two police officers had shown up at the hospital shortly after we arrived, and while Dex was filling out paperwork, one of them approached me.

"Hello, Ma'am, I'm Officer Bishop. Would you mind giving me

your statement and answering a couple of questions?" He smiled gently, "I know you've had a rough night but I promise it won't take up much of your time."

I nodded. He led me over to the seating area and brought me a cup of coffee, which I was incredibly grateful for considering that it was nearly three o'clock in the morning.

On autopilot, I went through the whole night, unable to stop the quiver in my voice and the slight shake of my hands as I described Steven's harsh grip on my throat, the frightening look in his eyes and the fear I had when I thought I might die.

"This Steven Chambers... you said he's your ex-boyfriend, correct?" I nodded, and he jotted my answer down on his report. "When was the last time you had any contact with him?"

"Not since May," I said. "I haven't seen or heard anything from him since I left New York. Well, not that I was aware of, anyway. He called from a blocked number a couple of times, but I didn't know it was him until tonight when he told me."

"Anything suspicious or unusual other than the phone calls?"

"Sometimes I felt like there was someone watching me... following me... maybe taking pictures? I thought I was being paranoid, though. I had no idea Steven would try and track me down."

"Has he ever shown this kind of aggressive behavior before?" he asked. "Or demonstrated violence toward you or anyone else?"

I thought about it for a minute and shook my head. "Not that I ever saw. I mean, he's a spoiled rich kid who's used to getting what he wants, but in all the years we were together, he was never violent. I never thought he was capable of something like this..."

A short time later, he finished with his questions. "I think that's all for now, Ms. Mason. If we need anything else from you, we'll call you down to the station, but for now you should go on home and get some rest. They're probably still collecting evidence at your apartment, and it might be a little overwhelming. Is there somewhere else you could stay for the night?"

"Yes, I can stay at my boyfriend's. He should be finishing up any minute now." I took a deep breath, needing to know one more thing before I could leave. "Um, Officer… what kind of condition is Steven in?"

"When we arrived at the scene, he was unconscious, but still breathing. He was beaten up badly, but from what I understand, he's likely to make a full recovery."

I was relieved that he wasn't dead, but most of that relief was for Dex. I didn't want him to face any kind of trouble for protecting me. I'd seen the pure rage on his face while he was hitting Steven, and there had been a moment when I wasn't sure if he would stop. Thankfully, I'd been able to pull him back. "What happens next?"

"He'll be charged with assault with a deadly weapon, criminal trespassing and harassment. As soon as the doctors discharge him, he'll appear in front of a judge for arraignment. Likely, he'll be released on bail until the hearing, but there's already a restraining order in place to keep him away from both you and Mr. Porter."

I wasn't too worried about Steven coming after me again. I knew that as soon as his father found out what he'd done, he would do more to keep him in line than any criminal justice system ever could. Not to mention, I had Dex, who would always protect me and keep me safe.

Officer Bishop handed me a card with his information. "If you need anything at all or have any questions, don't hesitate to call."

I thanked him, and a few minutes later Dex walked through the hospital doors, shirtless with a white bandage covering the wound on his abdomen. He had a small cut above his eyebrow and few bruises forming on his ribs, but was still as gloriously beautiful as ever. I ran over to him, burying my face in his chest as he pulled me close and said, "What do you say we get the hell out of here?"

When we got to Dex's house, he led me straight into his bedroom, helping me out of my clothes before slipping one of his soft tee shirts over my head. After tucking me under the covers, he dropped a kiss to my forehead. "Go to sleep, baby. I'll be right in."

As tired as I was, I didn't fall asleep, and after a while I got up and went in search of Dex. I found him out on the balcony with his elbows resting on the railing and his head hung low. There was a glass of whiskey next to him and it was obvious that something was troubling him.

I walked out into the cool night air and came up behind him. He shifted his head slightly, but didn't turn around. Stepping closer, I wrapped my arms around his waist and began trailing kisses along the hard muscles of his back.

"I almost lost you tonight," he said with a deep sigh. "If anything had happened to you... God, if he'd hurt you... I would have killed him. I still want to fucking kill him."

"But you didn't lose me," I pointed out. "I'm fine, thanks to you."

"If I hadn't come back... Fuck, Liv... I never would have been able to forgive myself if I let something happen to you."

"You saved me, Dex." I rested my forehead on his back, pressing my body against his and absorbing his heat. "I was so scared I was going to lose you. I—I can't lose you, too. I need you... I love you."

He turned around and pulled me into his arms. "I love you, too. With every piece of my heart. I'm never going to let anything happen to you. Ever."

His eyes were full of fire, but not angry. They were heated with desire, and I knew he needed me just as badly as I needed him. I needed to feel every part of him, needed to reassure myself that he was there and was okay. Everything that happened earlier drifted away, and the only thing on my mind was getting wrapped up in him.

Crushing his lips against mine, he kissed me fiercely, protectively, possessively. With one kiss, he communicated everything he'd ever said to me, and all the feelings that couldn't be put into words.

He spun us around, setting me on top of the railing and guiding my legs around his waist. His hands wandered up my thighs, underneath the hem of my oversize tee shirt and up my back, leaving a trail of heat on my skin that resonated all the way into my core. Leaning down, I pressed my lips to each of his bruises, wishing that my touch could take away his pain and heal him. I kissed along his rippled stomach, over his hard chest, up his neck to his jaw, and finally back to his mouth.

He growled, the sound vibrating through his chest as he took my mouth and rocked his hardness against me. I moaned, dampness pooling between my legs as I clambered to bring him closer, anxious to feel him inside me. His hands gripped my bottom and he lifted me up, effortlessly carrying me inside and setting me on the edge of the bed. I reached forward and popped open the button on his jeans, my fingers grazing his arousal as I lowered the zipper. Grabbing his waistband, I slid his pants and boxers down, letting his thick erection spring free. It stood perfectly at my eye level and I couldn't resist pressing my lips to the tip, and when I took him into my mouth, he groaned loudly, cradling my head in his hands. I let my tongue slide along his length, tasting his smooth skin as my lips moved over him. My eyes remained locked on his, watching as his face twisted in pleasure and listening to the guttural sounds that escaped from his throat. Seeing what I did to him only turned me on even more, and I loved knowing how good I made him feel.

When I sensed that he was getting close, he drew back, dropping to his knees and pressing my back against the mattress. "Nothing, not even your sexy mouth, is going to keep me from coming inside you tonight."

His hands moved up my stomach, lifting my shirt as he worshipped me with his gentle touch, gliding over my hardened nipples as he stared down at me hungrily. Peeling my shirt off, his lips caressed my skin, teasing my breasts as his mouth moved down my body, retracing the path of his hands. When he reached my panties, he hooked his thumbs in the sides, dragging them down my legs and tossing them aside.

Kneeling in front of me, he ran his large palms up the inside of my legs, spreading them open. When his eyes met mine, they were ravenous. By the time his tongue pressed against my center, I was desperate for his touch, clinging to the sheets as I squirmed beneath him. His lips moved slowly, coaxing me with gentle pressure until I was right on the edge. Clutching his short hair in my hands, I tugged his mouth away from me and pulled him on top me.

"Nothing is going to keep me from having you inside me when I come," I whispered.

He grinned, letting his hips drop between my legs as he settled his body over mine. "Why didn't you just say so?"

In one movement, he thrust into me, hard and deep, halting when he was all the way inside. I cried out loudly, wrapping my legs around his waist as he slowly drew himself out and gradually pressed back inside. His movements were slow and unhurried, and every feeling was magnified. He was taking his time making love to me, whispering sweet things in my ear with each slow thrust, our bodies moving familiarly together, making me feel more connected to him than ever before.

His breaths became heavier as his pace began to increase and he lowered his forehead to my chest. "You feel so damn good, baby. I want to stay inside you forever."

Clutching him against me, I lifted my hips to meet his and grabbed his perfectly toned behind, pulling him deeper inside me, making me feel full and complete. I toppled over the edge, calling out his name with my release, and Dex soon followed, his warmth pouring into me as he swept his lips against mine. Our chests rose and fell against each other as we fought to catch our breath, our foreheads pressed together and our bodies still intimately connected.

It wasn't until Dex rolled to his side that we realized his wound was bleeding through the bandage. I quickly ran into the bathroom for a fresh one before cleaning the area around his stitches and applying new gauze.

"Oops… I'm guessing we didn't quite follow doctor's orders," I said, putting the finishing touches on my handiwork.

"Fuck the doctor's orders. Nothing could have kept me from you tonight." He grinned cleverly, "Besides, I like it when you play nurse for me."

Once his bandage was taken care of, we climbed into bed and curled up under the covers. His hard chest was pressed against my back and I could feel his warm breath tickle my ear. Outside, the sun was just beginning to rise with the start of a new day. Together we watched the colors of the sky change until we both drifted off to a peaceful sleep.

We didn't wake up until well past noon the next day, and we took our sweet time getting out of bed, lazily making love until our stomachs were growling with the need to be fed. We ate breakfast with Olivia perched on my lap, neither of us wanting to separate from one another, even for a short amount of time. Being close to each other helped remind us that we were together and we were safe. I was already plotting to figure out the best way to keep her here, because I had no intention of letting her go.

"I think it's about time you gave me a drawer or something," Olivia suggested, glancing down at the huge tee shirt she wore that was swallowing her up. "As much as I love wearing your clothes and going commando, it might be nice to have a few of my own clothes here."

"Hmmm…" I scratched my chin, pretending to think about it. "I was going to offer you an entire closet, but now that you mentioned going commando and reminded me how incredibly sexy you look in my clothes, I might have to rethink it…"

She laughed. "I don't need a whole closet! Just one teenie, tiny little drawer… pleaseee?" Wrapping her arms around my waist, she looked up at me with a smile that made my knees weak.

"Okay, fine. But it's going to be really hard to fit all your stuff in one drawer."

"Why would I need all my stuff?"

"So that you can move in with me," I said casually.

"Are you serious?" Her hands dropped to her sides, and her lips curled up in amusement. "Is this because of last night? Because I don't want to rush into anything just because—"

"That's not why," I interrupted, grabbing her hips and hauling her body against mine. "I've been thinking about it for a while now, and after what happened, I don't want to wait any longer. I don't want you to be alone in that apartment anymore, and I don't want to be alone in my house anymore. I want to fall asleep with you every night and wake up with you every morning. What do you say?"

She didn't say anything for what felt like an eternity, and her expression was unreadable. I was sure that she was going to tell me no, and then her face broke into a smile.

"Let's do it," she said.

"I fucking love you," I shouted happily, lifting her up off the ground. I nearly had her shirt over her head, ready to ravage her yet again, when I heard someone pounding on the front door. We looked at each other quizzically, and when I rushed over to open it, Rose barged inside.

"Oh my goodness, Olive!" She rushed past me toward Olivia and threw her arms around her, hugging her tight. "I heard what happened, and I've been worried sick about you. I had to see for myself that you were all right."

"Rose?" Olivia looked at her with surprise. "How did you already find out what happened?"

"It's a small town. That kind of news spreads like wildfire. And for crying out loud, enough with the 'Rose' crap already," she said, taking a seat on the sofa and pulling Olivia down next to her. "I am your grandmother. You may call me 'Grandma,' 'Grammy,' 'Nana,' 'Gram,' or whatever grannie name suits you, but Rose is off the table. Got it?"

Olivia smiled. "Fair enough, Gram."

While Olivia was in the kitchen brewing a pot of coffee, Rose turned to me. "Thank you for keeping my girl safe. That poor thing has gone through so much in her life. After fighting on her own all this time, I'm grateful to know that she has someone to fight with her. You're a good man, Dex."

I really liked Rose. She had a way of drawing people in and making them feel at ease around her. It was the same quality that Olivia had. "She's been saving me since the day we met, and I intend to protect her for the rest of my life," I told her.

"Is she going back to her place?" Rose asked with concern. "I'm not sure how I feel about her living there all by herself…"

"Well, we, uh… we kind of just decided that she would move in here with me." I really hoped that Rose wasn't the kind of grandmother that frowned upon living together before marriage. After all this bonding we were doing, I'd hate for her to smack me around.

"Good boy," she said. "I'll sleep easy at night knowing she's in good hands. Now that I finally got her back, I'll do anything to make sure I don't lose her again."

"You and me both," I nodded.

When Olivia returned with the coffee, I excused myself to give them some time alone to talk while I took a shower and got dressed. I wanted to stop by her place and make sure it was cleared of any and all reminders of last night. The last thing I wanted was for Olivia to be scared walking in there. I also wanted to check in on Amy and Sadie. They weren't there when Steven broke in last night, but they could have been. I would have to talk to Nate about adding a few extra safety measures at the house to make sure that nothing like this ever happened again.

I dropped a quick kiss to Olivia's cheek before heading out. "Are you sure you're okay with me leaving for a bit?" I asked. "I can do this another time if you want me to stay."

"I'm totally fine, I promise," she assured me.

"Go on now," Rose said, urging me out the door. "If any little punk tries to come anywhere near her, I'll take him out myself."

"How was it?" Nate asked as we drove back from my first group therapy session a few days later.

"It was nothing like I thought it would be... but in a good way," I said. "They really understood what I was going through, and a lot of them were going through the same thing. It's nice to know that I'm not the only one and that I'm not, you know, crazy."

The group had completely surprised me. I'd been expecting a bunch of injured and broken old war veterans, but most of them had been around the same age as me. Some of them had obvious injuries, while others were hidden, like mine. I thought that being in a room surrounded by military men and women would be daunting, but instead I felt accepted. There was a bond between all of us; a common thread in our pasts that linked us to one another. I hadn't planned on talking or sharing anything at that first session. I thought I'd simply sit back and listen, but for the first time ever, I actually *wanted* to talk about it, so I did. They had all listened, nodding along in understanding because they'd been where I was. It was reassuring to know that I wasn't alone in my torment and that there was hope to be had for someone like me.

Normally, when I was forced to talk about my time overseas, I felt like I couldn't be completely honest about the things that I'd seen and done, because "ordinary" people couldn't handle it or wouldn't understand. But with people who had seen and experienced the same horrifying things that I had, I didn't have to sugarcoat it or wash over the details. I'd been burying all that stuff deep inside me, giving it a permanent home where it played in my head over and over again, tormenting me day after day. Saying those things out loud had severed the hold that those memories had on me, helping me to regain control and release me from the demons that had been haunting me since my first tour overseas. I felt free.

I wasn't stupid enough to think that I was cured—I was far from it—but for the first time I felt like I was on the right track and was beginning to heal. I would continue attending group meetings and maybe even some individual sessions, and hopefully, someday the darkness inside me would fade.

We were nearly home, when Nate turned into downtown Charleston instead of crossing the bridge to Folly Beach.

"Mind if we make a quick stop?" he asked, parking the Camaro on the side of the street near a cluster of stores. "I put something aside for Amy's birthday next week, and I wanted to get your opinion before I buy it. It's my first time getting her a gift, and I don't want to mess it up."

"Okay, but I'm not exactly an expert on shopping for woman, so if she hates it, that's your problem."

I followed him into a small jewelry store and let out a whistle when I glanced around at the glass cases filled with sparkling stones and polished metal. Nate was not messing around with this gift.

"It's my birthday, too, ya know… Amy and me being twins and all… so, uh, what are getting me?" I teased.

He rolled his eyes dismissively and gestured me over. "Just shut up and come look at this, would ya?"

The necklace he'd picked out was a small diamond pendant on a silver chain. It was simple and beautiful, and I knew my sister would love it.

"Damn, that's actually nice. I was expecting something in the shape of a car or like some cheesy locket with your face inside, but you have surprisingly good taste. I'm impressed."

"You think she'll like it?" he asked nervously.

"Yeah, man. She's gonna love it."

While I waited for him to pay for the necklace and have the clerk gift-wrap it, I began strolling around the store and nonchalantly browsing the cases. I wasn't paying much attention to anything that I was looking at until a ring in one of the displays caught my eye. It had an old, antique look to it that made it stand out from all the big, shiny baubles that all seemed identical to one another. This one had a single gleaming diamond in the center and intricate detail on the sides, mounted on a delicate platinum band. It reminded me of the earrings that Olivia often wore, the ones she said belonged to her mother and had been passed down in the family. I couldn't help but think about how perfect that ring would look on her tiny little finger.

"Stunning, isn't it?" One of the clerks appeared on the other side of the case and pulled out the ring. "It's an antique from the 1920s, with a one and a half carat single cut diamond accentuated by exquisite filigree detail along the sides. Truly one of a kind and positively stunning."

She handed it to me, and I held it up, admiring the way the diamond reflected in the light. There was only one place this ring belonged.

"I'll take it."

chapter twenty-six

Olivia

"This can't be all you have," Dex said curiously, eying the few measly boxes of my belongings that I'd packed up to bring to his place. "Where's the rest?"

"That's it," I shrugged. "I only grabbed a few things when I left Steven's, and the rest is in a storage unit in New York."

He scowled at the mention of Steven's name, crushing his fists angrily at his sides. "I still can't believe they just let that bastard go. He could have fucking killed you."

"But he didn't," I said, wrapping my arms around him reassuringly. "We knew he would likely get released on bail, and the important thing is that he won't bother us ever again."

Steven's father had bailed him out and hired some big shot attorney to represent him. I knew that there was a good chance he would get off easy—money had a way of making things disappear, and Steven's family had plenty of it. Dex was furious about the whole thing, but I was surprisingly okay with it. A few days after it happened

I got a call from Mr. Chambers, Steven's father, who apologized for "the incident," and assured me that Steven was being "dealt with," and I wouldn't have to worry about him ever again. He'd also offered me compensation—in the form of $50,000—for the "pain and suffering" his son had caused me. I politely responded that he could keep his money, and all I wanted was for Steven to stay away from me.

"Yeah, well if I ever see his face again, he'll wish he was behind bars," Dex scoffed. "I let him get away once, but I damn sure won't give him another opportunity."

"I know you'll keep me safe, babe." I stood on my tiptoes, pressing a kiss to his lips. As his mouth moved against mine, I could feel his tension slowly begin to ease. When his body was relaxed against mine, I pulled back and looked up at him. "Now let's get these boxes in the truck so we can go home."

"I like the sound of that," he smiled, smacking my ass playfully as he moved to pick up one of the boxes.

It took all of ten minutes to load my stuff into the truck. As I was locking the front door of the apartment for the last time, Nate pulled into the driveway with his Camero, stuffed to the brim with bags and boxes.

"What's going on?" I asked him.

"Didn't Amy tell you?" he grinned. "I'm moving in."

I glanced at Dex, expecting him to be furious, but he didn't even seem surprised. "You knew about this?"

"Of course I did," Dex said. "It was my idea. I wanted to make sure that Amy and Sadie were safe here."

"Actually, I believe your genius idea was to install an alarm system," Nate corrected him. "I'm the one who suggested that I move in with them."

"But I'm the one who came up with the plan to re-connect the two apartments and make more space for you guys," Dex replied smugly.

"Enough!" I laughed, shaking my head at them. "I'm just glad it all worked out." As excited as I was to move in with Dex, the one thing that held me back was leaving Amy and Sadie behind. Now that I knew Nate was moving in with them, I felt a million times better about everything.

As promised, Dex had cleared out space in his closet for me, and even bought a new dresser for me to use. Of course, my sparse collection of clothing barely took up any space at all.

"I'm going to take you shopping," Dex told me as he lay on the bed and watched me unpack. "You deserve to have a closet overflowing with nice stuff. Beautiful things for a beautiful girl."

I smiled, "You don't have to do that." I hung up the last of my clothes, crawling over to him on the mattress and straddling his hips. Lowering my mouth to his neck, I trailed my lips over his skin and tasted him with my tongue. "I have everything I need right here."

Immediately I felt him harden beneath me, and heat pooled between my legs as he reached for my hips, pulling me against him. "I want to take care of you," he said.

"You already do." I dragged my tongue over his earlobe, breathing a soft moan that caused him to shudder beneath me.

"I want you to feel at home here," he choked out, slipping his hand underneath my shirt and sweeping his warm palm up my spine.

"I'll feel at home as long as you're here."

"What if I—"

I sat up, rocking my hips along his length, sending desire shooting through my veins. "What if you... what?" I teased, completely aware of what I was doing to him.

"Aw, fuck…" he groaned, clenching my body against his rock-hard arousal. "What if I… arranged to have the rest of your stuff sent down here from New York?"

I froze, looking down at him. "Really? You would do that?"

"Of course, baby." He brushed my messy hair out of my face. "But only if you want me to."

I smiled, nodding. I'd never had a permanent place to keep all my mother's things and the stuff from my childhood. I liked that I finally did, and that what we had was permanent.

"Good," he said. "Now that we've settled that…" He flipped me onto my back, grinding his hips into me as he pressed me into the mattress. "I've got other plans for you."

My shift that night at the Seaside ran late, thanks to a rowdy bachelorette party that kept us busy behind the bar, and it was well past one o'clock in the morning when I finally got back to Dex's. I hated coming home so late. Even though Dex had been doing a lot better lately with his nightmares, I still worried about him sleeping on his own and not being there to pull him out of it. All I could think about on my way home was finding him flailing and screaming in bed, a look of terror on his face.

Unlocking the front door, I quietly slipped inside and put my purse on the counter. I didn't hear any noise coming from the bedroom, but sometimes he suffered through them in silence, barely making any noise. Tiptoeing through the house, I slowly opened the bedroom door and crept inside.

I let out a sigh of relief when I found him sleeping soundly. His handsome face so peaceful, his powerful body relaxed and still. My heart swelled with happiness. I was so proud of him. For few minutes I just stood there, watching him. Admiring the beautiful, amazing man in front of me. Sometimes it was hard to believe that he was mine.

"Quit watching me sleep and get your sexy ass into bed," he grumbled sleepily. His eyes were still closed but he stretched his arm to the side, leaving a space for me to climb into.

I undressed quickly, crawling under the covers and tucking myself into him. I realized in that moment that there was nowhere else I would rather be, and nowhere else I would ever want to be.

"Surprise!"

I stood frozen in the doorway of my house, completely stunned to find all my family and friends waiting for me inside.

I glanced at Olivia next to me. "Did you do this?"

She just smiled. "Happy Birthday, babe."

The house was decorated in streamers and balloons, with a huge "HAPPY BIRTHDAY" banner strung up from the ceiling. Platters of food covered the dining room table, and the outside deck was set up with tables and chairs.

Amy was the first one to run over to me, flinging her arms around me in a big hug. "Happy Birthday, bro!"

"You too, sis," I said. "Were you in on this? Shouldn't you be getting surprised along with me?"

"I was supposed to be, but Nate spilled the beans a few days ago," Amy said. "So, I decided to get in on it with them."

"Some people just can't keep a secret," Olivia teased Nate, who had walked over with Sadie.

"I can't keep secrets from my girl," Nate said, pulling Amy close. She beamed up at him, looking happier than I'd ever seen her.

"I helped with the decorations!" Sadie announced proudly.

I lifted her up into my arms, laying a kiss on her chubby cheek before putting her back down. "You did an awesome job, Sadie girl. I love it!" Leaning over to Olivia, I dropped my lips to her ear, tickling her skin and making her shiver. "Thanks for this, baby. You're amazing."

"You deserve it," she told me. "But I can't take all the credit, your parents helped me out. Nate and Amy, too. We wanted you to have a really great birthday."

I wrapped my arm around her waist, pulling her against me. "Now that I have you, it's already the best birthday I've ever had."

She blushed slightly. "You're pretty sweet, Dex Porter. You know that?"

"Shhh… don't tell anyone," I whispered. "That's our little secret. Besides, I'm only sweet for you."

"I hope you're not getting all soft on me…"

"Hell no! Soft is the last thing you make me," I winked, squeezing her ass and making her flush even more. "I'd be more than happy to prove that to you later. Or, right now…"

Her eyes twinkled deviously. "As much as I'd like that, we should probably go enjoy your party. You have all night to do whatever you want with me."

"Oh, I plan to," I promised.

I made my way around, greeting everyone that had taken the time to come and celebrate with me. Olivia had gone all out. In addition to my family, she had invited Nora and Jake, Rose, and even a few of my high school friends that I'd stayed in touch with over the years. I thought I'd seen everyone when Chase appeared in front of me, grinning widely.

"Happy Birthday, Porter," he said, shaking my hand and patting me on the back. "Your girl called me last week to tell me about the party she was throwing for you, and I couldn't resist stopping by."

"Thanks for being here, man. It means a lot that you came all this way, especially when you're wife is getting ready to pop."

"Actually, she already popped. The little guy decided he couldn't wait any longer." Smiling proudly, he pulled out his phone and showed me a picture of his newborn son. "He's impatient, but healthy."

"Congratulations!" I said, examining the photo. "You did good, brother. He's beautiful."

"Maybe one of these days, you and that wonderful girl of yours will give him a little friend to play with, eh?" Chase teased.

"One thing at a time," I said, forcing a laugh as my heart rate sped up. The idea of being a father, of being responsible for another human being, made me panic. I'd never considered it a possibility before, so I hadn't given it much thought. With all my issues, and with all the terrible, cruel things I'd seen… I wasn't sure if someone like me should ever be a father. But when I looked at Olivia… when I thought about her stomach swollen from something we created, and pictured a little boy or girl with her blonde hair and blue eyes… I felt something different. It made me nervous, mostly, but deep down there was a fragment of excitement. Longing. There was a part of me that wanted that someday.

"I wish I could stay, but I should get back to Lila and relieve her of diaper duty," Chase said. "But maybe you and Olivia could come over for dinner sometime soon, meet the baby and all that."

"Absolutely," I said. "I can't wait to meet him."

Shortly after Chase left, everyone gathered out on the deck for cake, singing "Happy Birthday" while Amy and I worked together to blow out the candles. There was really only one thing left for me to wish for. I already had almost everything I could ever want.

After the sun had set and the sky went dark, we lit a fire on the beach and roasted marshmallows. Olivia sat on the other side of the fire, talking and laughing with Nora and Jake. I watched her across the bright orange flames, captivated by her carefree smile and bright blue eyes.

"Mind if I sit?" my dad asked, breaking me out of my trance.

"Not at all." I gestured to the seat next to me, encouraging him to join me. "Thanks again for doing all this. It's been a really great day."

"It was mostly Olivia," he said. "She's an great girl, that one. Anyone who can make you as happy as you've been lately is definitely a keeper."

I smiled, "You don't have to tell me that. I have every intention of keeping her for as long as she lets me."

"Atta boy," he said with a grin.

We were quiet for a few moments, but the silence was was plaguing me. He didn't ask me the usual questions, and for the first time I actually wanted him to. I needed to finally let him in.

"I uh, started going to counseling," I said, fidgeting uncomfortably in my seat. "Mostly group therapy, but I'll do some individual sessions, too. You were right about me needing to get some help, I just never knew how."

"How's it going?" he asked, not seeming too surprised, or maybe he just masked it well.

"It's been good... it's been really good. Sometimes it can be tough, but it helps to talk it through." I glanced over at him, regretting that I'd ever pushed him away when all he'd ever wanted was to be there for me. "I'm sorry that it took me so long to be honest with you about all this. I didn't know how to handle it, and I didn't want to disappoint you."

He turned to me, his face serious. "You could never disappoint me, Dex. Never. Not once, in twenty-six years, have I ever felt anything less than pride to have you as my son. I'm proud of you for all you've done for your country, for our family, and for yourself… for being brave enough to get help when you knew you needed it. That's not easy. But you're strong, and there's no doubt in my mind that you'll get through this."

"I hope so," I choked out, my throat tightening from his words. "For a while I think I just… gave up. I stopped fighting for my own life."

He glanced at Olivia on the other side of the bonfire. "Sometimes, all it takes is finding something to fight for."

"I'll fight for her for the rest of my life."

As midnight approached, marking the end of my birthday, all the guests were gone, and I finally had Olivia to myself. Sitting on the beach next to the fading fire, wrapped up in a blanket to shield us from the cool night air, I'd never been more content. I could spend every for the rest of my life doing the same thing, and I would never grow tired of it.

"Thanks for an amazing birthday," I said, nuzzling in the curve of her neck and dropping my lips to the spot just below her ear.

She turned around in my lap, winding her long legs around my waist. "Can I give you your present now?"

"You got me a present?" I asked. "What is it?"

She pulled down the straps to her sundress, exposing her pink, lacy bra.

"Me," she smiled deviously. "Want to unwrap it?"

"Fuck, yes," I growled, crushing my mouth against hers. I was hard in an instant, straining against my jeans and pressing between her legs. I could feel her damp warmth through the thin material of her panties, and I knew I wasn't going to last long. I'd been waiting for this moment all day, and I was already too worked up.

I dropped my lips her throat, trailing kisses down her collarbone and over her cleavage as I pulled her bra down, letting her breasts spill over the top. Her nipples pebbled in the cool air, and I covered one of them with my mouth, sucking it gently while teasing the other one with my fingers.

"That feels so fucking good," she cried out, clutching my head to her chest and grinding her pussy along the length of my cock.

I loved hearing dirty words tumble from those pretty lips.

"Sorry baby, I can't wait," I said, fumbling with one hand to get my pants undone, and shoving them down enough to free myself. "This is gonna be hard and fast."

Desire flashed in her eyes as she nodded, biting down on her bottom lip. Slipping underneath her short dress, I ran my hands up her smooth thighs until my fingers found the delicate lace of her panties and tore them off. Keeping my eyes locked on hers, I raised her up and positioned myself at her entrance, slamming her down hard and filling her in one swift movement.

She cried out in pleasure, lifting her hips and then dropping back down over me. I couldn't control the groan that escaped my throat as I moved within her tight, wet heat. Her legs fastened around my back as I clung to her hips, rapidly thrusting inside her until I felt her body clench around me. As soon as she reached her climax I followed, exploding inside her with a low growl.

Our breaths were heavy as she collapsed against my chest, tracing her delicate fingers up and down my spine. "Happy Birthday," she said softly.

"I'm not done with you yet," I grinned. "Not even close."

epilogue

Olivia

Our big day had finally arrived.

Well, actually, it was Myrtle's big day. After months of nursing her back to health and rehabilitating her, she was finally ready to be released back into the wild – along with two other sea turtles from the rescue center. I'd grown strangely attached to Myrtle. Ever since she came in on my first day at the aquarium, she had become my own little project. In a way, I was a bit sad to see her go, but spending her days in a boring tank was no way to live, so I was happy she was going to be set free.

I was amazed at how many people had come out to Folly Beach County Park for the release of the sea turtles. According to Frank it was a big deal for people around here. All my friends had even shown up – Amy, Nate, Sadie, Nora, Jake, Gram, Mr. and Mrs. Porter, and of course, Dex. I had mentioned the release event one night, never expecting anyone to actually be interested in coming out, but there they all were… giving up their Saturday to support me. I couldn't believe how lucky I was to have such great people in my life.

Eight months ago, I never expected my life to change so drastically in such a short period of time. More importantly, I never imagined that I could be so happy. For too long I was simply coasting through life, content to settle for what was easy and secure in order to keep myself from feeling pain. At some point along the way, I'd stopped feeling anything at all. Stopping by Steven's apartment that day, finding him with someone else, was the best thing that ever happened to me because it forced me to *live*. I'd learned that nothing good ever comes easy and life doesn't offer a guarantee. Life is full of pain and heartbreak, conflict and doubt... but there's also love and passion, joy and laughter... and it's the ups and downs along the way that make life worth living. It's not about cruising along a straight path, but about not letting the dips and twists take away from the thrill of the ride.

I was no longer content to just be content. I was no longer drifting through an average life. Now, I was surrounded by people who loved and supported me, and were always there for me. They had taught me the most valuable lesson of all – that not all family is bonded by blood. A true family is made up of the people who are with you through good times and bad, whenever you need them, regardless of DNA. Not because they feel obligated to, but because they *want* to be. My family tree may have been sparse, but I had all the family I would ever need, and more.

I'd brought my camera along to the beach, and I couldn't resist snapping pictures and capturing the happiness of the most important people in my life. Dex and Nate were chasing a screaming, laughing Sadie around on the beach while Amy stood back, observing them with a blissful smile on her face.

Also on the beach was Nora, sitting on Jake's lap with her back pressed against his chest while he whispered in her ear, holding her protectively in his arms. Dex and I had grown very close with them, and despite the fact that Nora and I had been friends and roommates for four years, in a lot of ways, we were only now truly getting to know each other. We had been mere shadows of ourselves during those years together in college, both of us trudging down the paths that we felt obligated to follow because we feared what would happen if we shifted our course. Fortunately, we had both found our way to where we were meant to be.

My grandmother was standing with Dex's parents, happily chatting away as if they'd known each other for years. Gram was like that, though. She had such a big heart and a kind soul, as well as a tough-as-nails attitude that I admired. We'd been spending a lot of time together since she came back into my life, and I was grateful for every day we shared. I was also starting to get to know my half-sister, Harper. We were taking it slow, one step at a time, but I hoped to eventually be part of her life in a real way. She was a great girl, I could already tell, and I'd been surprised at how open and welcoming she was to the idea of getting to know me. Part of me had expected her to have some animosity toward me because we shared a father, but she was nothing like that. I got the sense that she was closer to Gram than she was to her parents, and didn't spend a lot of time at her own home. Hopefully someday she would learn, like I did, that you choose your own family. You choose who matters to you and who you want in your life.

Strong arms enveloped me from behind, pulling me against a hard chest and interrupting my stream of thoughts.

"Hey, baby," Dex said, dropping a kiss to the curve of my neck.

Goosebumps tickled my skin as I sank into his welcoming grasp. "Hey, you," I said. My body still reacted to him the same way it did when he first touched me, and I would never grow tired of that feeling. The warmth he brought me, from even the simplest look or briefest touch, made me feel more alive than anything else could.

"I've barely seen you all day, I needed a fix. I thought that you moving in meant I was supposed to get sick of you, not miss you more… What are you doing to me, woman?" he teased.

I turned around in his arms and looked up to meet his gaze. "I'm all yours tonight, if you want me…"

"Oh, I definitely want you." His eyes flared with desire, burning into me as he lowered his mouth to mine. All of a sudden, I was counting the minutes until it was time to go home.

Living with Steven had been more of a chore than anything; something I put up with because it seemed like the logical thing to do. I'd always felt like I was suffocating being around him all the time, and frankly, I got fed up with him and his annoying habits. I would make excuses to get out of the house just so I could have some time alone.

It was nothing like that with Dex. With him, every day was an adventure. I never got sick of him and I missed him when he wasn't around. He put a smile on my face every morning, made me laugh when I was in a bad mood… and of course, satisfied me every night. He gave me space when I needed it, which wasn't often because the fact of the matter was, I was happier with him than without him.

We were open with each other about everything and there were no secrets or walls between us. No matter where we were, or who we were with, he always made me feel like I was the only one who existed to him. My heart was safe in his hands, and I trusted him with every part of me.

Dex was a regular at the group therapy sessions, and I couldn't be more proud of him. They really seemed to be helping him, and the change in him was incredible. He still had the occasional nightmare, but they weren't nearly as vivid and they no longer kept him up all night. The darkness that used to haunt his eyes was all but gone, and there was joy in them that I'd only ever caught glimpses of before.

Thinking about the future brought excitement and hope rather than fear and doubt. We were both healing. Healing from our pasts and helping each other move forward.

You can't escape the past. It's what makes you who you are and it remains a part of you. All you can do is accept it and move on. Choose to look forward instead of looking back. Make the past a part of your present and your future; a piece that you carry with you to remind yourself how you got to where you are and how far you've come.

Teddy's parents had been right when they said that the greatest kinds of friends are the ones who bring out the best in one another. That's what I had with Liv. She was my best friend, my confidante, my hero, my lover… my everything. We made each other stronger every day and together we could face anything.

Olivia's ring was hidden in my sock drawer. For now. It wasn't a matter of *if* I would ask, but *when*. The future was full of uncertainty, but the one thing I was sure of... was her.

She was my future.

Turn the page for a preview of Nora and Jake's story,
This Time Around,
available now...

THIS TIME
AROUND

Ellie Grace

Nora Montgomery left home and heartbreak behind in South Carolina when she moved to New York City after her high school graduation. Now, four years later, she returns home and is forced to confront the past she left behind, and the reckless boy who broke her heart. It's not long before the pieces of her past begin to blur with the present, and she realizes that the feelings she had for her first love never really went away. As old dreams resurface and new truths come to light, she begins to question the future she's always planned on.

Jake Harris has spent four years regretting the night he let her get away. When she finally reappears in his life, he is determined to win her back and prove how much he's changed. She might never forgive him for that night, but if he tells her the truth about what really happened, it will shatter the world she thought she knew. If he doesn't, he might not get a second chance. He's already lost her once and he won't lose her again.

They come from two different worlds that are threatening to tear them apart... can they make it this time around?

CHAPTER
ONE

Nora

When I first set foot outside the airport and got a taste of the fresh South Carolina air, I felt like I could finally breathe again. Like I'd been holding my breath underwater, and had finally reached the surface. I hadn't realized how much I'd missed being down here. Well... maybe I'd realized it, but I certainly hadn't let myself admit it. Over the last four years I'd become pretty accustomed to pushing my feelings aside; especially my feelings about home. I'd managed to stay away for as long as I could, but now the time was right. Besides, it would only be for a little while.

I spent the two hour drive with the windows down and the radio blaring in my rental car. Driving was one thing I had definitely missed. No one drove in New York City. Transportation consisted of flagging down cabs on the sidewalk or hopping onto the subway. Throw any kind of weather into the mix and forget it: you'd better be prepared to walk. After a few weeks in the city, and walking countless blocks in high heels, I'd learned to always carry flats in my purse.

Either way, no matter what form of transportation you used, you had to fight the hordes of people, all of whom were also in a rush to get wherever they were going. That was another thing; city people are always in a hurry, always moving. There never seems to be any time to just sit back and enjoy the ride before you're rushing on to the next thing. Perhaps that's why the last four years had gone by so fast.

In my hometown of Beaufort, South Carolina, things were completely different. It was a small southern town in the heart of Lowcountry, with a historic feel and the kind of scenic beauty that required you to slow down and enjoy it. Life seemed to move a little slower there, and I never truly realized it, or appreciated it, until I was thrown into the chaos of the city. New York was beautiful in its own way, but to me, it paled in comparison to the natural magnificence of the south. The feel of the cool coastal breeze on your face, the quiet shade of the towering live oak trees, and swinging off a rope into the refreshing water of the river on a hot day... there was nothing quite like it, especially in the city. At heart, I was still just a small town girl.

Regardless, my time in the city wasn't over yet. At last week's graduation ceremony I sat among the rest of my NYU classmates as we filled the endless sea of chairs, donning our violet caps and gowns, and baking under the hot sun as we waited to collect our diplomas. But, unlike many of my college peers who would be heading off to various parts of the country to begin the next chapter of their lives, my "higher education" chapter was still unfinished. When the summer was over, I would be heading back to NYU for my first semester of law school... and three more years of city living.

As I turned off the highway and crossed into Beaufort, all the relief I felt when I first got off the plane vanished and my stomach began twisting into knots. When I saw the oak trees draped with Spanish moss, the historic antebellum houses and the river lined with marsh, I was flooded with memories that made my heart ache. Now that I was actually here it was easy to remember why I fled to New

York and stayed away for so long. Everything about this place made me think of him.

Jake.

I took a deep breath in an attempt to calm myself down, and reminded myself why I was here. My best friend Susie was getting married this summer, and as her maid of honor, I was determined to help her with the preparations and spend as much time with her as I could before the big day. I had also agreed to keep an eye on my father's law firm while he and my mother were away.

The reminder that my parents wouldn't be home gave me some relief. At least I would have some time to myself and wouldn't have to put on a show the second I walked through the door. They assumed that the only reason I hadn't been back all this time was because I was so busy with school and my summer internships; which was they'd been so understanding about all the missed holidays, and having to come visit me in the city instead. They would never understand the real reason for my reluctance. After all, it had been four years. *Four damn years!* Frankly, I didn't really understand it myself. If someone told me that they'd avoided going home for that long after a breakup, I would probably have them sent in for a psych evaluation.

At least with my parents out of town I would have a chance to get a grip on myself and figure out how to handle being here. Besides, I had no idea what Jake was doing, or if he was even in town anymore. I could handle this. In a few short months I would be leaving Beaufort behind. Again.

Pulling into my parent's driveway, I could see that not much had changed. The home I'd grown up in was exactly as I remembered it – white with dark blue plantation shutters, and a two-story front porch that ran along the first and second levels– all of which was sitting beneath the tall oaks and magnolias. This had always been my haven, the one place I could always find peace. But even here I was haunted. Still, it felt good to be home.

I hauled my bags up the front steps and retrieved the spare key from its hiding place in the flower pot. After fiddling with the old lock for a few seconds, I swung open the front door and walked inside, pausing in the foyer to look around at the house I hadn't been in for so many years.

Aside from redecorating the living room and adding a few new pieces of artwork, it was mostly unchanged. I stepped into the den and inhaled the faint scent of cigar smoke that lingered in the air, even though my father had been away. The bookshelves were filled with the brown leather-bound law books that my father had inherited from his father before him, and the same elegant, clear glass bottles lined the bar, filled with pricey amber malts and whiskeys that my father sipped nearly every evening as he puffed on a cigar. Everything about this room reminded me of him, and I almost felt myself beginning to miss my parents. Almost.

I walked over to the old grand piano that sat in the corner and ran my fingers over the smooth wood, leaving a trail in the dust that had collected on it. I'd never once seen anyone play it, and I often wondered why my parents kept it there, sitting unused and wasting space. When I was younger I'd tried to teach myself how to play, but it wasn't long before I realized that the piano just wasn't for me.

After a few minutes of wandering around my childhood home, I brought my bags upstairs to my bedroom. Walking in, it was as though no time had passed. It was completely untouched and exactly as I had left it all those years ago. I knew that my parent's house had more rooms than they could possibly need, but after being away so long, I still half expected to find my stuff hauled out and replaced with gym equipment or a man cave, or something. It was nice that they had left it for me, and I was reminded of how much they cared about me. I knew they had missed me, and for a split second I started feeling guilty for being so relieved about their absence.

Dropping my bags down, I swung open the French doors to the balcony for some fresh air before lying down on my bed to rest. As I studied the floral pattern of the duvet that I hadn't seen since I was a teenager, I felt my eyelids began to droop closed. All the traveling combined with my emotional turbulence had left me exhausted.

"Noraaaaaa!!!!"

I awoke with a start when I heard a voice outside. I glanced out the window at the changing color of the sky as dusk began to fall.

"Nora Montgomery! Get down here now!"

Standing up groggily, I walked out to the balcony and looked below to see the familiar blonde hair and cheery smile of my best friend, Susie.

"SUSIE! What are you doing here?" I yelled down to her.

"Here to see my best friend, duh."

"Don't move I'll be right down," I said as I rushed back out through my bedroom and down the stairs to meet her.

Opening the front door, I greeted Susie with a big hug. "I thought you weren't coming back until tomorrow?" I asked her as we walked through the house into the kitchen.

"Ethan and I finished our packing early so we got in yesterday," she answered. "How does it feel to be home? I really cannot believe it's been so long since you've been back!"

"Yeah, it's been a long time." I went to the fridge and grabbed a bottle of white wine. "I've really missed it here," I told her truthfully as I poured two glasses.

We sipped our wine and caught up on everything from the few months since we'd last seen each other. Even though I hadn't been home since I left for school in New York, Susie and I always made time to spend together. She would visit me in New York, or I would make the trip to Virginia where she and her boyfriend Ethan (now her fiancé), had gone to school at the University of Virginia. We'd all been close growing up. Susie and I have been inseparable since the age of four, and Ethan and Jake grew up next door to each other. When Susie and Ethan got together in high school, it wasn't too long before Jake and I started seeing each other, too. After that we did just about everything together.

"Well, I have to get home to have dinner with my parents," Susie said as she stood up. "But you and I are going out tonight. No excuses!"

"Okay," I laughed. "But wouldn't you and Ethan rather have some alone time?"

"No way!" she said. "I think we can handle a night apart. Besides, he's already going out tonight with, uh… his friend."

I smiled at her attempt of a cover-up. As though I didn't know which "friend" she was talking about. Susie was good about not mentioning Jake. I had made it pretty clear that I didn't want to talk about him, and over the years she had stopped trying to bring him up in conversation. I was grateful for that. However, her little slip-up did reveal that Jake was still here in town, and hadn't moved away like I'd wished. Beaufort was a small town, and my stomach dropped at the mere idea of running into him. I'd known I would have to see him at the wedding–he was Ethan's best friend–but I'd hoped that I would have some time to mentally prepare before then.

"I'll pick you up at 8:30!" Susie yelled out her car window as she started pulling out of the driveway. "Wear something sexy!"

Jake

I took a step back to get a better look at my work. It wasn't much, but it was getting there.

Over the last few months I'd started to work on renovating my grandfather's fishing cabin. Well, it was more like a shack right now, but it wouldn't be when I was done with it. It had been falling down for years, and my parents had finally given me the go-ahead to work on it. I'd always loved this place. Even though the building was battered and run down, it was tucked away in the woods and sat right on the lake with a little dock for swimming and fishing.

Throughout my entire childhood and teenage years, I'd spent a lot of time in this place. But, as much as I'd enjoyed being here, I stopped coming a few years ago and hadn't been back until I started the renovation. When Ethan announced that he and Susie were getting married, I decided to finally fix this place up so I could let them use it. We had all spent a lot of time here back then, and I knew how much they loved it here. This place held a lot of memories... memories that still made my throat tighten and my chest ache, even after four years.

I met Nora during the spring of my senior year of high school, shortly after Ethan and Susie got together. Nora and Susie were a year behind us in school, so even though I'd seen her around, I didn't know much about her. All I really knew was that she was a Montgomery—rich, smart, privileged—definitely not the type of girl that would hang around a "bad boy" like Jake Harris. Not that I'd ever done anything really bad, just stupid teenage boy crap. But it was a small town, and when someone labeled you a bad seed it stuck and everyone had a tendency to believe it.

When Ethan first tried to get Nora and me together I had scoffed and told him he was crazy. *"Why would I want to get with a snob like that?"* I'd said. As much as I loved Ethan, I wasn't going to pretend to be interested in some random girl just so we could all hang out together. Not my style. Especially not when there were a shitload of other girls I could be giving my attention to. Ones that were much more my speed. Why have just one girl when you can have lots of girls? That was my philosophy.

Then, one especially hot day in April, Ethan and I decided to come up here to the fishing cabin. We were hanging out on the dock drinking beers when he told me that he'd invited Susie and Nora. Before I had time to protest, I saw them coming out of the woods and heading our way. Ethan ran over to Susie but Nora just kept walking towards me. Without saying a word to me, she pulled her tank top over her head and shimmied out of her cutoff denim shorts, revealing a tiny black bikini underneath. She walked past me to the edge of the dock, dove right into the water, surfaced, and then swam back over and gracefully climbed out. I'd been watching her since she arrived, and as she spread out her towel and sat down, I couldn't take my eyes off her. She glistened in the sun as beads of water slid down her tan skin, her rich brown hair falling down her back and clinging to her perfect body.

She was the most beautiful thing I'd ever seen.

When her hazel eyes finally met mine, she flashed me a grin and said, *"So, Jake Harris... are you just gonna sit there and stare, or are you gonna offer me a beer?"*

I couldn't help but smile as I remembered it.

From that moment on, I was totally hooked. I'd known she was different. Nothing like I'd assumed, but still unlike any girl I'd ever met. Within minutes, I'd grabbed my phone to text whichever girl I had plans with that night and cancel. I didn't make any more plans after that, and I stopped noticing other girls altogether.

Until that point, I'd never really pursued a girl before. At least not for anything more than a couple dates or a hookup, so I'd had no idea what I was doing. All I knew was that I wanted to be around her. I wanted to know her.

Unfortunately, I had no clue how to go about it. The girls I was used to were easy… in every sense of the word. Nora was different. She didn't hang all over me, making up excuses to touch me any chance she got, or bat her eyelashes and laugh at everything I said, even when it wasn't remotely funny. Instead, she called me on my bullshit, teased me when I deserved it, and didn't flinch about getting a little dirt under her fingernails. She challenged me. And I loved it.

I had resorted to tagging along with Ethan and Susie like a pathetic third-wheel anytime I thought she might be with them. I could tell she didn't take me seriously, not that I could really blame her. I'd dated or messed around with half the girls in town, and had never been with one person for longer than a week or two. I knew that I would have to do something to make her realize that I wasn't just messing around with her, and in order to do that I needed to spend some time alone with her.

Since she never would have agreed to go out with just me, I had to beg Ethan and Susie to help me out. After making fun of me for quite a while – *"Jake Harris needs help getting a date? Oh how the mighty have fallen!"* – they finally agreed to make "plans" for all of us to hang out at the cabin, and then never show up so that I could have a chance to be alone with Nora.

The day of our "date" had finally arrived, and everything at the cabin was set up perfectly. I'd planned it all out, spending most of the day getting ready. I'd strung twinkle lights along the path to the water and along the dock, and found an old radio in my dad's garage. There was supposed to be some kind of meteor shower that night, so I'd brought blankets and set up lawn chairs so we could watch it. I didn't know shit about romance, but I thought I'd done pretty damn good.

When Nora walked down to the dock, I'd handed her the flowers that I'd picked from my mom's garden. I could still remember the look on her face. I'd never seen anyone look so confused... but there was a hint of excitement in her eyes when she started to realize what was going on. Moving in real close, I'd looked down at her and said, *"So, Nora Montgomery... are you just gonna stare at me, or are you gonna give me a chance?"*

By some miracle she had actually decided to stay, and we sat down at the end of the dock with the radio on, staring up at the sky as I took her hand and entwined my fingers with hers. I don't remember anything about what was going on in the sky that night, but I didn't care. I barely took my eyes off her. At some point she'd turned to me, and our eyes met. Without saying a word I'd leaned over and kissed her. After that, we'd been inseparable.

Just thinking about it made my chest constrict, filling me with agony. So, I pushed the memories aside and started packing up my tools. Ethan was meeting me at my apartment in an hour, and I was in desperate need of a shower. A night out would be good for me. I'd been so busy with work and classes over the last few months that I barely ever left the house unless it was to go to a construction job or a class on campus. Now that I was finally finished with school, I couldn't wait to unwind a little bit.

Ethan and I went down to the waterfront to grab some food. As we sat in the booth waiting for it to come, he held his beer up.

"Here's to you Mr. Architect," he said. "I never thought I'd see the day."

"That makes two of us," I chuckled. "And here's to the future groom."

"Hear, hear!"

We clinked our beers together. It was strange to think about how much we'd grown up. Ethan had been my best friend for as long as I could remember, and it seemed like just yesterday we were stealing beer from the neighbors and getting in brawls with the idiots at school. Despite how much had changed, sometimes I felt like I was permanently stuck at the age of eighteen.

Ethan on the other hand, was gearing up to marry his high school sweetheart and he couldn't have been happier. After we graduated from high school, he had taken a year off to stay in town while Susie finished her senior year. Then, they'd both gone off to college together; somehow managing to beat the odds and stay true to one another. Ethan had proposed to her over their Christmas vacation, and frankly, I was surprised he'd managed to wait that long. He'd wanted to put a ring on her finger for almost as long as he'd known her.

In a lot of ways, I envied what they had together. It seemed so stable and uncomplicated. Sure, they'd faced their struggles throughout the years, but they'd always managed to come out stronger on the other side. For them, love had always been enough. If only it was that simple for everyone.

"So, what's next?" Ethan asked. "Are you thinking about joining a firm, or are you gonna work on your own?"

"Still figuring it out," I said. "There aren't many architectural firms nearby, so it would mean branching out. I'd love to work on my own, but I've gotta get some projects under my belt first, and even then, who knows if I could actually generate any business here. You know how people are in this town… So, for now I'm still working with my dad, and maybe soon I'll get some projects going."

My dad worked in construction, and since I'd been working with him on jobs for as long as I could remember, I already knew a lot of contractors and architects in the area. Unfortunately, Beaufort was a small town, and most people here still saw me as the troublemaker I'd been when I was growing up. Especially the wealthy folks. If I was smart, I would get out of here and start fresh someplace else, but I couldn't bring myself to do it. Not yet anyway. I felt like I was tied to this place, and I couldn't really understand why.

"How's the wedding stuff going?" I asked, changing the subject. "Has Susie turned into bridezilla yet?"

"Not yet, but she's been so preoccupied with final exams and moving back down here that she hasn't had time to start freaking out. Now that we're here and she's giving it her full attention, I'll probably have to run for cover eventually."

After we ate, Ethan and I walked down Bay Street to find a place to settle in and grab a few drinks. When we passed one of the local favorites, The Landing Bar, we saw that a familiar band was playing, so we decided to check it out. I was two steps from the door when I heard the gentle strumming of a guitar, followed by a voice that halted me in my tracks. I'd recognize her voice anywhere.

When I got inside I saw Nora sitting on a stool up on the

makeshift stage, strumming the guitar as she sang "Wagon Wheel." The girl loved to sing… and I loved listening to her sing. So much of our time together had been spent with her singing and playing guitar while I just laid back and enjoyed it. I'd always told her that she had the most beautiful voice I'd ever heard. She still did.

Cowering behind the other people standing in the bar, I kept my head low and watched her. She looked exactly the same, and still made my mouth water. She was wearing a short pink lacy dress with her brown cowboy boots. Her long brown hair came down in light waves, and her eyes sparkled. She lit up the entire room. When Nora was around it was impossible to notice anyone but her.

I couldn't believe she was here, and being around her made me ache with longing. Even though I'd expected her to be around for the wedding, I didn't think she would here so soon… and nothing could have prepared me for seeing her here now.

Available now in ebook and print!

acknowledgements

To the readers: I cannot thank you enough for taking the time to sit down and read my book. With so many amazing books out there to choose from, I truly appreciate you giving mine a chance. I started writing because it's something I love to do, but I had zero expectations. I never would have imagined that so many people would actually read my words, and I am forever grateful!

A huge thank you to Autumn Hull, of The Autumn Review and Wordsmith Publicity, for all her wonderful advice and for helping me out along the way when I had no idea what I was doing. She was the first person to read my first book, and I had no idea what to expect, but her enthusiasm and encouragement gave me the confidence to move forward with it.

Tawdra Kandle and Stacey Blake, for all their hard work with the editing. They fit me into their busy schedules and really went the extra mile to help make this book better.

Angela McLaurin of Fictional Formats, for her wonderful interior design and formatting, and for putting up with me throughout the process!

Sarah Hanson of Okay Creations, for her amazing work on the cover. Her designs are incredible, and I was beyond excited when she found time to do mine.

To all the bloggers out there who signed on to my blog tours, and took time to read and spread the word about my books, thank you!

Last but certainly not least, my family, who have always supported me and been there for me no matter what. Especially Will, who is my biggest cheerleader, even when it means being neglected because I'm busy trying to write.

about the author

Ellie is a reader, writer and overall book lover. When a story popped into her head that she couldn't seem to shake, she decided to pursue her childhood dream of becoming a writer, and released her debut novel *This Time Around*. Now, she spends much of her time dreaming up new characters and stories to write, or curled up with her Kindle reading books by her many, many favorite authors.

To connect with Ellie:

Facebook:

https://www.facebook.com/elliegracebooks

Twitter: @elliegracebooks

https://twitter.com/elliegracebooks

Website/Blog:

www.elliegracebooks.com

Also by Ellie Grace:

This Time Around

27383860R10169

Made in the USA
Charleston, SC
11 March 2014